A
NOËL
KILLING

Center Point
Large Print

Also by M. L. Longworth and available from Center Point Large Print:

The Curse of La Fontaine
The Secrets of the Bastide Blanche

A
NOËL
KILLING

a provençal mystery

M. L. LONGWORTH

CENTER POINT LARGE PRINT
THORNDIKE, MAINE

For Ken and Eva

CHAPTER ONE

Debra Hainsby took extra care getting dressed that morning. She chose one of her best outfits: a colorful, fitted wool jacket that *sort of* looked like Chanel. She had bought it at Ross Dress for Less back in the States, and wore it with a bright green wool blend skirt that matched one of the stripes in the weave of the jacket. It was early spring, a cool breeze moving in, so she hoped she wouldn't be too hot. Looking at herself in the mirror she was pleased, glad to have kept her slender figure even after the birth of her two children more than ten years ago.

She was excited not to be working at the bilingual school today, surrounded by grumpy teachers and noisy kids, but instead spending the day with her boss, Alain Sorba. They'd be visiting the human resources offices of two of the region's biggest employers. "Our dog and pony show," Sorba had joked. Debra put on her pearl earrings, a gift from her mother on her wedding day, and realized that Sorba wasn't really joking when he said dog and pony show: His private bilingual school, which accepted kids from kindergarten right through to grade twelve, relied on local companies that hired expats who arrived in France with generous foreign salaries. Who'd be crazy enough to throw their non-French-speaking kids into the old-fashioned rigorous French school system when there was a bilingual school in town, complete with tennis courts and a swimming pool?

An hour later she was sitting in the passenger seat beside Sorba, enjoying the elevated view in the German-made SUV, a car that her sister back home would call a gas guzzler. But Cheryl lived in California and ate only organic foods, a luxury that Debra and her husband, Cole, and their kids couldn't afford. The thought of Cole and their financial troubles—which had existed almost since the day she was given the pearl earrings—made her stomach knot up, and she turned to concentrate on what her boss was saying.

"Most of these expat families have more than one kid, so we offer a reduced rate from the second child on," Sorba said, gesturing with his hands as he drove the big black car.

Debra, recently hired as Alain Sorba's executive assistant, sometimes heard the teachers whispering about him, mimicking the way he spoke with his hands flailing around. They were just jealous, Debra had quickly decided, that the son of a Marseille fisherman now owned the school where they all had to work as hourly wage earners.

"The companies don't like paying tuition, so every little reduction we offer helps," Sorba went on. "Anyway, they're stuck!" he said, now laughing. *"Pas de chance, les cons!"* He hit the steering wheel with the palm of his right hand. *"Les cons!"*

Debra smiled politely, knowing that *con* was a swear word, and not quite sure what it meant. Something like stupid, she thought. She opened a folder on her lap, trying to be professional. "Our first meeting is with HeliIndustries," she said in careful French. Even though Alain Sorba owned a bilingual school, she wasn't sure if he spoke much English. Hence her participation at these meetings today.

"The world's largest helicopter maker," Sorba said, still smiling. "And as our luck would have it, they're located right here in Marseille, just down the coast from where my dear papa had his boat and *cabanon*!"

Yes, Debra thought, they were lucky that Marseille and Aix were only a twenty-minute drive apart, and that while Marseille had a few important companies, most foreigners preferred to live in sleepy, quiet Aix. She certainly did. "Oh, your father has a *cabanon*?" Debra asked, trying to make small talk. "A sea view! What a dream!"

"It certainly was," he said, now laughing again. "A shack that he put up in a weekend and that I sold to a Parisian television producer for five hundred thousand euros!"

Debra cringed, trying to imagine that kind of

money, and how much it would help with Cole's travel business. It made her angry with Cole; why couldn't he figure out how to make money, when even an old fisherman could swindle a suave Parisian? "I added the new color photos of the school's gardens," Debra said, pointing to the folder. "And I think we can safely tell the HeliIndustries people that our new science lab will be constructed by the end of this school year. I spoke to the architects yesterday."

"Excellent!" Sorba said. "Good work, Debra. What would I do without you?" Debra felt a burst of pride and tried not to smile.

"Plus our new science lab will be a great draw for the parents who work at Iter," she continued. "I'm at work on their presentation right now."

"Oh, yes, Iter! The new nuclear power research station," Sorba said, briefly taking his hands off the wheel and rubbing them together. "I love nuclear power! *Les cons*!"

"And the employees are given international diplomacy status so they don't pay income tax," she added, leaning toward her boss as if passing on secret information. She had picked up the income tax fact while eavesdropping on two math teachers complaining about how little they earned at the bilingual school while having to pay income tax on top of it.

Sorba said, "No income tax? All the more money for the expats to spend here in Provence!"

"But Iter will be located north of Manosque," Debra said. "That's an hour from Aix, but a lovely part of the Luberon."

Sorba rubbed his chin. "Rats. Some of the families will want to live up there, given the price of housing in Aix."

Debra bit her lip, now feeling guilty that she had mentioned how far the nuclear plant was.

"I know!" Sorba said, glancing at her and smiling. "We'll offer free bus service from Manosque to our school for the kiddies! That way the moms can stay at home and do their yoga."

"Wouldn't that be too expensive?" Debra asked, picturing the life of a woman who didn't have to work and just go to exercise class and lunch with girlfriends.

Sorba touched the side of his head. "We'll charge them higher tuition," he said. "That's why we never publish the tuition costs on our website. Besides, they're not paying taxes, so they can afford it. It all comes out in the wash, Debra, and we'll even make money in the deal. I have a meeting later this week with Aix's mayor; I'll make sure to talk to her about Iter."

Debra looked out the window, thinking of the mayor's office. She imagined, correctly, that it had ceiling frescoes. She thought that Alain Sorba, in his custom-made dark suits, with his handsome face and booming voice, would be a dramatic addition to the mayor's luxurious office.

Three hours later Alain Sorba was navigating his giant car down the narrow streets of Marseille's oldest neighborhood. "I can't believe you haven't been to the Panier!" he bellowed, charged up on what had been a very successful meeting with the multinational helicopter executives. HeliIndustries was expecting a new slew of engineers from Munich and Texas in the next few months. Along with their families, naturally. Debra was happy, too; she had a feeling that her presentation to HeliIndustries was top-notch, and that she had impressed them.

"I've always been a little shy of Marseille," Debra said, watching the pastel-colored stone walls come within an inch of her window.

"Spoken like a true expat! I'm going to take you to lunch at a place that's known only by the locals. They don't take reservations; in fact, they don't even have a telephone." He miraculously squeezed the car in between two metal poles embedded in front of a derelict centuries-old building. "I never pay for parking," he said as they got out and he locked the doors. "Waste of money that is."

Debra looked up at the building and saw that it wasn't as neglected as she had thought; there were flower boxes in the windows, and the pale blue shutters looked lovely against the yellow ocher walls.

"The restaurant owner's name is Étienne," Sorba said as they walked up a narrow hill. "He was a buddy of my old man; they used to fish together. And I hope you like pizza and calamari."

"I love both."

"Good, because that's the only food on the menu."

Debra almost stopped walking. "Seriously?"

"Yep," he said. "And there will be a queue outside the door."

"Are the calamari prepared in the Marseille style, with only garlic and parsley?"

Sorba shot her a look. "You know a bit about local food! I'm impressed!"

Debra's heart fluttered at the praise.

As Sorba had predicted, when they arrived at Chez Étienne there were five or six people waiting outside the front door. Debra thought she heard English; so it wasn't only locals who came here, like Alain had said. Sorba took her by the waist and gently pushed her through the front door.

"*Étienne! Mon ami!*" he bellowed.

"*Putain!*" an old man wearing a white fishing cap said as he walked up to Sorba and gave him the *bises*. "And who is this lovely creature?" Étienne asked, giving Debra the *bises* as well. She blushed, feeling like she was already a regular. Sorba introduced Debra as his executive secretary and Étienne led them to the bar. "We'll have a table for you in a few minutes," he said. "In the meantime, have a pastis on me."

Debra was thankful that she liked the licorice taste of the aperitif, although she would rather have had a glass of rosé. "Is pastis all right?" Sorba asked, as if reading her mind.

"Pastis is fine!" Debra replied quickly.

Sorba smiled and leaned in toward Debra, his shoulder brushing hers. She realized he wasn't actually very tall, though he carried himself in such a way that his presence certainly felt imposing. They didn't have much choice but to stand close, as there was already another couple hovering at the tiny bar, and the harried waitresses were running back and forth, annoyed that Étienne kept sending people to the back of the restaurant to wait.

"Third table to the left, by the window," Sorba whispered to Debra. "The mayor of Marseille and his entourage." Debra's eyes widened and she tried not to stare. It was one thing to have Alain know the mayor of Aix, but to know the mayor of France's second-largest city was something else. As if on cue the mayor looked up and waved to them. Sorba yelled across the restaurant, "Jean-Charles! Save some calamari for us!"

"Sorba, next time get here by noon!" the mayor called back, tapping his watch. Alain and Debra laughed and Étienne came and told them that their table was ready.

"Well, I guess there's no menu," Debra said as they sat down.

"Nope. The pizza comes first, then the calamari." Sorba ordered a pitcher of rosé and a bottle of sparkling water. As he placed the order and said hello to two men at the next table, Debra quickly checked the messages on her cell phone, which was buzzing in her handbag; it could be a work issue, and here she was with the owner of the school. Sure enough, there was an email from the head of Iter's HR department, asking if their small high school offered the International Baccalaureate.

Sorba turned to her and poured her a glass of rosé.

"Do you know everyone here?" Debra asked, laughing and feeling very comfortable.

"Just about," Sorba replied, winking. "Either we went to school together, or played soccer together, or our parents were friends."

Debra gestured to her cell phone and told Sorba about Iter's request.

"*Merde*," he said, taking a sip of rosé. "Who arranges that? The Brits?"

"Yes," Debra confirmed, although she was just guessing. "I think we have to arrange it through Cambridge University."

"Good," he said, pouring them both more rosé. "You go ahead and arrange all that. Do whatever it takes. I'll buy the bloody curriculum if I have to. We'll just—"

"Charge them more tuition?" Debra asked.

"You learn fast!" Sorba cried, touching his wineglass to hers.

The pizza arrived and Alain served them each a piece. Debra was famished—she hadn't realized how hungry she was. The pizza was fantastic, although the crust was much thinner than American pizzas. Sorba must have seen her huge grin as he said, "If you think Étienne's pizza is good, wait until you taste the calamari."

Debra wanted to pinch herself; if Cheryl could only see her now, fitting right into this typically Marseillais scene, with the mayor just a few tables away. She loved the food, the dry wine, the happy chatter of the patrons, and Étienne, who slowly moved between tables, talking with clients while resting one of his large tanned hands on each person's shoulder.

"Try to book an appointment with Iter next week," Sorba said.

"No problem," Debra answered.

"And do you know what we'll do before the meeting?"

"No, what?"

"I'll take us clothes shopping," Sorba said. "A cousin of mine owns Marseille's best clothing boutique; they do men and women. We'll both set ourselves up with some fine threads, and Iter won't know what hit them. You've got to look prosperous at these meetings. Not like some poor fisherman's son, eh?"

At that moment Étienne came by and invited them on his sailboat the following Sunday. Sorba clapped his hands. "You should see Étienne's boat, Debra," he said.

"Why not?" Debra said. She felt giddy from the wine and the company. "I'd love to come!" Cole could stay at home with the kids. This was a work outing, anyway.

CHAPTER TWO

six months later

France Dubois didn't like the Place des Cardeurs. Sometime in the nineteenth century dozens of buildings were razed to create the vast square, and it was now too big, almost forlorn, as if a meteor had landed and created a big hole in the center of Aix. But perhaps it was better this way, with the narrow, cramped houses gone, and she shuddered thinking about the medieval conditions where large families once shared two or three poorly lit rooms. She was lucky, living alone in her spacious apartment in the Mazarin. No, lucky wasn't the right word. Fortunate. Privileged, even.

It was mid-December and the Christmas fair was on; the square was full of white tents, most of them selling what France considered uninteresting gifts. She tried to smile as she passed by the tents, as she felt so sorry for the young woman who made brightly colored, too-expensive soaps and the middle-aged man who carved smiling animals out of olive wood. Did they appreciate her smile, or did they care only about making a sale? She hoped that some of her fellow Aixois liked their wares enough to make a purchase or two.

France walked on, knowing that no one really saw her in the maze of shoppers. She was a single woman of thirty-five years, short and thin, with mousy midlength brown hair. She had no interest in fashion (she was too careful with her money), and so she could not stand out by wearing outrageous colorful clothes, as other plain-looking women sometimes did. Her neighbors on the rue Cardinale politely said *Bonjour, Mlle Dubois* when they saw France, but she was quite sure they didn't know her first name. They appreciated that she lived alone—no rowdy parties with loud music, no little children running up and down the halls over their heads— and had no further interest in her. France was the perfect neighbor.

She stopped at a tent lined with wheels of cheese on display, each one poked with a little red, white, and green flag. *"Buongiorno!"* a tall, wide-shouldered man called out to her from behind his makeshift counter, in this case a folding table draped in a red tablecloth. He asked if she'd like to try the cheese.

"Si, grazie!" she replied. The Italian winked as he passed her two thin pieces of Parmesan on a sheet of waxed paper. She smiled and nodded as she nibbled at the nutty cheese, wishing she had a little white wine to wash it down with. "I love Perugia," she said in accented Italian.

"Oh, you've been to our city?" he asked.

"Twice," she replied. "With my parents." She didn't add *when they were alive*. She attempted a joke about all of the law offices she had seen in Perugia's old town, each one with a heavy carved wooden door and bronze plaques. "Perhaps that's why Perugia is Aix's sister city in Italy," she said. "Our law school here is one of the oldest in France, so we've always been a town of lawyers . . ."

"Yes, who knows?" the Italian said, laughing. He gave her a chocolate from Perugia and she thanked him, giving him her business card. He tried not to grimace as he read her employer's name, Église Protestante d'Aix, and she quickly reassured him that she was not trying to convert him. "Our Christmas carol sing-along at the cathedral is on Sunday evening," France said. "Each year we invite Aix's sister cities to participate and bring along food that we all share at an early dinner after the service." Again, at the mention of a service, the Italian winced. "Not really a service as such," France explained. "More like a concert, with Anglo-Saxon Christmas carols."

He nodded, smiling. "English Christmas songs? We will be there, with our food!"

France thanked him and was about to give him the address when she caught herself, laughed, and pointed to the cathedral's octagonal steeple, visible over the red tiled roofs. "That's it, over there," she said. "If you could be at the hall, which is around the corner to the right of the front door, at five o'clock, that would be great. The service . . . concert . . . is at five-thirty, and we'll all have dinner together after that."

"The other sister cities," he said, winking again, "they will be bringing their food, too?"

"Oh, yes," France answered. "I'm just about to go and confirm with the others. Some of them have been coming to Aix for years."

"Food from Bath!" he said, slapping his thigh. "And Philadelphia!" He bent over, laughing.

"The English desserts are really quite good," France tried to explain, but she was drowned out by his laughter. "What's important is that we're all together, sharing," she went on, but gave up as a woman he seemed to know came into the tent and he addressed her in Italian, still laughing. France whispered a thank-you and moved on, embarrassed. She hoped he wouldn't make the same kind of scene on Sunday.

She took a piece of paper out of her purse and put a checkmark next to "Perugia." "Carthage, Tunisia" was next on the list, and she spotted the tent, swathed in earth-colored cotton fabrics and white-and-blue pottery.

The Tunisian man waved; he remembered France Dubois from last year, as she had bought an expensive olive wood salad bowl and commented on how much she loved its marbled contours. He remembered the concert, too, and how his eyes had welled up with tears at hearing the songs and voices fill the cathedral.

They reintroduced themselves, and spoke about this year's concert. He shook her hand and promised to bring food.

"I remember your cookies made with rose-water," France said. "They were my favorites, M Abdelhak."

"Please call me Mehdi. Did you not like the pistachio ones?" he asked.

"Oh, yes! They were my second favorite."

"More than the baklava?"

France laughed, sensing that he was teasing. "I loved the baklava, too." Although, if she remembered, Mehdi's baklava was drier than the kind she had eaten in Greece. She preferred it the Greek way, oozing with honey.

She lingered, running her hands over a pale blue cotton bedcover. It would be perfect in early summer, when sometimes a sheet wasn't enough. France always had cold feet. "Hand woven," Mehdi told her, holding up a section for her to examine.

"I'll think about it," France replied, smiling. "I'll see you on Sunday."

She walked along, smiling now. The sun was shining, and the Aixois had come out in full force as it was lunchtime. Voices and laughter filled the square, along with the occasional friendly bark of someone trying to sell something. Her stomach growled, and her hunger pangs increased as she approached the tent for Philadelphia, where a queue had already formed. Now would not be the time to talk to the Americans about the carol service, as they, a sister and brother, if she remembered correctly, were busy serving up their hot steak sandwiches. She hadn't had the nerve to try them last year. "Philly cheesesteaks!" the American man called out. "World-famous Philly cheesesteaks right here in Aix-en-Provence!"

Across the way from the Philadelphia tent sat the British tent, from Bath, tended by two elderly women who looked bored. France could easily see why Bath had been chosen to be a sister city to Aix: They both had been Roman spa towns. "Why, hello," one of the women said, the smaller and rounder of the two, when she saw France. "We remember you from last year, don't we, Eunice, dear?"

"Of course we do," Eunice said, setting aside her knitting. "Your name is France. Easy enough name to remember, isn't it, Sally?"

France smiled, touched that they remembered her, and thankful that they had just reminded her of their names. She thought the name Eunice was perfect for an elderly British woman who knitted, but thought the name Sally belonged to a teenage girl, and not to a tiny, plump woman with white wispy hair. Eunice, on the other hand, was tall and wide shouldered, with black hair that France decided must be dyed.

"Have you come to cheer us up, dearie?" Sally asked. "We've been dreadfully quiet this morning. We don't serve hot sandwiches and beer like the Americans and Germans."

"But your desserts are so delicious," France said truthfully. "You'll be busy this afternoon, I'm sure."

"Have an Eccles cake," Eunice said.

"Oh, thank you." France took it and bit into the flaky pastry. The filling oozed into her mouth, a caramel-like richness of light brown sugar, egg, raisins, and lots of butter.

"Is the cathedral hosting the carol sing again?" Sally asked. "We so enjoyed it last year."

"Yes," France said, holding her hand under her chin to catch the bits of pastry that had not quite made it into her mouth. "We'd love it if Bath could participate again."

"Oh, we certainly will," Sally said, clasping her hands together.

"Your English is really very good," Eunice said.

"Thank you," France replied. "I speak it every day, at the Protestant church here in Aix, and studied it at university."

"Is it Anglican, your church?" Sally asked. She could not hide the hope in her voice.

"No, it's multidenominational," France answered.

"You'd need High Anglican, Sally, dear," Eunice said, shaking her head.

"Oh, I suppose you're right." Sally sighed. "It's why I quite like the Catholic masses here in France. That, and the new pope."

France saw Eunice's eyes widen in dismay at the mention of Pope Francis and she tried to hide her grin. "I'll see you on Sunday, then, at five o'clock in the reception hall, just like last year."

"Oh, we wouldn't miss it for the world," Sally said.

"It's going to be a momentous occasion," Eunice said, almost sternly.

France thanked them and left, wondering what Eunice could have meant by "momentous." It didn't seem like the appropriate word to use when describing a Christmas carol service. She rubbed her tongue along the back of her teeth, realizing that she had missed other flavors from the tart, including allspice and lemon. Or was it orange?

Marine Bonnet hopped up and down, trying to stay warm.

"I really do wish he'd stop announcing his cheesesteaks," her mother, Florence, said, a little too loudly. "It's obvious that's why we are all standing in this line."

"Well, Sylvie promised me they were worth the wait," Marine answered.

"Sylvie!" Florence huffed. "I didn't know that Sylvie Grassi is an epicurean!"

"Look at the poor women from Bath," Marine said, motioning to the British tent, trying to change the subject. "They have no shoppers."

"No one is interested in their royal family mugs and calendars," Florence said. "The Windsor family members are a bunch of German inbreds who live off the British taxpayer—"

"Maman! Did you not sleep well last night?"

Florence shrugged. "Your father snores too much." She was about to say something else when she noticed France Dubois. "Do you see that girl speaking to the women from Bath?"

"Yes," Marine said. "Although she's hardly a girl. She must be almost my age."

"Well, she carries herself like a girl. Anyway, I know her; her name is France Dubois. She's some kind of secretary at the APCA."

The line moved about a foot and Marine and her mother stepped forward. "The APCA?" Marine asked, her stomach growling.

"The Anglo Protestant Church of Aix. We are helping them with their Christmas carol service this Sunday."

"Oh, I love that service," Marine said. "I'm going to try to drag Antoine with me."

Florence snorted. "Antoine Verlaque at church? I can't imagine—"

"He's not a heathen, Maman, just agnostic."

"Hm. I suppose that if his grandmother was English, he'll at least know the words to the songs."

"Exactly," Marine said, relieved. "Is your choir assisting?"

"A dozen or so of the choir members. The Protestant church's reverend, they call him Reverend Dave," Florence began with a snort, "asked us to help. That's where I met her." Florence tilted her head in the direction of France Dubois, and Marine watched the young woman try to daintily eat a flaky British pastry.

"She looks very sweet," Marine said.

Florence said nothing and kept watching. "In the theology faculty I knew others like her. France Dubois types."

They were now second from the front of the line, and Marine stretched her head to watch the American flip the steaks on a makeshift grill. She wouldn't tell Antoine, a food snob, about the bright orange melted substance that dripped out of the sandwiches. "Oh? What type is that, Maman?"

"Those meek-looking marginal types. You don't notice them at first, but they watch what's going on from a distance. Nothing gets by them."

"Wallflowers?"

"Yes, but you were never associated with those types, Marine, so you wouldn't understand."

"I think I do understand," Marine tried to argue. She was about to add something about a former

27

classmate whose name she could no longer remember when she stopped. She knew now that her mother—the headstrong, widely published, now-retired professor—was confessing; she herself had been a wallflower. She knew little about her mother's youth, except for her academic successes, naturally. Marine was about to ask about her mother's high school, located in a small town in the southwest, when she realized they were at the front of the line.

"Hello!" a male voice bellowed before them. "Welcome to Philly cheesesteak heaven!"

"Thank you!" Marine heard herself yelling back in English.

"*O Mon Dieu*," Florence whispered, pulling Marine closer to her. "Is that bright orange stuff supposed to be cheese?"

CHAPTER THREE

Antoine Verlaque had mixed feelings about Christmas, and it didn't help his mood that the Cours Mirabeau was now lined with little wooden Alpine-style chalets selling trinkets. Having just had a long, drawn-out meeting in a café with a courtroom lawyer, going over a case that involved a botched kidnapping of the wealthy wife of a Parisian businessman who owned a home in Aix, he felt a headache coming on. Too much espresso and not enough water, his wife, Marine, would tell him.

He looked at his phone—it was after twelve and he was hungry. Stopping on the sidewalk, he pulled out his cell phone and dialed Marine. Shoppers knocked into him with their oversize bags that advertised the latest "in" shops; this year it seemed to be Sandro and Maje, whatever those were. Women's clothes, he presumed. Next year another brand would be *le must*, and the Sandro and Maje clothes would be taken to Emmaus or simply thrown out. His headache increased and his mood fouled; he really hated Christmas, he decided. He stepped aside, closer to a building, to get out of the shoppers' way.

As he waited for Marine to pick up, he watched one of the chalet sellers arrange tiny blown-glass animals on velvet pads. Verlaque winced and turned away, instead busying himself by reading the plaque at number 3, where, on October 10, 1799, Napoleon dined, only to leave quickly after dinner, disappointing his hosts, who had no doubt hoped to entertain the dashing young Corsican for a longer period.

"*Oui*, Antoine?" Marine answered just as he was about to give up.

"Where are you?" he asked. "It's so loud I can barely hear you."

"Well, hello to you, too."

"Sorry. I'm on the Cours."

"Oh, that explains your mood," Marine said. "Have you picked out what you want for Christmas?"

"I'd like a new mayor who doesn't allow this . . . this . . ." He trailed off, gesturing at the scene before him, and Marine laughed.

"Listen, Antoine, I'm in the middle of lunch with Maman," Marine said. "On the Place des Cardeurs, that's why it's noisy. Is this important?"

"No, no," he answered, knowing now that he'd have to eat alone. "I'll see you at home after lunch. Say hello to your mother." He hung up and began walking up the Cours, remembering Napoleon would be back through Aix in 1814, disgraced, on his way to exile at Elba. There would be no downtown dinner for him that night, thought Verlaque, but a quick stop at an auberge north of Aix that was now a pizza restaurant.

Verlaque watched the crowd amble up and down the boulevard, some stopping to browse the chalets. A well-dressed couple stopped to look at one—this one selling *santons*—and he guessed, from their black cashmere wool coats and expensive boots, that they were Parisian. The woman turned her head slightly toward Verlaque and he recognized her, as did a few of the pedestrians who stopped to whisper to one another. She was Margaux Perrot, the actress. They bought a few *santons* and walked away, arm in arm, toward Verlaque.

"Antoine?" the man said when they were about two feet away.

"Léo?" Verlaque said, guessing the name and hoping he was right. Was it Léo from Bordeaux law school?

"I heard you were in Aix," the man answered, holding out his hand. "You're now Aix's examining magistrate, right? Oh, I'm sorry. This is my wife, Margaux."

"Pleased to meet you," Verlaque said, shaking her hand. He wondered if he should add something like *I love your work,* but in truth he hadn't seen very many of her recent films, which tended to be romantic comedies.

"We were buying some *santons* for our crèche," Margaux said hurriedly, as if embarrassed.

"That's the one authentic Provençal item you'll find for sale here," Verlaque said, because, if truth be known, he had a soft spot for the miniature figurines that represented the varied personages of nineteenth-century Provence—the cobbler, the winemaker, the laundress, the ironmonger. "I went to law school with Léo," he added.

"I don't know about you, Antoine, but that's a distant memory for me," Léo said. "Are you free for lunch?" he asked, turning to his famous wife for a nod of approval.

"Oh, yes, what a good idea," she answered. "You two can get caught up that way, and I'll listen in and take notes."

Verlaque laughed, charmed. "As a matter of fact I am free, and happen to know of a good restaurant right behind us. But I'm not sure you'll find anything interesting, Mme Perrot, in our escapades as law students."

"Léo doesn't tell me anything about his past," she said. "So any little tidbit will do."

Verlaque then remembered his old friend's full name—Léo Vidal-Godard—and some tidbits, as his wife had referred to them, about Léo's life after Bordeaux law school: various business ventures, some having more success than others; a few marriages and divorces; and perhaps, if he remembered correctly, a court case. He wondered how long they had been married.

Verlaque pulled open the door to the Café Mazarin and said something to Frédéric, the head waiter, who led them upstairs to a small wood-lined dining room where luckily there were two small tables free. Frédéric quickly pushed the tables together and discreetly whisked away the fourth place setting and pulled out a chair for Margaux.

"It's charming here," Margaux said, smiling.

"My friends call it the office," Verlaque answered. "We often meet downstairs for coffee before the day begins." As Mme Perrot studied the menu, Verlaque was able to steal some looks at her face, which seemed to have been chiseled out of pale white marble, accentuated by her bright blue eyes and dark red lipstick.

Frédéric reappeared and, as Verlaque had suspected, Margaux ordered a large salad and sparkling water, while he and Léo had the daily special, a ham hock with lentils.

"So who are your office mates?" Margaux asked, leaning forward.

Verlaque stared at her, surprised. Did she want to know about his colleagues at the Palais de Justice? His secretary, the posh Mme Girard? He then laughed, realizing she was referring to the café downstairs. "My best friend, Jean-Marc, a courtroom lawyer; our commissioner of police, a guy named Bruno Paulik; and my wife, Marine, who was until recently a law professor."

"Until recently?" Léo asked. "Did she give up on law?"

Verlaque smiled, stopping himself from saying *like you*.

As lunch wore on, the conversation shifted to Aix real estate, as Margaux and Léo had recently relocated from Paris to Aix. Verlaque asked them why, but couldn't get an answer that made any sense to him. Surely Margaux Perrot's work would keep her in the capital? Mme Perrot also admitted that her children from a previous marriage, ages thirteen and fifteen, were less than thrilled by the move.

"Maybe Sacha will manage to *not* get kicked out of the high school here," Léo said, smirking.

"Sacha is my fifteen-year-old," Margaux explained, visibly embarrassed. "He has . . . trouble with authority."

Verlaque tried to give a sympathetic answer, unimpressed with Léo's insensitivity. It seemed that Sacha would not be getting any male guidance from his stepfather. Margaux changed the subject back to real estate and Verlaque's mind wandered further on the question of male role models. His own father would have scored about a three out of ten, by his estimation; his paternal grandfather, Charles, more like a seven. Charles could have scored higher, but he was too busy running the family's flour mills, and he did come from a generation where men simply did not play with children. Nevertheless, he'd had a big impact on Verlaque in the limited time they did spend together. His maternal grandparents died when he was very young. How would he score if he was ever in that role, especially to a young boy, he wondered? He tried to return his attention to Margaux and Léo as they bickered affectionately about housing prices, but the question stayed with him, lingering in the back of his mind long after the subject had passed.

France Dubois tried not to stare. Especially since everyone else in the café *was* staring. She knew the woman was an actress, but suddenly couldn't remember her name. The waiter set down the plat du jour, and she regretted choosing it. She would be able to eat the lentils, but how in the world would she be able to finish all that ham? France raised her hand and the waiter came back. "*Un verre de rouge, s'il vous plaît,*" she said. A glass of red wine would help, as she was still cold from her walk through the Place des Cardeurs that morning.

The wine would bring the bill up over what she normally allowed herself for lunch, and she'd have to use at least two of her restaurant vouchers, and then some cash, to pay. But, she rationalized, she sometimes didn't use the restaurant vouchers at all, but brought leftovers from home for lunch, saving the vouchers to use at the butcher shop. She smiled, glad to be living in a country where employers and the government shared the cost of a lunch, even if her vouchers were worth only seven and a half euros each. It meant that people went out for lunch more often, restaurants were busier, and she even thought it helped the downtown businesses. If you were out for lunch, you might also pop into a shop and buy something.

She cut into her meat, which fell easily off the bone. It had been cooked with the lentils in red wine and carrots, and was salty and delicious. Perhaps she'd be able to finish it after all. She continued watching her fellow diners, trying not to look too long at any one table. The film star had her back to France, but she had a good view of the two men the actress was eating with, one of whom France assumed to be her husband or boyfriend, for every so often he would take her hand. He also served himself wine twice, without offering any to the other man, and France found herself frowning in distaste. She checked herself, looking down at her lentils. When she glanced up again, the three of them were laughing, but not a hearty laughter. More of a strained one. Their friend, the other man, looked from the actress to her husband with his dark eyes, as if assessing them. Who was he? An old friend? Or perhaps their lawyer . . . wealthy celebrities always had strings of lawyers and accountants working for them, didn't they?

France sat back and took a sip of wine, enjoying herself. She had been watching people and making up stories about them for years, even when her parents were still alive. Sometimes it depressed her, as if she were creating a life of fantasy for herself. But today she let herself savor it, like a guilty pleasure. She was in a good mood; perhaps it was the spirit of Christmas, and the kind words she had exchanged at the Sister City fair with the English women and the Tunisian. She'd go back in the afternoon to talk with the Americans and Germans when they weren't so busy serving lunch. She tore off a piece of bread and thought of the Italian, unsure whether she liked him, when one of the men eating next to her pounded the table with his fist. She jumped and tried not to look over, concentrating on dipping the bread into the red wine sauce.

"Don't worry," the man beside her said in French with a heavy American accent. "You're always worrying."

"One of us has to," his dining partner, whom France could see, answered. He was French, and young, perhaps in his late twenties or early thirties. Even in winter his face was very tanned. "You never think of the finances. Somehow you believe that the money will always appear, and everything will turn out okay."

"And it always has," the American answered. She could see him throw his hands in a wide gesture in her peripheral vision.

France glanced over as she reached for her

water glass; both men were slim, and the younger one looked like an athlete, as his arms had the sinewy look that France did not at all care for. That would explain his tanned face. A skier? A biker? Neither man drank wine.

"I see it will be up to me," the Frenchman said, leaning toward the American, "once again."

"You don't have to do anything," the American said. "My new ideas are going to work their magic."

The Frenchman snorted in response, pushing his half-eaten salad away from him.

"You're not finishing that, Damien?" the American said. France could see his fork now piercing bits of lettuce and green beans from the athlete's salad.

France, embarrassed for him, buried her head in her book. She wanted to see the American's face, as she recognized his voice. The expat community was small enough in Aix, and he obviously lived and worked here. Many of the expats—especially the Americans—came to the church where she worked.

She looked up just as the waiter came into the room, and she signaled for the bill. The film star and her companions were gone.

"You really get on my nerves, Cole," the younger man said, folding his arms across his chest and sitting back.

France froze, tightly gripping her fork. *Cole;*

she *had* recognized the voice. It was an unusual enough name. He must be Cole Hainsby, the local businessman; she thought he ran some sort of Provence travel company. France knew his wife, Debra, who volunteered at the church. She couldn't remember where they were from; the American Midwest, perhaps. France had never met Cole, as he often had guided tours to give on the weekends. But she certainly knew who he was.

She had spoken to Cole on the telephone, and didn't like his voice. He spoke too quickly, too chirpily, not really listening to her replies. And he was too friendly, and too chatty, even though they had never met. She remembered imagining the big wide grin in his voice as they spoke on the phone. She thought there was an English word for people like him: a phony. He also told France twice, and unnecessarily, that they lived in Saint-Marc-Jaumegarde, a wealthy suburb of Aix.

She quickly gathered her things, now embarrassed to have overheard their conversation. Her hands were shaking. She hoped Cole Hainsby wouldn't recognize her if they ever did meet. As she walked down the stairs to pay her bill at the well-known zinc-topped bar, she felt her face flush. She realized she would be meeting Cole Hainsby this Sunday, at the Christmas concert. He and Debra were this year's hosts.

CHAPTER FOUR

Verlaque looked at the olive orchard and remembered that someone had once said olive groves were God's first temples. But he couldn't remember who. A poet? A politician?

There were fifteen trees, three rows of five, which had been planted ten years previously by his friend Jacob, who sold them the house. It looked easy enough to harvest the fruit, he thought as he looked around, as most of the trees were only about six or seven feet tall; though they would need a ladder to reach the olives on some of the upper branches. He ran his hands along the silvery leaves, delighting in their smoothness. He wouldn't even need gloves; this would be his kind of gardening.

Marine's car pulled up the pebbled driveway and she got out and waved. Verlaque watched her approach him, tall and slender but with a strong, purposeful stride. She wasn't Florence Bonnet's daughter for nothing. In fact, Marine had inherited qualities from both her parents. Her politeness and calm nature came from her father, a retired general practitioner; her quick intellect and drive from her mother, who for years ran the faculty of theology at Aix's university. "I see you've put the nets down,"

Marine said after giving him a kiss. "Good job. Now what?"

Verlaque shrugged. "Bruno was too busy to tell me," he said. "He put the nets and buckets in the back of my car and sped off. Do you think we shake the tree?"

Marine looked up at the blue sky shining through the branches. "That seems awfully harsh, doesn't it? Although olive trees must be the sturdiest trees that exist. They've survived thousands of years of frosts, droughts, parching sunshine . . ."

Verlaque reached up and shook one of the branches and they watched as three fat black olives fell to the ground. "I really don't want to shake it any more than that."

"You're such a softy," she said, kissing him again. "What have we done, buying a house in the country?"

Verlaque laughed. "Listen, we've both been to very good law schools and held down prestigious jobs. So we must be able to figure out how to harvest some olives."

"The green ones mustn't be fully ripe yet," Marine said. "That's why they're hanging on." She reached up and pulled at one, examining it in her hand. "They really are beautiful."

"And so will their olive oil be." He ran his hand along one of the branches, gently pulling at the olives as he went, and a dozen fell to the ground. "There you go!"

Marine did the same, and they worked side by side, in silence, for ten minutes. The net at their feet became littered with green and purple olives. "Antoine, you're stepping on them!"

"*Merde!*"

"Let's gather these ones up and put them in a bucket," Marine said, dropping to her hands and knees.

"It will take forever at this rate," Antoine said, reluctantly following her to the ground.

"But that raking motion we were doing with our hands seemed to work."

"Ah! The rakes!" Verlaque said. "Bruno was angry with himself that he forgot to bring the rakes for us. He said they're these little mini plastic rakes, like kids use at the beach."

"Oh, those would have been useful." Marine sat up and said, "I've just thought of something. I'll be right back." She got up and marched over to the house as Antoine continued to pull olives off the branches, careful where he was putting his feet this time. He looked over at the other trees and couldn't imagine finishing even this tree before it got dark out. It was certainly more cost efficient to buy olive oil straight from the mill. But he continued on, and after a few minutes he was lost in thought, enjoying the sensation of the soft leaves running along his hands.

"Ta-da!" Marine said, now at his side and holding up two small wicker baskets, each with large handles. She handed one to her husband. "We'll gather up the olives in these, and then when they get full, we'll dump them in the buckets."

"Great thinking."

Marine hooked the basket on her left forearm, leaving her right hand free to pick. Verlaque, not to be outdone, found a stubby knob on one of the branches and hooked his basket onto it, leaving both hands free. He held his hands up for effect. Marine laughed. "Let's try to finish at least this one tree before dinner," she said. "Once we get going, I'm sure it will go quickly."

They began picking again, and in less than fifteen minutes both wicker baskets were full. They chatted about their day as they went, and Marine made Antoine laugh with her description of her mother eating a gooey Philly cheesesteak. "The funny thing is, it was really good."

"Of course it *tasted* good," Verlaque said. "That's the problem with fast food."

"Well, I wouldn't really call it fast food!" she said, although Verlaque looked unconvinced.

"You'll never guess who I had lunch with," he said.

"Margaux Perrot?" Marine grinned.

Antoine stopped picking and turned his head toward Marine, surprised. "How in the world?"

"Sylvie saw you leave the office—the café, that is—with Perrot and a man."

"You really can't do anything in Aix in secret."

Marine shook her head, smiling. "So what is she like?"

"Very affable. Her husband, Léo, was a friend of mine at law school, who seems to be one of those guys who every two years has a new business that's bound to fail. The latest is some quarry in North Africa; Tunisia, I think."

"Oh, dear," Marine said. "Margaux must be very patient. What were they doing in Aix?"

"They live here now," Verlaque said. "The exodus from Paris—"

Marine sighed, thinking of the days before Parisians had moved en masse to her town. "Do they have kids?"

"Margaux has two teenagers from her first marriage. They go to some private school north of Aix."

"Private!" Marine said, stopping to pick up a fallen olive. "Why on earth private? The public ones are better."

"I know," Verlaque said. "But her son has been kicked out of public school, so it's an expensive private school for him."

Marine pulled more olives off a branch and watched them drop into her basket. "Kids," she said. Taking a breath, she added, "They must be a lot of worry." She looked over to see Verlaque's reaction, but he continued to pick.

"Yeah, especially spoiled rich kids," he said,

"which is what I was, I suppose, but somehow I came out all right."

"That private school is bilingual," Marine said. "I've heard people talk about it. It's outrageously expensive."

"That's perfect," Verlaque said, "as the kids' father is some American film producer."

Marine said, "Stay still for a second. I'd like to take a photo of you working the land."

"Stop teasing me."

She reached into her coat pocket and pulled out her phone. "Antoine, smile and look over here." Verlaque did as he was told. Marine fussed with her phone, squinting at its tiny screen. She then held it away from her, pointed at Verlaque, waving her index finger in the air before deciding which button to finally press. He laughed and looked at his beautiful wife, whose wavy auburn hair was framed by the silver leaves and blue sky. "It's really quite good," she said, looking at the photograph on her screen. "I'll get it printed and framed for your father for Christmas."

There were so many things he wanted to say at that moment. He had mixed feelings about Christmas and family celebrations; about his father, who lived in Paris with a much younger art historian; about his dead mother, with whom he had never been close; and about his estranged brother. But Marine was already heading into the

45

house to preheat the oven—they were going to eat a small roast beef—so he merely gathered up the net, carefully picking up the stray olives and throwing them into one of the large black bins Bruno had lent him. He placed the baskets and the net on top of the impressive pile of olives in the bin and carried it around the side of the house to a stone outbuilding that housed tools and the summer patio furniture. It was now dark, and by the time he walked into the house he was quite cold. He watched Marine cut narrow slices into the beef with a knife, knowing she would insert a sliver of garlic into each one. She bent over, concentrating, not humming as she usually did when she cooked. He knew why; it was the same reason he had a lump in his throat. Her comment about children had been about them, about their marriage, and it had not gone unnoticed. But he had not answered her.

Did the Aixois ever work, or go home, or sleep? thought Gerhard Rösch as he quickly opened a new pack of paper plates and stacked them on the table in front of him. His neighbor in Tübingen (who had been to Aix the Christmas before and visited this very Sister City fair) had suggested that Gerhard apply for a permit to sell his cheese, sausages, and dumplings. Gerhard, although exhausted, was thankful. It had been excellent advice, as he and Anna desperately needed the money. Nobody in Aix would know that all they owned in Tübingen was a snack shack.

Gerhard knew his products were good, but business back home had suffered since the high school moved into a brand-new building four blocks farther away from his popular snack shack. The high school students had been faithful customers for years, and he and Anna loved to tack up postcards from former students who had graduated, gone to college, traveled (hence the cards), then settled down to work and, sometimes, a family life. Their own sons, Edmund and Clovis, were both in college, both training to be dentists; and just at the time when they needed financial assistance from their parents, Gerhard and Anna had had their lowest annual intake in their twenty-five-year career.

A small queue had formed in front of their tent and he saw that Anna was smiling, listening intently, as her French was much better than his. She turned to him and spoke in quick German, with the lilting accent of her native Black Forest, and asked Gerhard to serve two orders of dumpling soup. He picked up two paper bowls—relieved that they had brought the more expensive, thicker ones with them—and ladled the soup, knowing the French clients would be happy with his dumplings, a recipe passed down in his family for generations.

Gerhard looked up and saw a young woman

across the way, standing erect against a lamp pole, watching him. It was France—he couldn't remember her last name—the girl from the Anglo church, although she wasn't a girl at all; she was at least ten years older than his sons. He had agreed that afternoon that he and Anna would contribute to the dinner at the cathedral, even if it cut into their earnings. He didn't want to be the only sister city to refuse. Was she staring at him, or at Anna? He couldn't quite make it out, with the steam from the dumplings and the glare of the bright Christmas lights. And then he saw the American—the young man who couldn't stop yelling about his steak sandwiches—walk up to France and say something in her ear. She backed away, and the American followed her, grabbing her upper arm. France grimaced and shrugged him off, walking quickly through the crowd. Gerhard froze, not knowing if he should run after her and see if she needed help, or go and rough up the American, who was now walking back to his own tent, hands in his coat pockets, smiling.

Anna had also seen France watching their tent, despite the queue. And while Gerhard was perplexed, Anna wasn't at all.

CHAPTER FIVE

As Damien Petit drove, he tried not to let Cole Hainsby anger him. Or let Cole's actions frighten him. What was Cole thinking, going to *them* for money? Just last month the magazine *Le Point* did a feature article on the Corsican mafia in the South of France and it scared the wits out of him.

Damien pulled his car up in front of the Hainsbys' house, glad they were meeting here this evening. He liked Debra, and kind of felt sorry for her, stuck with Cole. As a bachelor, Damien was always grateful for a home-cooked meal, and Debra was one of those expats determined to master every single dish in the French gastronomical repertoire.

"*Bonsoir!*" Cole called from the open front door.

Damien smiled, thinking perhaps he had been too harsh on Cole. Besides, Americans who signed up for their tours liked his kind of enthusiasm. Didn't they? "Hello," Damien answered, handing Cole a bottle of local red wine.

"Hélène Paulik," Cole said, reading the label. "A woman!"

"Yes! Imagine that!" Damien replied, realizing he was now speaking as loudly as Cole and was teasing him slightly. Damien walked into the living room, where he was glad to see a fire lit in the fireplace. It was cold out—his nose was freezing, a sensation he hated—and the wind was blowing. He grew up in Nice, and the cold winters in this part of Provence had always surprised him. Here they couldn't even grow lemon trees.

"The kids are upstairs," Cole said, taking Damien's coat. "They ate already."

Damien thought of his family back in Nice, and the fact that they had always eaten together, even during the week. He was about to ask if that was an American habit, not to eat together, when Debra came out of the kitchen, wiping her hands on a tea towel.

"They couldn't wait, sorry," she said. "Plus since we'll be talking about the tours tonight, I let them eat this once on their own. Besides, they both have too much homework."

"That's fine," Damien said. "Tell them I say hello."

"Kids!" Cole hollered. "Come down and say hello to Damien!"

Damien heard loud footsteps and remembered that kids always ran, never walked. Mary— Damien guessed that she was about thirteen— gave him the *bises* and Sean, who was a year younger, shook his hand. They ran back upstairs as quickly as they had come down. "Let us know when you're serving dessert, Mom," Sean said from the top of the stairs.

Debra smiled and shrugged. "Lemon tart."

"The French way," Cole cut in, "without the meringue."

"Oh, yum," Damien said, thinking of the lemon tree in his parents' garden in Nice that would now be covered in fruit.

"Cole, serve Damien a glass of white wine while I preheat the plates," Debra said.

Damien's stomach growled at the glorious smells coming from the kitchen. "Thanks," Damien said when Cole handed him a glass of wine.

"I have a great idea for a tour," Cole said, sitting down.

"Really?" Damien helped himself to some salted almonds from a bowl on the coffee table. He supposed it was okay; he was hungry and Cole hadn't offered him any.

"Wait until I'm there, Cole!" Debra called from the kitchen. *Did she need to approve all of Cole's ideas?* Damien wondered. And so they chatted about Aix, complaining about the ongoing construction and then changing the conversation to Marseille's soccer team's recent winning streak.

"A table!" Debra said a few minutes later, coming from the kitchen carrying a large baking dish with oven mitts.

"Coq au vin," Cole said, rubbing his hands together.

"Cole, can you open the wine that Damien brought?" Debra asked as she disappeared back into the kitchen.

"Right!" Cole jumped up from the table, muttering to himself about where the corkscrew was.

"On the side table!" Debra called.

Damien smiled, glad he wasn't married. Debra, it seemed to him, had changed so much over the past year, even the past few months. It was like she had matured, wizened. No, toughened. He watched as Cole opened the wine bottle and poured what Damien considered to be too much wine into each glass. Debra came out of the kitchen carrying another dish. She sat down and looked at the wineglasses and sighed. She caught Damien looking at her and smiled as she served him a piece of chicken with mashed potatoes.

"Purée," Damien said, smiling back. "This is one of my favorite dishes, Debra, and yours looks velvety smooth."

"*Du beurre, du beurre, et encore du beurre,*" Debra said.

Damien laughed. "Escoffier, *bien sûr.*"

"Who's that?" Cole asked.

"A nineteenth-century food writer," Debra replied. "A food tour," she continued, tasting the chicken and deciding she had gotten the ratio of red wine, stock, mushrooms, and salty bacon perfect this time. "Wouldn't that be interesting? Many international food writers have lived in Provence at one time or another."

Cole wiggled his nose, eating the food but, Debra could tell, not truly tasting it. "I have a better idea." He set down his fork and looked from Debra to Damien.

Debra said, "Cole, the business is losing money—"

"This is going to blow you away," Cole said, his eyes wide with excitement. "A salt tour."

"Tasting salt?" Damien asked, coughing.

"The ancient salt route," Cole went on. "They've been moving salt around here for two thousand years!"

"That's true," Damien said. "And it might have been exciting back then, with the Roman roads and bands of thieves hiding along the route, but I'm not sure today's traveler"—he was careful not to say *tourist*—"wants to see that."

Cole continued as if he hadn't heard. "We could start in the Camargue, where they're still harvesting salt, then head along the coast and go as far as Ventimiglia in Liguria, then head up into the mountains, following the route. Even Hannibal used it to his advantage."

Debra tilted her head to one side. "And could salt be a theme in the food you'd be eating along the way? Just last week I tasted the most amazing *dourade* cooked whole in a crust of salt."

Cole looked up. "Where was that?"

"In Marseille," Debra said quickly. "We were there for work."

"Food could be a small part of it," Cole said. "But we'd mostly picnic along the way. Kind of do a rough-and-tumble thing, like in the old days."

Debra and Damien exchanged looks. "Do you mean the Middle Ages?" Debra asked, not hiding her frustration.

"Without cutlery?" Damien added.

"I haven't worked out the details," Cole said, not registering Damien's sarcasm. He held his hands up in the air. "I'm a history nut! I plead innocence!"

"Please serve Damien some more wine," Debra said flatly.

"Cole," Damien said, leaning forward. "The business, as Debra said, is faltering. We hardly have any tours booked, and not much interest coming in on the website." He wondered if Debra knew about Cole's little arrangement with the Corsicans and swallowed nervously.

"It will pick up!" Cole insisted.

Damien raised his voice. "This is serious. I've invested my inheritance from my beloved great-aunt to set this up. I honestly don't think that North Americans will sign up to visit the salt road while having to eat on the cold, damp ground along the way."

"Damien's right," Debra said, half feeling sorry for her husband's ridiculous naïveté. "Your clients will want to go to nice restaurants, see some historic and cultural sites, mixed with some shopping, buying the kinds of local products that you can't get back home."

"That sounds perfect," Damien said, trying to get Cole's attention. "And I've had requests from cycling enthusiasts asking about that kind of tour. With a van up ahead, carrying the luggage."

"The counts of Provence had the salt monopoly throughout the later Middle Ages," Cole went on, "all the way up into Piedmont. Then the lords of Savoy became involved, but I'm a little fuzzy on that bit—"

Debra stopped listening, and instead concentrated on the taste of the wine-soaked chicken, wishing herself elsewhere. Damien swirled some wine around in his mouth and tried to pick out the flavors: Earthiness was all he could get at the moment. The earthy taste of his grave, he thought drily, after the Corsicans come to them to recoup their loan.

In downtown Aix a very different evening was taking place: an aperitif among four girlfriends in the snug salon of Fanny Jacquet. If customers at her bistro felt like they were at Fanny's home, then that was because her apartment had the same interior, filled with bright colors and potted ferns.

She had a fetish for ferns. The walls were painted dark red, or radicchio, as Fanny insisted on calling it. The small sofa was green velvet, and two mismatched armchairs, both blue but in two different shades, sat opposite the sofa separated by a glass coffee table from the 1970s.

Rachida Hammoudi was the first to arrive, and she looked around the apartment as she always did, wondering how anyone could stay sane in such a place. Her own apartment, just around corner on the rue Emeric David, was a haven of calm, inspired by a trip to Stockholm and a series of three boyfriends who had been, respectively, Swedish, Finnish, and Danish. She worked in a busy pharmacy on the Cours Mirabeau, and when she went home she wanted to be surrounded by creamy colors, white candles, and beige throws (in natural fabrics, of course). Indoor plants were tacky, too, she thought; when did you ever see them in a posh interior design magazine? Never. Rachida sat down on the sofa and began busily arranging magazines on the coffee table into a neat stack while Fanny prepared snacks in the kitchen.

"Dida, I know you're tidying out there!" Fanny called from the kitchen as she spread sautéed onions onto freshly made dough. With her finger she picked up anchovy fillets one at a time and laid them around the onions, making a pinwheel pattern.

"Just making some room," Rachida mumbled, holding the magazines and wondering where to put them. She shrugged and shoved the magazines under the sofa.

Fanny set the tart aside, turned on the oven to preheat, and came out of the kitchen carrying a corkscrew and a bottle of chilled white wine. "Can you open this?" she asked, handing both to Rachida. The doorbell rang and Fanny walked over and picked up the receiver. "Hallo, Jennifer," she said, "third and last floor." She hung up and said to Rachida, "That's Jennifer, an American friend. Who knows when Brigitte will get here."

"Brigitte's always last," Rachida said as she popped open the wine bottle. "She has to put the kids to bed. Does Jennifer speak French?"

"Of course!" Fanny answered. "She makes those wonderful cakes for me at the bistro."

"Oh, I know," Rachida said. "Or should I say my hips know."

Fanny looked at her tall, elegant friend with admiration, not envy. Rachida ate like a teenager but never gained weight. She was always envious of Rachida's thick, curly black hair and flawless brown skin. Fanny knew, though, that people who looked like Rachida had other worries to contend with in this old-fashioned community.

It wasn't long before Jennifer arrived and introductions were made. Rachida loved Jennifer's curly red hair and freckles, and was impressed that a reverend's wife would wear a short skirt and silk blouse from the shop Sandro, her own current obsession. "You speak such good French," Rachida said, topping up Jennifer's wineglass.

"Thanks," Jennifer said. "I spent a year in France as a university student—right here in Aix, as a matter of fact."

"Just like Bradley Cooper!" Rachida and Fanny cried in unison, Rachida feigning a swoon.

Within ten minutes Brigitte Plantier had arrived as well, looking frazzled. "Wine, please, any color," Brigitte said as she flopped down on the sofa next to Rachida.

Fanny served pieces of the warm tart on small antique plates.

"Is it a *pissaladière*?" Jennifer asked. "I've never made one."

"So easy," Fanny said. "Do you like anchovies?"

"Oh, yes," Jennifer lied. She took a bite, knowing that she could wash down the hairy fish with a gulp of white wine. She chewed, noting a salty flavor, but nothing too fishy. Jennifer passed a plate of thinly sliced salami to Rachida, who held up her hand.

"Not for me, thanks," Rachida said.

"Oh, I'm so sorry!" Jennifer said. "Pork, right?"

Brigitte snorted. "No pork, but she drinks like a fish."

"I make certain concessions," Rachida said, grinning and grabbing a handful of cashews.

"How many children do you have, Brigitte?" Jennifer asked, since it was clear to her that both Fanny and Rachida were single.

"Two. And you?"

"Two as well," Jennifer said. "Do you work?"

Brigitte took a big gulp of wine. "Yeah, I teach French literature at a private high school."

"The Four Seasons?" Jennifer asked.

"Yes! Do your kids go there?"

"No, they're both at École Sallier."

"Good for you," Fanny said. "That's what I'd do, too, plunk my kids right into a French school."

"Throw them in the deep end," Rachida said.

Brigitte and Jennifer exchanged smiles, taking in the advice of the two nonparents.

"Would you ever teach in a public school?" Jennifer asked.

"I didn't get my French teaching papers," Brigitte said. "I was living in Montreal—my husband, Yves, is Quebecois—and after we got married we moved here to be closer to my family, when I was already pregnant with our first child. The second came along a year after, and I just never had the time to take the exams, and so even though I have a master's degree in French lit, I'm at the mercy of Alain Sorba."

Jennifer nodded, not letting on that she knew

Sorba through her husband's church. "Teachers are better off in the public system here?"

Brigitte guffawed. "Fewer hours, better pay, and a good civil servant retirement."

"Plus here in France, the students who get sent to private schools are brats," Rachida said.

"Dida," Fanny said. "Now, now."

"It's basically true with most of the French students," Brigitte said. "But my international students are brilliant." She thought of Mary Hainsby, in particular.

Fanny excused herself to retrieve the next course from the kitchen—a mushroom soup with cream and chervil, her new favorite herb—and the conversation turned to the latest Paolo Sorrentino film that Jennifer, relieved, had seen at one of the two downtown art house cinemas. "I'll bring out a second bottle of wine," Fanny called from the kitchen.

"More like the third," Brigitte called back.

"Three already?" Fanny asked, poking her head around the corner. "Everyone is on foot tonight, right?"

"Yes!" the other three answered in unison.

"Oh, I almost forgot to tell you! I saw Margaux Perrot the other day," Rachida said. "Walking up the Cours with her husband and our examining magistrate."

Brigitte said, "Her kids go to the Four Seasons."

"Judge Verlaque was looking glum as usual," Rachida continued.

"Maybe your magistrate doesn't like the chalets, or Christmas," Jennifer offered.

Fanny reappeared carrying a tray with four bowls of soup. "I'm with you on the chalets. Anyway, Antoine Verlaque eats all the time at my bistro and he's anything but glum."

"And I went to the same high school as his wife," Brigitte said. "How's that for small-town gossip?"

"My head is swimming," Jennifer said.

"I'm sorry, I didn't prepare the soup as I usually do, with a pastry crust on top," Fanny said as she distributed the bowls.

"Well, that's it, I'm leaving," Rachida teased, tossing her napkin on the coffee table.

"What were you doing all day?" Brigitte asked, laughing. "You could have at least bought premade pastry at Monoprix."

Fanny's hands shook from laughing as she passed around spoons and cloth napkins. "I have never . . . in my life . . . bought premade pastry. I wouldn't even know where to find it."

"In the refrigerated section by the milk and butter," replied Jennifer and Brigitte in unison.

CHAPTER SIX

It was a sunny, cold morning as the Reverend Dave Flanagan walked, his hands in his pockets, whistling "All Things Bright and Beautiful." He enjoyed walking from his apartment in La Torse, just east of downtown, to the church; he was relieved that a furnished apartment came with the job, and that it was easy walking distance to the city center. The Protestant church of Aix-en-Provence was located on a small street to the east of the much larger church La Madeleine. It wasn't a spectacular building, having been built in the late nineteenth century for local Anglicans—mostly English—who lived near Aix. The church, with its single nave, held more than two hundred celebrants.

He stopped on the rue des Bretons to read, painted on a wall, an old sign that he had vaguely noticed before, but now he was able to pick out a word, as the sun was shining directly on the faded letters: STREET, in English. He looked up, squinting, and was amazed, as not only one word but the entire text was in English. He switched songs, to a Christmas carol, "Hope Was Born This Night," humming as he took a photograph of the sign with his cell phone. "This street off-limits for American and Canadian soldiers," Dave said aloud, pausing on each word as he managed to decipher the much-faded letters. "Why on earth?" He shook his head, confused.

"*Mais oui,*" a voice sounded behind him. "*Interdit aux soldats Américains!*"

"*Et les Canadiens apparemment!*" Dave said, smiling at an old man now standing beside him. "But why? *Pourquoi?*"

The old man, his small face red from the cold, pointed up to the building, which to Dave's eye looked like any other old apartment in Aix. "*Une maison close!*"

"A closed house?" Dave repeated. He didn't understand what *close* meant in French. Was it an adoption of the English word? He made a gesture with his hands, crossing them into an X. "Closed? *Fermée?*"

The old man laughed, grabbing Dave's forearm. "*Mais non!* Not at all closed!" He laughed again. "Very open!" He then made his own hand gesture, that of a shapely, very buxom woman.

"Good Lord," Dave said. "A bordello? A brothel?"

"*Mais si! Un bordel!*"

Dave, pleased with his French, knew that *si* was a very emphatic "yes." He also now realized what it meant when his French colleagues used the expression *un bordel* when they thought Dave's office was too messy. "But why no foreign soldiers?" he asked.

"Le Claridge was one of Aix's best brothels," the old man said in rapid-fire French. Dave found himself leaning in, trying to understand, fascinated. "Their clients were Aix's elite, and they didn't want rowdy foreign soldiers disturbing, um, their tranquility."

"Was it legal?"

"Certainly! Until 1946. There were five brothels in Aix, and hundreds in Paris."

"Is that so?"

"But don't worry," the old man continued. "Your boys had somewhere they could go."

"Oh?" Dave asked, shocked.

"Les Milles! La Pioline."

"You mean where the supermarket is?"

The old man laughed. "Have a good day," he said. "It's going to get colder later in the week."

Dave reached out and shook the old man's hand, which he had politely removed from his leather glove. "Thank you for the history lesson," Dave said.

"Aix is full of surprises," the old man said. "You just have to look around. I live down the street, and most people walk right by that old painted sign. You didn't."

Dave smiled, warmed by his words. "I'm sometimes a little too curious," he said. "I'm often late for things!" He looked at his watch and laughed; it was already 9:30 and he was to host a lunch meeting with some of the parishioners who would be helping at the Christmas service on Sunday.

The old man smiled and saluted, walking away. Dave watched him, admiring his straight posture and elegant wool coat and hat. He looked up at Le Claridge, which now had flower boxes in the windows and white lace curtains. Could the old man have been in Aix before 1946? Dave did a quick calculation; if the man was in his eighties or nineties, he would have been born around 1925. That would have made him about twenty years old just before Le Claridge was closed. The reverend shuddered and walked on, amused and disturbed that his new friend could have been a client. Or perhaps his father was? Could he have been sent out by his mother to fetch his father? "Go now, son, and get your father for dinner! He's at that damn Claridge again!" Dave began to hum, trying to get that disturbing scenario out of his head. But he would have fun telling Jennifer, his wife, about the sign and the old man's story. She was much more liberal than he was. She even liked French cinema.

Jennifer Flanagan helped France Dubois carry plates and cutlery from the kitchenette into the Protestant church's small but frequently used dining hall. The organizing committee was about to meet to discuss the quickly approaching carol sing at the cathedral. As the pastor's wife, she really didn't have to do this, but Jennifer enjoyed helping out when she could, especially since the carol sing was one of her husband's biggest days of the year.

"Sorry, France, but I'm moving a little slowly today," Jennifer said. "I was out with some girlfriends last night." She was about to add some details but then realized that she might be hurting France's feelings; she wondered, did the quiet France Dubois have friends? What would she have thought of the evening at Fanny's?

"It's so kind of you to come and help," France said, with no trace of jealousy or sadness. "The Hainsbys are here, as are the McGregors and M Sorba."

"Alain Sorba?" Jennifer asked, thinking of Brigitte and her job at Sorba's private school. "Why?"

"Some of the kids from the bilingual school are helping out during the service and afterward at the Sister City dinner."

"Oh, that makes sense," Jennifer said. She was about to ask where the bread was when they both heard a glass break out in the dining room.

"I'm so sorry, France," Debra Hainsby said as she came rushing into the small kitchen. "Cole was gesturing as he spoke. . . . It was a wineglass. . . . I'll get it."

"They're under the sink," France called over her shoulder as she walked into the dining room

66

and set down the quiche on a large wooden table that she and Reverend Dave had carried into the middle of the room. "Quiche Lorraine, everybody!"

"Does it have bacon?" Cole asked.

"Yes, of course," France answered, trying not to show her exasperation. She wanted to add *quiche Lorraine always does.*

"Why, Cole?" Jennifer asked as she walked into the room carrying three baguettes. "Don't you eat meat?"

"I'm a vegetarian," Cole answered.

"Since yesterday," Debra Hainsby added as she walked back into the room carrying the broom and dustpan.

"Let me help you with that," Dave Flanagan said, bending down on one knee and holding the dustpan for her.

"There's a tomato and basil quiche, too," Jennifer Flanagan said. "I'll go and get it."

"Being a vegetarian will be difficult for you in France," Alain Sorba said.

"Oh, I don't think so," Cole answered, grabbing a handful of peanuts and throwing almost half of them in his mouth. A few stragglers fell to the floor. Sorba winced. "Especially here in Provence."

"That is true," Sorba said slowly, in heavily accented English. "There is a lot of fish here."

Cole Hainsby shook his head back and forth.

"You don't eat fish, either?" Sorba asked, his dark eyes wide with amazement.

"No, never liked the taste."

"Well, you'll save a lot of money eating that way!" Jim McGregor said.

"Jim, you sound a little too much like a Scotsman," his wife, Claudie, said in accented English, holding him by the arm. France looked at Claudie McGregor and saw, from her smiling face, that she was joking, teasing her husband. It seemed to France that Claudie, despite being *une* Aixoise by birth, had acquired the dry humor of the British.

"Well, this morning's meeting was very useful," Reverend Dave announced, picking up a bottle of red wine. "So I suggest we all have a little tipple, to congratulate ourselves on what I believe will be a fantastic Christmas service this Sunday."

"Real wineglasses," Alain Sorba said, holding one up and admiring it. "I'm impressed."

"I insisted," Jennifer Flanagan said. "When we arrived here, there was a stack of plastic ones in the kitchen. Not only are they bad for the environment, but they change the taste of a wine."

"Hear, hear!" Jim McGregor said, lifting up his glass. "A very sound investment you've made for our little church."

"*Jamais*! *Jamais*!" Claudie McGregor said, shuddering. "I could never drink wine from plastic, even if it is not a very fine wine, *non*?"

"I'd like to thank you for passing the torch to us," Cole Hainsby said, pointing his glass in the McGregors' direction, not noticing the red wine swirling dangerously close to the top. "Debra and I are thrilled to be hosting the carol sing this Sunday."

"No need to thank us," Claudie McGregor said, pursing her lips.

France knew what Claudie meant; the decision had not been theirs. Cole Hainsby had hassled Dave so much that the newly appointed reverend finally conceded. The McGregors had been hosting the service for years.

"You will be wonderful," Alain Sorba said, looking at Debra Hainsby.

Debra smiled and looked up at Sorba, blushing.

France, mildly embarrassed, began serving the quiche while Dave poured out the wine, or sparkling water for those who preferred. Jennifer stepped up and began helping France, and they chatted about the sister cities as they served. Jennifer commented on how generous the cities were, to both attend the service and then contribute food for the dinner afterward. "Oh, yes," France said. "The Italians were especially excited."

Jennifer laughed. "I wouldn't have expected anything less than that kind of enthusiasm coming from Italians. Are the Americans helping out?"

"Yes."

Jennifer looked at France, expecting her to say more, but she was simply twirling her glass around in her hand, watching the wine slide down the sides. She certainly was an oddball.

France finally said, "The Germans were rather reserved, almost as if they were undecided."

"I don't want to say that that sounds very German," Jennifer said, "the same way I just made a cliché about Italians."

"I've met very generous, outgoing Germans," France said.

"Oh, so have I," Jennifer said, nodding. "It's their first time in Aix, isn't it? Perhaps they're shy, or they don't know what to expect."

"Yes, I thought the same thing," France said. "Not everyone likes the idea of going to church, either."

"But it's really more about singing carols, and being together," Jennifer said.

"Yes, I know, but sometimes—"

"Cole!" Debra Hainsby called out. "That's not your plate!"

France held tightly on to her own plate and glanced at Jennifer, who returned her look with a gentle smile and a shrug of the shoulders.

"You really have to be more careful," Debra Hainsby said, sighing. "You were eating off of Jim McGregor's plate!"

"Well, I just set my plate down on the table two

seconds ago," Cole said. "I got them mixed up."

"That's no problem, no problem at all," Jim McGregor said. "My fault for setting my plate down next to yours, as I was greedy and wanted to pour myself more wine."

"Your plate had the quiche Lorraine on it, Jim," Claudie McGregor said. "You didn't see it, Cole?"

Alain Sorba let out a forced laugh and said, "Musical plates!"

Debra Hainsby set her empty plate down on the table with a loud bang and turned on her heel and fled, sobbing.

CHAPTER SEVEN

Damien Petit carefully set his bicycle down on what looked like clumps of wild thyme. He could smell its lemony fragrance, or at least he thought he could; it was mixed with pine needles and other wild herbs that made up the garrigue. Taking off his small backpack, he lowered himself onto the dry ground and rested his back against a pine tree. He looked at the looming Mont Sainte-Victoire, Cézanne's obsession. The craggy white mountain was still about a fifteen-minute bike ride away, but given its size it looked much closer. It was almost as if he could reach out and touch it. He opened his pack and took out a ham sandwich and began eating, thinking of Cézanne and how the artist would walk daily, even into his sixties, the route that Damien had just biked. Damien would like to have such an obsession—sure, he loved sports, and he had figured out how to make a living out of them— but was he consumed like Cézanne? No, he knew he wasn't.

As he ate, lamenting the fact that *boulangeries* never added mustard to their ham sandwiches, he thought of Cézanne's paintings, and the fact that he had never liked them—or *appreciated* them— until a former girlfriend dragged him into a small museum in Paris and he found himself in front of a Cézanne landscape. He couldn't move. Up until then, Damien had seen only a handful of Cézannes, and they were still lifes and portraits. The painting before him—he had continued staring even after his girlfriend had moved on—was a small forest opening onto a grove of dark green pine trees, with the blue sky peeking through and the red earth below. The painting's label explained that it was a scene in Le Tholonet, the village he had just ridden through, now home to Swiss millionaires and Parisian CEOs. But the view was much like where he now sat. Damien had grown up in Aix, and it was the first time he had seen a landscape so familiar to him but, transformed onto canvas, made different. It was beyond realistic; although the colors and shapes were true enough, they were exaggerated, as they often are in Provence. The greens so green, the blue sky so bright it hurt your eyes. It was majestic.

And that's what bothered him so much about working with Cole Hainsby. Cole didn't have the capacity to see—to really see, or be moved by— art. Damien knew that he was still learning (the girlfriend no longer in his life), and there was still much he didn't know, or had never seen. But he now knew that he was capable of understanding. Cole was too jumpy; he couldn't keep still long enough to concentrate. And his head was always racing onto the next idea—usually a bad one, Damien now knew, too. But Damien, much like many of their clients, had been charmed by Cole, taken in by his enthusiasm. That was part of the problem: Cole was enthused by everything. He had no guidelines, no barriers. Once you got to know him, his enthusiasm wore on you. Damien saw that Debra Hainsby was exasperated by her husband. He sighed, knowing that he was, too. His cell phone rang and he looked down at it, annoyed. It was Cole.

"Hi, Cole," Damien said as he stared straight ahead at the mountain.

"Where are you?"

"I'm taking a bike ride around Mont Sainte-Victoire," Damien said. "Remember? I told you I was going to do that today."

"Oh, right. Listen, you need to come back to Aix. I have some ideas about tours in the Languedoc we can do."

"Cole," Damien said, trying to stay calm, "the Languedoc is a beautiful place, but our specialty is Provence. We should stick to one region. It makes us more credible."

"No, we're missing out—"

"Besides, I can't come back to Aix now as I haven't gone around the mountain yet. I'm timing it for our experienced bike tour."

"The Cévennes is a really great area, too. Very undiscovered—"

Damien held his phone out and looked at it. Had Cole just heard any of his points? "Cole, I agree that we need to talk, but not about future tours in regions we know nothing about. We need to talk about the meeting you had last week. I'm still not happy about it."

"What meeting?"

Damien now let out an audible sigh and looked around before he answered. He was about to speak when a sudden paranoia that his cell phone might be tapped made him stop. "You know the one," he said. "And don't say their name on the phone!"

Cole said, "They're great guys. You have no idea—"

"No, no, Cole. They are not great guys."

"You've never met them!"

"I've heard about them," Damien said. "I grew up in Aix. They're Corsican, they're—" Again, he looked around, but no one had driven by for ten minutes. There were no sounds except the birds and the wind. "They're . . . dangerous. You can't just go to those kinds of guys and ask for a business loan."

"Why didn't you say something last year, when I told you about it?"

"Because, Cole, you didn't tell me you went to the *Corsicans* for money. You said *friends*. How was I to know? And now your *friends* want us to pay, right?" Damien looked at his phone again,

75

now frightened. Could they be listening to the conversation? They were capable of that. They were capable of much worse; he read about their escapades in *La Provence* all the time. "I told you at the time we should go to our bank for a loan. But you didn't listen."

"Well, you needn't worry as I've calmed down Jean-Paul and Michel—"

"Idiot! Don't say their names!" Damien yelled. "Calmed them down? How on earth?" He looked up as he heard a car drive slowly up the road, its tires crunching as they rolled over the dried pine needles.

"I said we had a new plan—"

"We?"

"Yes, they know all about you."

Damien's mouth felt so dry that even if he knew what to say, which he didn't, the words wouldn't be able to escape his mouth. The car had now stopped. It was a black BMW two-door sedan. Damien swallowed again, and looked at his bicycle. Could he outrace a BMW? No, as he had brought his road bike and not the mountain bike. He could hear Cole chatting away, but all his concentration was focused on the car, the make and color he had always associated with criminals in Provence. He couldn't see how many people were in the car, as the windows were tinted. Of course. He reached for his water bottle, his hands shaking. "I'll call you after I get home and shower," Damien said, trying not to stutter.

"Okay, hurry up, then," Cole answered.

Damien hung up and started to put his lunch wrappings in his backpack. The BMW driver's window slowly opened a few inches, not enough for Damien to see inside. He began to whistle, pretending that he hadn't even noticed the car. The engine was now turned off and the driver slowly opened his door. A black-panted leg with a shiny black dress shoe poked out. Damien began to sweat; this was not the attire of a hiker or a sightseeing tourist. He began to breathe deeply and make a plan. He was in shape, probably much better than the Orezza brothers combined. But that wouldn't help him if they were armed. The leg hadn't moved, and he could now hear a voice. A deep male voice.

Damien was about to stand up when the driver of the BMW finally emerged. He was tall and broad shouldered, wearing a suit and tie, but he looked older than Damien had imagined the Corsican brothers to be. At least twenty years older. It was difficult to make out his features, as Damien was too afraid to stare.

The man was about to close his door when he stopped and reached back into the car and picked something up off the seat. He closed the door and began walking toward Damien, holding the retrieved item in the crook of his arm. Damien got up, now prepared to run through the woods.

He could surely outrun them. He planted his feet, feeling his toes dig into the ground and his calf muscles tighten. When the man was about ten yards away, Damien braced himself, turning his body, prepared to sprint. Then the passenger door opened, and a woman slowly emerged, wiping her brow. An old woman.

"Excuse me," the driver called out to Damien in heavily accented French. He held up what he had been so carefully cradling in the crook of his arm. It was a map. "*Sprechen Sie Deutsch?*"

CHAPTER EIGHT

Antoine Verlaque sat in the living room, in his favorite armchair, with his feet resting on the coffee table. He stretched, relaxed, thinking about the Sunday lunch he and Marine had just finished and enjoyed very much. They had done the market shopping together early that morning, then come back to their Aix apartment to cook. Each had chosen a dish out of a book of farmhouse recipes that Verlaque had inherited from his grandparents, the pages stained and some slipping away from the binding.

Marine had chosen a *garniture* of fresh chestnuts, walnuts, fennel, and onions; it had taken the two of them, and a careful reading of the cookbook, to rid the chestnuts of their tough outer shells. "Passing the bar was easier," Verlaque had joked. But they found that heating the chestnuts in hot oil separated the shells from the meat in a matter of minutes, and when they had cooled Marine was able to peel them, removing the shell and the inner skin. The result was delicious—Marine had been worried that it would be lacking a strong flavor, but that's what they both ended up liking so much about the dish: its delicacy. The pearl onions and fennel blended in beautifully—with the help of chicken stock and butter—with the two types of nuts.

Verlaque's selection was faster to prepare but, in his opinion, hardly easier: crispy sautéed potatoes fried in duck fat. "I have to rinse the potatoes," he had complained, adjusting his reading glasses so that he could see the recipe's small print, "twice."

"Mm-hm," Marine replied as she stirred her walnuts. "Why is that?"

"To rid of them of their starch, so they won't stick to the pan."

"That's sounds like a good idea, then," Marine said.

"And I salt and pepper them only *after* they've browned," Verlaque said. "Otherwise they'll become soggy."

"Who would have thought that potatoes could be so complicated?" Marine said, grinning. She had had no idea that her husband could find a cookbook so absorbing. But he always surprised her.

"That last note is written in by hand," he went on, holding up the cookbook, "by Emmeline."

"How sweet," Marine said, looking at his English grandmother's careful cursive penmanship. "She was so refined; she fit in equally well in Paris high society and in the Normandy countryside."

"Do you think we're doing well in the country?"

"You can hardly compare the Aix countryside to Normandy," Marine said, setting down her wooden spoon. "There aren't many farmers here."

"Millionaire winegrowers."

"Exactly," Marine said. "It was fun sleeping here in the apartment last night, and walking to the market."

"I thought so, too," Verlaque said. "I miss the apartment. But just wait until the warm weather, we can go swimming every day at the house. During the winter, downtown always seems better. By the way, why am I cooking two dishes, and you only one?"

"Because it will take you no time at all to fry the pork chops," Marine answered. "What will you fry them in?"

Verlaque had shrugged and then picked up the jar of duck fat he had bought at the butcher's.

Marine had laughed. "Ask a stupid question . . ."

The meal had been delicious, and he wished he could now smoke a cigar, but, even as a cigar lover, it would be unfair to Marine given that the windows were closed. He sighed and sat up straight as Marine brought him an espresso and the sugar bowl. "Thank you," he said, taking some sugar with an impossibly tiny spoon that Marine seemed to love. "Aren't you having one?"

"I just did," Marine said. "You dozed off there."

"Did I?"

"Yes, but only for ten minutes or so. We have to go soon—"

"Where? On this quiet Sunday afternoon?"

"The Christmas service," Marine replied. "Don't tell me you forgot about it."

Verlaque groaned.

A stream of people flowed up the pedestrian street leading to the cathedral. Verlaque frowned as Marine took his arm.

"It's going to be lovely," she said. "My mother is looking forward to seeing you. And so is Philomène Joubert. You remember her, my former neighbor, and she sings in the choir with Maman . . ."

Verlaque snorted. "The wild women of Saint-Jean-de-Malte."

"Behave."

"How will I chat up your mother and Philomène if they're busy singing in the choir?"

"The dinner afterward," Marine replied.

Verlaque stopped. "What dinner?"

Marine pulled him toward the front doors of the cathedral, where a group of people had formed, waiting to go in. She continued, with artificial glee, "I got us invited to the celebratory dinner after the service!"

"That's not even funny."

Marine laughed.

Verlaque said, "I was planning on a nice quiet dinner with you."

"Aren't you sick of being with me all the time?"

Verlaque kissed her forehead. "Never. I want you all to myself."

Marine smiled, but something in her ached. She thought of their olive harvest a few nights earlier, and the nonconversation they had about children. She looked at her husband, who was reading a plaque to the right of the cathedral's door. "Come on, the line's moving," she said. "I want to get a good seat."

"All right, Madame Bossy," Verlaque replied, quickly finishing the plaque's text. "Did you know this about Cézanne?"

"Know what?"

"That toward the end of his life he stood outside the cathedral after Mass on Sundays and gave out money to the poor—"

"Mmm," Marine muttered as they walked in. "It surprises me for some reason that Cézanne would go to Mass."

"Well it didn't actually say that he went to the Mass," Verlaque said. "Only that he gave out money afterward. It also specifies that it was at the end of his life. Maybe he was getting nervous, wanting to get on the good—"

"*Bienvenue!*" a cheery voice rang out, and the young woman responsible gave each of them a thin booklet and a small white candle on a paper plate. "Please don't light the candle until told, and hand the song booklet back to us at the end of the service!"

"Okay!" Verlaque replied with exaggerated enthusiasm.

Marine poked him in the ribs. "Let's go get a seat," she whispered, pulling his hand.

"The church is packed," Verlaque said as they walked up the far right aisle, scanning the pews for a free spot. "It's like Midnight Mass—"

"It's even busier than that," Marine replied. "As we still have forty-five minutes before the service begins."

"What?!"

"Maman warned me of the crowds, so I got us here early."

Verlaque sighed. "I should have brought some poetry to read."

"You can study the song lyrics."

Verlaque looked at his wife, who was grinning from ear to ear. "There," Marine said, pointing to a small vacant spot in the middle of a pew about halfway up the aisle. "*Pardon!*" she said as she made her way for it, past a dozen people who were already sitting down. "*Pardon!*"

Verlaque shrugged and followed. "So sorry," he said in English.

They squeezed together in a space big enough for one and a half people. Verlaque leaned in to Marine and said, "Everyone's so cheery here, even when we made our way across all their legs just now. That's the Anglo-Saxons for you. The French would have been grumpy, giving us a hard time—"

"We are French," the woman next to him said.

Verlaque turned to her. She was a handsome woman in her sixties, sitting next to a man, perhaps her husband, who was bent over studying the songs.

"I'm so sorry," Verlaque said.

She smiled. "We've been coming to this service for years. You'll see; many of us are locals here today. It's just such a wonderful opportunity to sing Christmas carols."

"I agree!" Marine said, leaning over Verlaque so that she could see the woman.

"Well," Verlaque said, shooting Marine a look with a raised eyebrow, "I guess I'd better start looking at these lyrics. Since the service isn't starting for another forty minutes."

Marine looked at her watch. "Any minute now," she said. "Look! Here come Maman and the rest of the choir."

"Where's your father today?" Verlaque asked. "How did he get out of this?"

"He's at a medical conference in Lyon."

"Retired doctors still go to conferences?"

"When they're all-expenses paid, with lunches and dinners in Lyonnais restaurants, they do."

"Of course. Especially given your mother's cooking."

Marine laughed, despite herself.

"While you were studying the congregation,"

Verlaque said, "I memorized all of the songs, plus had a look around the church. Do you see those three tiny windows cut into the stone wall behind us? Up about two stories?"

Marine turned her head and looked behind her, and up. "Above the chapel of Saint Roch?"

"If you say so, yes," Verlaque said, annoyed that Marine knew the name of the chapel. Saint Roch was Aix's patron saint. "Any idea what they're for?" He crossed his arms, waiting.

Marine looked back to him and then scanned the crowd again. "They were for the sick, so that they could come to Mass but be cut off from the rest of the congregation. In case they were contagious."

She turned again to have another look at the three oddly shaped openings. "Wait a minute!"

"What?"

"I just saw someone up there."

Verlaque quickly looked around. "I don't see anyone."

Marine shrugged. "It was just a flash. Perhaps it was nothing."

"Oh, look, something's finally about to happen," Verlaque whispered. "The head honcho's taking the mic."

"The cathedral rector," Marine corrected.

"Welcome, everyone!" the priest's voice rang out. "It is an honor for me, and the congregation of this glorious cathedral, to share our space with the Anglo-Saxon community today in this celebration of the Lord's birth. Leading the service will be my esteemed colleague from Aix's Protestant Anglo-Saxon church, Reverend David Flanagan, who insists I call him Reverend Dave—" Laughter broke out among the congregation and the priest paused, smiling. "I'd also like to thank the choir of Saint-Jean-de-Malte. This has always been a magnificent celebration, and each year I am amazed that so many people from so many different countries and backgrounds come here to pray, to sing, to be with their neighbors. Those of you who haven't been to this service before will know what I mean when we sing "The Twelve Days of Christmas." And so in these days of Europe closing in on itself, and closing its doors to those who try to escape hardships, escape war, escape poverty, let us remember this day, when we sang together no matter our differences . . ."

"Whoa, our padre's getting political," Verlaque whispered.

"Yes! Take that and shove it, Marine Le Pen and your Front Nationale," Marine whispered back.

The priest went on, "And now I'll take a step back and enjoy sitting here as a spectator. Please, Reverend Dave," he said, gesturing to his spot in front of the lectern, "it's all yours!"

Thunderous applause broke out, as much for the priest as for the young Protestant reverend, Verlaque thought. He looked around at the packed cathedral and whispered to Marine, "This must have been what Sundays looked like not so long ago."

"You mean a full church?"

"Precisely."

"And it's warm in here for once," Marine whispered. "All these people . . ."

"There can't be that many expats in Aix," Verlaque whispered back. "Or I would have known about it."

Marine smirked. How would he have known about it? Just because he's the examining magistrate? "Foreign university students," Marine replied. "Here on the Erasmus exchange. I would always have a few sign up for my history of law class."

"Of course—"

The Reverend Dave said a few words of welcome and then introduced the masters of ceremony, Cole and Debra Hainsby.

"Please stand for our first song, "Joy to the World," found on page three of your booklet," Cole said.

Debra Hainsby then repeated the instructions in French. Verlaque rolled his eyes and whispered, "Is the whole service going to be bilingual? It's hardly necessary. I'm sure everyone here knows how to say 'page three' in both languages."

Marine held her fingers up to her lips and opened her songbook.

• • •

An hour later the ambiance in the cathedral was euphoric to Marine. She couldn't imagine anyone not enjoying this service. She glanced over at her husband, who was listening intently to Reverend Dave's sermon, which was, like the priest's, centered upon inclusiveness and openness to others. She smiled as she thought of the young immigrant from Mali who in May had scaled an apartment building in Paris to save a toddler hanging precariously from a fourth-story balcony. When interviewed, the young man, evidently ill at ease with his new fame as a hero, simply shrugged and said that he climbed the balconies without thinking of himself, or the danger involved, but only of the child. The next day he was invited by the *président de la république* to the Élysée Palace and was given immediate citizenship, and a job as a firefighter. *Take that, Front Nationale*, Marine thought for the second time that afternoon. *There's room, and a role, for everyone here.*

The reverend ended his sermon and the Hainsbys returned to the lectern. "And now, the moment you've all been waiting for," Cole Hainsby said, " 'The Twelve Days of Christmas.' For those of you who have been at this service before, you know how it goes. We'll divide the congregation up into twelve parts. Twelve groups of countries, that is. France, the US with Canada, the UK with Ireland, Italy, Spain and Portugal, Germany and its German-speaking neighbors, eastern Europe including Belgium and Holland, Australia and New Zealand, China and Japan, Africa . . . sorry folks, I know it's a continent but we only have twelve slots . . ."

Verlaque groaned and whispered, "*Quel con.*"

"Shhh, Antoine," Marine scolded, though she privately agreed.

Cole Hainsby went on, "The Middle East and Israel . . . behave, you two! Haha! And, finally, Scandinavia."

"We'll repeat the order once again," Debra Hainsby said, her face red. "And we'll call out your country as we sing. When your country is called, please stand!"

Despite Cole Hainsby's tasteless jokes, the song was a huge success, with citizens around the world proudly hopping to their feet to loudly sing their line of the song. Marine pulled at Verlaque when he stood a second time during the third verse, when the UK was called. "Antoine!" she hissed. "You already stood up with the French!"

"My grandmother! Emmeline!" Verlaque replied, louder than he meant to.

Marine and Verlaque clapped as the group of veiled women to their left stood up and sang during the Middle East verse, and the Swedish family behind them joined in afterward.

By the end of the song the whole congregation

was laughing and chatting, so much so that Reverend Dave had to wait a few minutes for everyone to quiet down. "Well, that was certainly a success!" he bellowed. "And now it's time for a more solemn moment, as our celebration is at an end. The lights of the cathedral will be turned off, as it's now dark outside, and your candles will be lit by ushers passing up and down the aisles."

A dozen men and women began to walk through the church, handing a lit candle to the person at the beginning of each row, who then passed it down their row, so that everyone could light their own candle. In less than ten minutes hundreds of candles were lit and the lights were switched off. Marine gasped at the beauty of the scene.

"Please stand," Reverend Dave said. "We will sing 'O Christmas Tree,' found on page—"

"Seven," Verlaque said as he quickly stood up, tossing his songbook on the bench. "I know this one by heart!"

Marine beamed as she listened to her husband's out-of-tune baritone. She knew he must know the lyrics thanks to Emmeline. The congregation sang two verses, and then the music faded away. Reverend Dave said, "And now you may sit down, and I'd like to ask the German-speaking members to stand and please sing us a verse in German."

About fifty Germans, Austrians, and Swiss, scattered around the cathedral, stood up and sang loudly and clearly. Marine's eyes filled with tears. A few rows up she recognized the German couple from the Sister City market, singing with what looked like bravado. Verlaque put his arms around her and pulled her close. "It's so much nicer in German," he whispered. Marine nodded in agreement. Verlaque raised an eyebrow as he saw Reverend Dave check his cell phone and quickly leave by a side door. Couldn't the call have waited?

Cole and Debra Hainsby stepped up to the lectern as the song ended. "Thank you all for attending this glorious service," Cole said. "The lights will come back on in a few, then you can extinguish your candles." He continued, "On your way out, please don't forget to hand in your song—"

"He's so annoying," Marine whispered, tuning out the emcee. She turned to Verlaque, who was playing with his candle, running his hand back and forth over the flame to the amusement of a small boy in the pew ahead who was watching, spellbound.

CHAPTER NINE

Noise from the cathedral's dining hall boomed across the courtyard as Marine and Verlaque walked across, arm in arm. "You're glad you came, I take it," Marine said, squeezing his arm.

"Yes, thank you," he answered. "I didn't know what to expect—"

"Which causes fear—"

"Certainly not!" Verlaque said, laughing at himself.

"The food smells wonderful," Marine said as they passed through a set of large wooden double doors. The scene before them was just as festive as—if not more than—in the cathedral. Dozens of candles lit the large space, along with electric wall sconces. A row of six or seven long tables lined the back of the hall, each covered in a white tablecloth and laden with food. Groups of people Marine didn't know stood awkwardly behind each table. "The sister cities," she whispered. "My mother told me that many of them offered food for tonight."

"That's so kind," Verlaque said.

"Let's get a glass of wine," Marine suggested. "Then I'm going to go and say hello to Maman." They walked across the room, carefully zigzagging through groups of chatting people, to the wine table. Verlaque beamed as he saw Olivier Bonnard, one of his favorite winemakers, pouring out glasses of red. A few years back, Verlaque had helped Olivier by solving a case of missing historic vintages, stolen from his cellar.

"M Bonnard," Verlaque said, shaking Olivier's hand.

"Antoine!" Bonnard answered. He handed Verlaque a glass.

Verlaque turned to where he thought Marine should be, but she had been stopped by her mother and Philomène Joubert. Verlaque smiled, glad to have evaded their attack.

"What's new at Domaine Beauclaire?" Verlaque asked, taking a sip and nodding appreciatively.

"Winter. A time of rest," Bonnard said. "We just got the branch cuttings done last week. Victor's coming home from his first semester at university next week. He absolutely loves it."

"Congratulations," Verlaque said. He liked Victor, a boy who, despite the fame of Domaine Beauclaire, was *bien dans sa peau*. "He's studying enology, right? Montpellier?"

"*C'est exact.*"

"And Elise?"

"She's over there," Olivier said, pointing across the room to his handsome wife. "I'm donating the wines tonight, and she lent out a load of fancy serving dishes from her shop."

"So that's why the hall doesn't look like a church basement," Verlaque said.

Someone reached across Verlaque's chest and grabbed a glass, striking up a conversation with Olivier about the wines, so Verlaque moved away from the table and began looking around the room. He was happy, and to his surprise, he was happy during the Christmas season. The joy of the carol sing seemed to hang in the air. People toasted one another and laughed. No longer shy, the guests had formed a line at the food tables, and the Sister City guest cooks were spooning food onto porcelain plates. They no longer looked out of place as they laughed and gestured, mingling with the guests. Now very hungry, he looked for Marine, but she was still in the throes of listening to some tale from Mme Joubert, whose head came up to Marine's shoulder. He turned to his right and saw the Hainsbys, their heads pressed together, neither smiling. Embarrassed, he quickly looked away and saw a young woman staring at him. He thought he might know her and was mildly unsettled by her regard.

"Did you get me a glass of wine?" Marine asked.

"Oh, you managed to get away?" Verlaque asked. "Here, have some of mine." He handed his glass to Marine and returned his attention to the young woman, but she was gone.

"Maman and Philomène have some serious bees in their bonnets," Marine said, taking a sip. "Wow!" She held up the glass up and looked at it in the light.

"It's Olivier Bonnard's."

"That explains it."

Verlaque asked, "What are they on about?"

"Oh, how the Protestant service was fine and all, but lacking in theological references."

"I thought Dave did a fine job."

"Me, too."

"But I didn't like those emcees," Verlaque continued. "They spoke to us like—"

"We were simple."

"Exactly. Is that a thing in the Protestant church?"

"I shouldn't think so," Marine said. "There are many kinds of Protestant churches, and each one is different. Just like our churches."

"No, Catholic churches are all the same," Verlaque said, rolling his eyes.

"Now, now."

"Let's get some food," Verlaque suggested. "I'm starting with the Germans and working my way down in strength."

"You mean fat content," Marine said. Verlaque opened his mouth to protest but then Marine added, "I hope they made their spaetzle." She charged on ahead, and Verlaque had to swerve around two old men to keep up with her.

• • •

"We're lucky we found spots to sit down," Verlaque said, ripping off a piece of bread and dipping into some eggplant Parmesan the Italians had made. "Made with Tuscan olive oil. You can see its gooey green goodness running out the sides."

Marine asked, "Did you try this?" pointing to a Pecorino cheese with tiny streaks of black running through it.

Verlaque took a piece and put it in his mouth. He closed his eyes and leaned back, his hands on his stomach. "Truffles."

"It's like a drug," Marine said. "It must cost a fortune. What generosity."

"Yeah, and we'll all be lined up tomorrow morning at their food stand. Good marketing, I'd say."

A woman on Verlaque's right got up and someone else sat down seconds later, his plate piled high with food. "May I join you?"

Verlaque turned and saw the cathedral's deacon, or rector, or whatever he was, smiling at them.

"Père Fernand," Marine said, holding out her hand. "Please do." They shook hands and she introduced Verlaque as her husband.

"You're the examining magistrate," the priest said, shaking Verlaque's hand. "Marine's mother has told me a lot about you."

"That's right," Verlaque said. "That was a lovely service."

"Yes, I thoroughly enjoyed it as well."

Marine asked, "Did you attend the service last year?"

"Oh, yes. They began this tradition six years ago. I've been to all of them, of course."

"The candlelit moment," Verlaque began. "Did they do that last year?"

"Yes," Père Fernand answered. "Although I'm not sure of the song. It's such a dramatic way to end the service. I thought that only we Catholics did drama."

Verlaque smiled. He took a bite of a deep-fried *boulette*, smiling in delight. "Fennel, but with spice—"

"*Karbar bès*," the priest answered. "I'm a big fan of Tunisian cuisine. The spicier the better."

Verlaque eyed Père Fernand's ample stomach and put him down as a fellow *fin gourmet*.

"I'm going to look up the recipe for these *boulettes*," Marine said, wiping her mouth with a paper napkin. "They can't be too difficult to—"

"Cole!" a woman's voice rang out.

"Oh, dear," the priest said, grimacing. "Did someone have too much of the Domaine Beauclaire?"

"Cole! Please, is there a doctor here?!"

"It's Debra Hainsby," Marine said, standing up to see over the heads of Antoine and Père Fernand.

Voices and the scuffling of feet echoed throughout the hall.

"I'm a doctor!" a male voice called out. "Let me through, please!"

Verlaque held Marine's hand and squeezed it. There was nothing they could do, he felt, but sit there and hope the American was just having some kind of dizzy spell or upset stomach, and not something more serious.

Père Fernand mumbled, "Excuse me," and got up, slowly walking to where a small crowd had formed, gathered around the outstretched Cole Hainsby.

"Cole!" Debra Hainsby called out once more, as she began weeping. Verlaque let go of Marine's hand and got up from the table, making his way over as people began moving away from Cole Hainsby, their hands in their pockets, one or two of them quietly crying.

Verlaque arrived and knelt down. A man whom he recognized as a choir member and a doctor friend of Marine's father leaned over the American's body. The doctor looked up with recognition when he saw Verlaque. He shook his head. "He's gone," he whispered.

"What happened?" Verlaque asked.

"I wouldn't want to guess," the doctor answered. "As I didn't see what happened until he was here, lying on the floor. I'm a general practitioner; Jérémy Forestier." They shook hands and Verlaque looked over at Debra Hainsby, slumped over in a chair, surrounded by people. "It could have been a heart attack," the doctor said, leaning in closer to Verlaque, "or heart failure."

"I've called an ambulance," Reverend Dave said, kneeling beside them. He put a hand on Cole Hainsby's shoulder. "Heart attack?" he asked, seeming unable to look away from the body.

"It looks that way," Dr. Forestier answered.

"Here's the emergency response team," Dave said. "I'll go and help Père Fernand."

Verlaque looked over at the tables. "Where was he sitting?" he asked, getting to his feet.

Dr. Forestier stood up and pointed. "There, the second table down, in the middle. I was closer to the end."

Two young women stood at the end of the table, one of them holding a large tray while the other stacked plates and cups on it. They kept glancing at each other, as if by cleaning they would be helping in some way. Most of the other guests stood around in groups, talking quietly, or not saying anything at all.

"Thank you, Dr. Forestier. I'll go and have a few words with Mme Hainsby," Verlaque said. "My grandfather had a heart attack at an event much like this one, in Normandy . . ." He listened to his own voice trail off, unable to finish his sentence. What words of condolence could he say to the now-widowed Debra Hainsby? But he felt that, as a senior city employee, he should at least introduce himself and offer what comfort he could.

Verlaque was about to get up when the doctor leaned in, drawing Verlaque close with an arm on his shoulder. "I don't want to raise unnecessary alarm bells, but there's something odd—"

"Go on."

"The dead man has a skin rash," Dr. Forestier said. "Although he may have already had that. I didn't know him. But he also had what looked like burns around his mouth."

"That's not a symptom of a heart attack, is it?"

"No," the doctor replied, looking around the room as he did. "It's more a sign of poisoning. Please let me know what conclusion the coroner comes to." He handed Verlaque a business card and they shook hands once more. Verlaque watched the doctor cross the room and exit through the green door.

Verlaque turned around and walked the other way, pulling up a chair beside Debra Hainsby. "Are you all right, Mme Hainsby?" Verlaque asked in English. "My name is Antoine Verlaque and I'm the examining magistrate here in Aix. That's like a—"

"A judge," she replied, looking at him with a vacant stare. "But you take an active role in crime solving with the police. I've read French crime fiction." She buried her head in her hands. "Our children . . ."

101

"Are they here?" Verlaque asked, aghast. Had they just seen their father die?

"No, they're on a weekend ski trip with their school," she replied, looking up at him. "How will I tell them? They were so disappointed to miss this service." From her tone, the irony was not lost on her, nor was it lost on Verlaque.

Verlaque tried to focus on making her as comfortable as possible. He could hear voices around him, and people moving. He heard the doors being opened and what he knew to be the ambulance. "Can I get you anything?" he asked.

Debra Hainsby shook her head.

"Was your husband ill?" he asked.

Debra shook her head. "Never. He didn't even get colds."

"Did heart attacks run in his family? They do in mine."

"No," she whispered. "Cancer, yes, but the Hainsbys all have strong hearts. What just happened?" she asked, wiping her eyes with a tissue. "He kept complaining of a raging thirst, and had me feel his forehead a few times. He was burning up."

"We'll know more soon," Verlaque said. "Did he complain of anything else? A tightening of the chest? Or an aching sensation in his chest or arms?"

"No."

A friend of Debra's approached them, putting

her arms around her shoulders. "Let's get you home," she said.

"No, I want to go with the ambulance," Debra replied, trying to get up.

Verlaque and the other woman helped her to her feet. "Debra, do you want me to go with you?" her friend asked.

Mme Hainsby shook her head. "No, thank you."

Her friend turned to speak to someone else, and Debra took hold of Verlaque's arm. "I wasn't a good wife," she said, barely audible.

The atmosphere in the dining hall was as hushed as one would expect. People spoke in whispers and hovered at the edges of the room, as if they thought it in bad taste to continue eating or drinking. Père Fernand stood in front of one of the food tables and raised his hands. "My friends," he said, looking around the room. "What just happened, in God's home, has shocked all of us. I'd like to thank you all for your discretion and attention to Mme Hainsby. I'd also like to take this opportunity to thank our sister cities, who have generously supplied food for this evening's dinner. Please, continue eating if you so wish, and if you could clear your tables afterward that would be a great help to our volunteer clean-up crew. Now I'd like to properly introduce this gentleman on my left, Maître Antoine Verlaque, who is Aix's examining magistrate. Please give him your utmost attention. Thank you."

"Thank you, Père Fernand," Verlaque said. "Please do not be alarmed by this request, but since by chance I was here during M Hainsby's death, I'd like to ask you each to leave your name, address, and telephone number with two police officers who will be standing at the door. This is a precautionary measure only."

"What's going on?" a man standing in the far corner of the room asked. "Why can't we just go home now?" Various other people mumbled in agreement.

Verlaque raised a hand, his palm facing outward. "Please don't worry. I repeat, this is only a precautionary measure. M Hainsby's death was very sudden, and there's no reason for me to believe that it was not a natural one, but since you are all here now, this would make things much easier once the cause of death is determined." Verlaque looked at the crowd and saw a few puzzled faces, and heard more grumbling, so he repeated his request in English. He stepped away, thinking he'd very much like a glass of wine.

"You look like you can use one of these," a voice said, handing him a glass of Olivier's red.

"*Merci*, Mme Bonnet," Verlaque said, smiling, as he took the glass from his mother-in-law. Florence Bonnet stood beside him, holding a plate in her hands.

"I think you may have frightened some of the people here."

"Yes," Verlaque agreed. "I'm not sure I handled that very well."

"You did what you had to do. It's unusual to see such a young man keel over like that," she said as she dipped a carrot stick into some hummus and surveyed the room. "Usually it's those old folks," she added, gesturing toward a group of white-haired women.

Verlaque shot her a puzzled glance, as he knew that Mme Bonnet was in her midseventies. Before he could recover she said, "Seventy is the new fifty."

He laughed. "That's great news."

"I read it in *Elle*," she continued. "At the dentist's office." She pointed the carrot stick at him. "What happened to that emcee, exactly? I saw you talking with Forestier."

"It's a bit of a mystery," he answered, doing his best Gallic shrug. "It looks like a heart attack."

"Do you and Forestier think he died of something else?" she asked.

"No, no," Verlaque said, looking desperately around the room for Marine.

Mme Bonnet said, "Agatha Christie's favorite murder method was poisoning."

"I didn't know you read Christie." Had she heard their conversation? He now remembered seeing her standing just behind Dr. Forestier when they were speaking over Cole Hainsby's body.

"When I was young," she answered. "Hiding in my room."

"Same."

"Same what? You read Christie, or you had to hide to read her books?"

"Same, I read Christie," he answered. "I didn't have to hide; my parents didn't care one way or another what books I read."

Florence knew, via Marine, the story of his cold, much-absent parents, and raised an eyebrow in acknowledgment. She said, "We weren't permitted to read popular books. Only classics, preferably in Greek or Latin, or the saints' stories."

Verlaque smiled. He didn't have to say *it served you well;* it was understood in the way she had said it, as her voice had had a tiny ring of pleasure and satisfaction. Florence Bonnet had had a stellar education and career.

"During dinner I happened to observe that young man who died," she went on. Verlaque tried not to cringe, mad at himself that he hadn't been quick enough to change the subject. "He was in front of me in the queue and was flittering around like a butterfly. Such a chatterbox. And he kept trying the food while he was still in line, then helping himself to more."

Verlaque looked at his learned mother-in-law,

as usual not surprised, but dismayed, at her love of gossip. He nodded and wondered, for the first time, if Cole Hainsby could have been a drug user. "He had a good appetite, eh?"

"And how! People kept refilling his plate."

"The Sister City hosts?"

"Yes, and various friends of his who kept coming up to him, egging him to try this and that. His wife even force-fed him some deep-fried thing. He really was holding up the line! Philomène thought she was going to faint from hunger!"

Merde, Verlaque thought to himself. It sounded like chaos, the perfect chance for an opportunistic killer. He then checked himself; he was jumping to conclusions. An autopsy would be done; until then he shouldn't be worrying. But he couldn't get the strangeness of the whole event out of his head, and the doctor's words *rash* and *burns around the mouth*. He studied the faces around the room, as Florence complained about the city's recent decision to change all the bus routes. "That's him," she said, causing Verlaque to turn his head to look at her.

"I beg your pardon?"

"That big guy over there," she said, again gesturing with another half-eaten carrot stick. "He looks Italian, or maybe Corsican. Anyway, he's new money." She wrinkled up her nose and went on, "I saw the emcee's wife talking with him."

"Debra Hainsby is her name. And?" Verlaque tried to stay patient with Florence Bonnet's primness, and her nosiness.

"I see your look. I know that it's not unusual for a married woman to speak to another man."

Verlaque smiled. "Indeed."

"But it *is* rather unusual for a woman to eat off of another's man's plate, and to drink from his wineglass."

Marine had been watching her mother and husband, imagining their conversation and trying not to laugh, when a young woman approached and held out her hand. "You're Dr. Bonnet's daughter, aren't you? My name is France Dubois. I work at the Protestant church here in Aix."

"*Enchantée*," Marine said, shaking her hand. She assumed that France Dubois knew her mother and not her father. Marine quickly assessed the young woman, remembering her from the Christmas market. Mlle Dubois—Marine supposed France was unmarried since she wore no rings of any kind—would have been a perfect candidate for a makeover. She immediately suppressed the idea, although she meant no harm in it. She imagined herself as an older sister, or cousin, perhaps, choosing more flattering clothes for France in one of Aix's many clothing shops. They'd giggle, then go out for a drink to celebrate, or ice cream. "That was very upsetting, what just happened," Marine said, realizing she'd taken a bit too long to say something. "How are you doing?"

"Oh, I'm fine," France replied with a wave of her hand.

"Did you know him?"

France seemed to hesitate before answering. "Only in passing."

Marine looked at her, curious. France didn't seem upset; perhaps the young woman saw the look of bewilderment on Marine's face, as she wiped her forehead, sighed, and said, "Sorry, I'm very tired. I organized this dinner, you see. It's been quite a lot of logistics."

"Congratulations on a job well done. Everything was delicious, and the room is transformed."

"Thank you. I do hope people feel like they can stay and continue eating," France said, scanning the room. "The desserts from England are wonderful, although there's probably too much butter in them. But the latest studies now say that butter's good for us!" France giggled and Marine felt herself warming to her.

"I've stopped reading those studies," Marine replied honestly. "Just eat meals made from good fresh food three times a day."

"Well, you're certainly doing something right, if you don't mind my saying." France's face turned slightly red, but she went on, "You're the kind of person who could probably teach someone like me a thing or two about style!"

It was now Marine's turn to turn red in the face. She hoped it didn't show. She was sometimes superstitious around religious people, which she took France Dubois to be. She worried they could read minds, or have magical powers. She put it down to reading too many biographies of the saints when she was a young girl. "Well, I'll go and do my bit at the dessert table," Marine said. "Thank you for the compliment and the food tips."

"My pleasure," France replied.

Marine could feel the young woman's eyes on her back as she turned and walked away.

CHAPTER TEN

Neither Verlaque nor Marine slept well. They had come home separately, Verlaque staying at the cathedral past midnight, in part to speak to Père Fernand and make sure he was well, and in part to watch the last of the carol sing organizers. At 3:00 a.m. Verlaque switched on the light beside his half of the bed, tired of both of them tossing around. "Should we read a bit?"

"Was I keeping you awake?" Marine asked, leaning on her side, facing him.

"No. I thought I was keeping you up."

Marine leaned over and switched on her light and picked up a book, a mystery set in Venice.

"Did you know that your mother was eavesdropping on my conversation with Dr. Forestier this evening?" he asked.

Marine laughed. "She's an expert at that. What did she hear?"

"Forestier said he was only guessing, but Hainsby showed more signs of someone who had died of poisoning than of a heart attack victim."

"Do you think Hainsby was a drug user?" Marine asked. "He did have that kind of frenetic energy, from the little bit I saw of him."

"That occurred to me, too." Verlaque looked at the cover of her book with its stock photo of a gondola in a blue night. "Armchair traveling?"

"Mm-hm."

"I heard a report on France Inter that that author doesn't live in Venice anymore. Too many tourists."

Marine set the book down. "You're killing me. I always thought we'd retire there. Do you think that could happen here?"

Verlaque looked at her over his reading glasses. "In Aix? Nah. Our mayor will have paved over the whole city in concrete by then, so no tourists will want to come." He made quotation marks with his fingers and said, "Improvements."

"You're right," Marine said, smiling and turning back to her book.

The next morning Verlaque awoke before the alarm. He looked at the clock; it was 6:45 a.m. He decided to get up and have a coffee in town, and let Marine sleep in. He felt like walking and thinking about the strange Sunday they had had. He threw on some clothes and brushed his teeth, trying to be silent, and ten minutes later he was downstairs in the street.

All was quiet. He headed toward the cafés on the Place Richelme to get an espresso and take a look at that day's edition of *La Provence*. Once there, he stood at the bar and watched the fishmongers set up their market stand, wondering where or how they found the strength to do that every day, all year long, in rain and sun and, especially in Provence, wind. And yet they seemed happy. Locals, mostly senior citizens up at the crack of dawn, passed their stand and waved or stopped to chat. A city worker, dressed in bright green coveralls, smoked a cigarette with one of the fishmongers, and Verlaque watched them as they gesticulated and laughed. He imagined they talked about soccer. Thank God for *le foot*, he thought, allowing millions of men the world over a subject of conversation.

Three espressos and two croissants later, Verlaque headed for home to have a quick shower and shave. There wasn't much interesting in *La Provence*, except for an expensive quarter-page ad for the Four Seasons bilingual school. A few days ago he hadn't heard of the school; now it seemed to come up every day.

He ran up the four flights of stairs to their flat, pretending he wasn't tired, pretending he was in shape. As he turned the key in the lock he had to stop and catch his breath, breathing deeply for a few seconds.

"Hello, beautiful," he said quietly as he walked through the doorway. Marine was in her dressing gown, with her back to him, staring at the espresso machine. She turned slowly and nodded, her eyes bleary.

"Oh, dear," he continued. "Go back to bed and I'll bring you a cappuccino." She gave a small wave, barely lifting her right hand to chest level, and shuffled down the hall toward their bedroom. Verlaque whistled as he busied himself with the coffee, knowing the whistling would annoy her. He grinned.

"Cappuccino, croissant, and a glass of cool water," he said as he carried the tray into their bedroom. He set the tray on Marine's lap and stood up. "I'm going to have a shower, then I'll go make you another coffee."

"Thanks," Marine said. "Why aren't you exhausted?"

"I ran into one of the young officers at a café. He gave me a little pill and told me to have it with a Red Bull."

"What?!" Marine sat up straight, jiggling the tray.

"I knew that would get you going!" He laughed as he left the room, and was still laughing as he undressed and turned on the water.

"Jerk," Marine mumbled as she scooped up the remaining milk froth with her index finger.

Thirty minutes later they were both showered and dressed, sitting in the living room. "You look very chipper," Verlaque said. Marine wore a deep red cashmere turtleneck with black woolen pants that were cropped just above the ankle and black high heels. He knew that this was a writing day for her; she always dressed up when she was going to write. Marine normally wore classically cut clothes with little or no jewelry. But today she

114

wore a thick gold chain necklace that shimmered off the red turtleneck. It touched him, as the necklace had been his mother's.

"Thank you," she said. "And thank you for the breakfast in bed."

"Don't mention it." He looked at his watch. "I should get going soon. But tell me, what did you think about last night?"

They spoke of how much they had enjoyed the ceremony.

"And after, at the dinner?" Verlaque asked. "What did Wallflower tell you?"

"Wallflower? That's interesting."

"What is?"

"That's what my mother calls her, too," Marine answered. "Her name is France Dubois and she works for the Protestant church. Not much. We need to start thinking about Christmas."

Verlaque groaned.

"I know it's not your favorite holiday," Marine said. "But we've invited your father and Rebecca, and my parents, so we do need to think about the meal and some gifts." Marine set her coffee cup down. "Antoine," she began. "Our Christmas can be a happy one."

Verlaque got up and walked over to the living room window, watching an old woman walk up their narrow street, a market basket hung over her forearm. "Christmas reminds me of my mother," he said. He took a deep breath and continued,

"Both of my parents, actually. And the lousy job of parenting they did."

Marine stayed sitting so as not to break his concentration, however much she wanted to go and embrace him.

"There were some Christmases when Maman wouldn't even be there," he went on. "So my father would flail around and take us last-minute skiing, along with one of his model girlfriends, or drop us off with Emmeline and Charles, who would be delighted, don't get me wrong, but who would overcompensate. If my mother was there the odd Christmas, she and Father would argue. So as soon as I moved out of the house I got into the habit of avoiding Christmas altogether. I'd make sure I was on an airplane on December 24, destination anywhere, as long as it was far away. Tokyo, Tel Aviv . . ." He paused, rubbing his chin. "Give me another city that begins with a *T*."

Marine snorted. "Toronto."

"Thanks."

Marine got up and walked across the living room and put her arms around Verlaque.

"Have a good day, my love," Verlaque said as he held Marine. "I'll see you tonight." He kissed her, drinking in her smell . . . *roses?* . . . delighting in the warmth of her body. "I won't be late," he said.

Marine stood against the window, watching Antoine put his coat on in the hallway. He opened the door, waved, and left. She picked up her coffee cup and carried it into the kitchen, thinking of Antoine Verlaque and all of the things he had done before she met him. She knew that she couldn't ask him about his past without putting him on the defensive; he just clammed up. But she was curious all the same. She shrugged, putting the cup in the dishwasher, and thought to herself that it wasn't important. But she had a clear image of a younger Antoine—no gray hair and a little more svelte—walking through a foreign city, one very much like Tel Aviv, with a sea and rows of palms, and she was curious, with a little pang of yearning.

The first thing Antoine Verlaque did once inside his office was to make an espresso. The second thing was to fill out the necessary form to order an autopsy of Cole Hainsby's body, by demand of the examining magistrate, thus avoiding the need to wait for Debra Hainsby's permission. He took it to Mme Girard—his secretary, who seemed to be away at the moment—and laid it on her spotless desk. He looked at the framed photograph of her three smiling children, now all grown up and out of the house. "*Trois, bien sûr*," he mumbled. Most people he knew, if they had children, had three; the state child benefits reached their maximum with the third child. He went back into his office, closed the door, and picked up the phone to call Bruno Paulik.

Five minutes later the commissioner was in Verlaque's office, gently holding an espresso cup in his large hands. As Paulik sipped his coffee Verlaque told him of the previous evening's events. "I know we don't have much going on here at the moment, which is a blessing," Verlaque concluded, "but do you think I'm overreacting?"

Paulik set his empty demitasse on the edge of Verlaque's desk and folded his arms. "A guy in his early forties can die very suddenly," he said.

"I know."

"I had a cousin . . ."

Verlaque tried to hide his smile. He folded his arms on the desk and leaned forward, ready to hear yet another story about one of the Paulik cousins from the Luberon. Both of his parents came from families with more than ten children, so Paulik had hundreds of cousins and hundreds of stories.

"Yvan," Paulik said. "Fell over dead at the age of thirty-six one afternoon after having eaten cassoulet for lunch."

Verlaque, who loved the meat and bean dish from the southwest, said nothing but did raise his eyebrows. Many cassoulets, he thought, were heavy enough to invoke a heart attack.

"But it wasn't a heart attack," Paulik continued. "His heart just stopped, the doctor told us. I think Yvan was brokenhearted."

"Seriously?"

"Yep. He loved a girl from Gordes, who just a few months previously had gotten pregnant and married one of those village assholes that always seem to exist. A bully in school."

Verlaque nodded. "We had those kinds of guys in Paris, too."

Paulik went on, his voice rising, as it always did when he told a story. "His parents—he still lived at home—found all kinds of letters Yvan had written but never posted to this girl. They burned them."

"This is tragic," Verlaque said. "It's like Ugolin in *Manon des Sources*."

Paulik nodded and let out a grunt. "Yeah, Yvan even looked like a young Daniel Auteuil, too."

Verlaque smiled, picturing the actor in the 1980s film version of *Manon des Sources*. It was one of the things that fascinated him as a young man, with Provence and its rich characters.

Paulik went on, "Yvan was a wiry little guy, just like Auteuil. Could run like the wind." He stopped and smiled.

Verlaque knew that if small, wiry Yvan was being teased by the bullies from Gordes, his cousin Bruno would have protected him. Bruno Paulik: well known in the Luberon for his rugby skills, and well known to Verlaque for his calm and gentleness. "If it wasn't so early I'd suggest we toast Yvan with a little rum," he said, motioning with his head to a cupboard under his bookshelves where he kept a bottle of seven-year-old Havana Club, two glasses, and all of his cigar paraphernalia.

Paulik, knowing what was in the cupboard, said, "Rain check."

When the commissioner had gone, Verlaque sat back down and thought about what had just happened: He goes to a Christmas concert, his first one, and a man dies after the concert. No wonder neither he nor Marine could sleep last night. Why was it bothering him so much? Was it memories of Grandpapa Charles, falling over during a Lions Club dinner near their country house in Normandy? With a glass of his favorite wine in hand, Verlaque had heard an elderly neighbor report a few days later. Or was it Dr. Forestier's words of the rash and burn marks and Florence Bonnet's gossiping? Yes, there was something in his mother-in-law's story that nagged him.

He got up and reached into his coat pocket, taking out *La Provence*, which he had folded in two. He sat back down and laid it out on his desk, turning to the full-page bilingual school ad. Resting his head in the palms of his hands, he studied the small black-and-white photographs. Each one depicted the students and faculty having a wondrous time at this school that Verlaque imagined cost more per year than his law school.

120

Adjusting his reading glasses, he studied the third photo. The students were giving some sort of recital outside on a stage, and a bit of the first row of spectators could be seen. Debra Hainsby sat there, watching the students and smiling. Her right shoulder touched the man next to her—he, too, was smiling, but at Debra, not at the students. It wasn't Cole Hainsby. Verlaque lifted up the newspaper and looked even closer; he recognized the man as the supposed "Italian or Corsican new money" that Florence Bonnet had pointed out in the dining hall. In the next photograph, Aix's mayor was giving the school's director some kind of award for good citizenship. In the caption their names were given: the mayor's name Verlaque knew well, and the school's director was cited as Alain Sorba. He was the same man who last night had shared his plate and glass with Debra Hainsby, and the same man sitting next to her at the students' show.

CHAPTER ELEVEN

Aix's coroner, Dr Agnès Cohen, called Verlaque at 10:00 a.m. "What are you doing?" she asked. "Am I disturbing you?"

Verlaque had spent the previous hour writing down all the reasons he suspected foul play in Cole Hainsby's death. He also spent a good deal of time looking out his office window onto the small street below, where a constant stream of cars slowly drove by, each hoping to get one of rue Mondar's few parking spots. He wondered how long the rue Mondar would last before the city's construction teams attacked it, under the guise of the mayor's improvement schemes.

"Paperwork," he replied to the doctor. He looked up and could see the rounded dome over the chapel of Les Oblats, and beyond that, the tall pointed spire of Saint-Jean-de-Malte. The sky was the same clear blue that children used when depicting it in drawings.

"I have the test results," she said, "which I'll send over by courier. But I thought you might like a heads-up."

"Go on."

"The dead man died of poisoning. His liver burst."

Verlaque winced and began pacing the room. "What kind of drug was used?"

"Ah, one which I seldom use, but many people use every day or every other day. No prescription needed." She paused and Verlaque could hear her chewing something. *Pain au chocolat*? Croissant? "Doliprane."

"Acetaminophen?"

"Yes, the painkiller."

"How is that possible?"

"Eight pills of one thousand milligrams strength will do the trick," she replied, now sipping something. Coffee? Water? "It's very easy. I'll leave it up to you to decide if it was self-administered or if someone put it in his food."

"You can't tell?"

"Nope."

"Seriously?"

She paused before answering. "I'll need more time, but can't promise anything." She hung up before he could thank her.

"Doliprane?" he mumbled. "Who dies from an overdose of Doliprane?" He opened his middle desk drawer and saw the familiar little yellow box. He also kept a box in the glove compartment of his car, and he knew that Mme Girard had a box in her desk, too. He had once had to ask her for one.

He picked up his cell phone and called Bruno Paulik, filling him in and suggesting they have lunch together. His next phone call was to the

APCA; he'd visit them before bothering Debra Hainsby. Who knew where she was right now? He dreaded the idea of her next task: telling her children that their father was dead.

It was cold and sunny as Verlaque and Paulik crossed the square in front of the Palais de Justice, turned left onto the rue Chastel, and walked into Chez Fanny's, a bistro they both loved. It was run by a friendly blonde who years ago sold her flat and real estate business in Paris to relocate to Aix. Her food, simple and hearty, was made with organic and locally sourced ingredients. Paulik spotted an empty table for two and put his coat and scarf across a chair to save it while they ordered at the counter. Fanny said hello and, ever discreet, kept it to herself that she knew that the two burly men who had just walked in were a judge and a police commissioner.

Paulik scanned the chalkboard and ordered a *pan bagnat* from Nice, something Fanny always had available.

"What's the plat du jour, Fanny?" Verlaque asked, squinting to read the menu.

"Daube," Fanny answered, flipping a white linen tea towel over her shoulder. "I made it with white wine, not red."

Verlaque raised his hand. "Sold!"

"Wait a second," Paulik said. "I'll change my order and have the daube as well."

"What?" Verlaque asked, looking at Paulik and then grinning at Fanny. "You don't want a healthy tuna salad on bread?"

"It's cold out," Paulik said, shivering for effect.

Fanny laughed. "The beef stew will warm you up. Go ahead and sit down. I'll bring it over."

"Red wine!" Verlaque called out.

"*Ça marche!*" Fanny answered. "I'll bring you a carafe of water, too."

Paulik sat down, his forearms resting on the table. "The Protestant church is around the corner, isn't it?"

"Yes. I called to make sure some of the key people from last night will be there this afternoon. I spoke to the reverend, who didn't think it odd that we would want to speak to them."

"Because they don't know we are questioning them," Paulik suggested. "Yet." Paulik looked out the windows of Chez Fanny. One or two people walked by, and across the street was an historically listed mansion with an elaborately carved stone doorway. "I like this street, always have."

"Me, too. We're so close to the Place des Prêcheurs and yet it's so quiet here."

"Maybe too quiet for Fanny's liking."

"Gentlemen," Fanny said, setting two bowls of beef stew on the table. "The bowls are hot."

"Thank you," Paulik said, turning up the sleeves on his shirt.

Fanny's assistant brought two carafes, one with tap water and one with wine, and set them between the men.

"Anything else?" Fanny asked. "Besides bread, which I'll bring in a second."

"The APCA," Verlaque said, motioning outside by nodding his head toward the window.

"On rue Lacépède," Fanny said, her hands on her hips. "I get a lot of customers from there. And one of the congregation, the minister's wife, in fact, just started making my chocolate cake, and pecan pie. American style."

"Has anyone from the church been in today?" Verlaque asked.

"Just Jennifer—the baker—delivering the cake and pie. But we were both frazzled; it's a Monday morning, so we didn't speak much."

Paulik looked over at the counter, where half of a pie sat under a glass dome, butter oozing out its sides. "Where's the cake?" he asked.

Fanny pointed to the far end of the counter. "There are two pieces left," she said. "Jennifer calls it chocolate death."

Paulik turned back around and looked at Verlaque, eyebrows raised.

"You'd better set those aside for us," Verlaque said, grinning.

Fanny laughed, wiping her hands on her apron. "Okay. I'll go get your bread."

"I have a feeling the chocolate cake will give

us a bit of a jolt," Paulik said, dipping into his daube.

"Better than Red Bull, eh?"

"*Que diable*?" Paulik asked, setting down his fork. "You would never drink that stuff, would you?"

"Certainly not," Verlaque said, taking a sip of wine. "Not when you can drink this," he added, holding up his glass.

"There's a restaurant in Venice," Verlaque said. "The chef's wife is the baker. Diane. She's from Texas—"

"Is there a point to this anecdote?" Paulik asked as they turned the corner onto rue Lacépède. He bent his head down to avoid the wind. "It's gotten colder out."

"Diane makes that same kind of chocolate cake."

"In a Venetian restaurant?"

"In one of Venice's *best* restaurants," Verlaque said. "In my opinion."

"Well, I'm glad we skipped the coffee, is all I can say." Paulik rubbed his stomach, which Verlaque thought a bit over the top. Sure, the cake had been rich and sweet, but no sweeter than a slice of Opéra, or a mille-feuille.

"Fanny obviously didn't know about Cole Hainsby's death, did she?"

"No, but maybe she's not that connected to the expat community."

They stopped in front of the church, and Verlaque looked at his watch. "We're right on time."

They rang the buzzer just below the bronze plaque that read APCA and a voice answered, "Please come in." The door clicked open and they entered, Paulik careful to close the door behind him. Before them was a medium-size office of about three hundred square feet, Verlaque estimated, crammed full with three desks, bookcases, and two trestle tables piled high with books and papers.

Reverend Dave came forward and shook their hands. "Welcome to our mess," he said in English.

A woman in her late thirties, tall and slim with red hair pulled back, came forward to shake their hands. "I'm Jennifer Flanagan, Dave's wife," she said in French. She looked at Verlaque and continued, still in French, "I saw you at the dinner last night, but I was distracted, trying to take care of Debra."

"Of course," Verlaque said. "That's quite understandable. It was shocking for all of us."

"Your French is very good, Mme Flanagan," Paulik said.

"*Merci*," she said. "I was a French literature major at university, and did a year abroad here in Aix, believe it or not, at the Vanderbilt extension—"

"Rue Cardinale," Verlaque said. "I know the building."

"Jennifer's from Tennessee," Dave inserted.

Verlaque nodded. Did Dave think he didn't know that Vanderbilt University was in Nashville? "I must confess," Verlaque said. "We just had the pleasure of tasting your chocolate cake at Fanny's." He shot Paulik a look.

"Oh, I hope you enjoyed it," she said. "I got up this morning extra early to bake it, but my heart wasn't in it, I'm afraid."

"I completely understand," Verlaque said.

"You said you'd like to talk to us about Cole," Dave said, rubbing his hands together nervously. "May I ask why? I'm not sure how we can help. . . . It's true he was a member of this church . . ."

"I had a telephone call from the city coroner this morning," Verlaque said. "M Hainsby did not die of a heart attack, as we all thought last night. He died of poisoning."

"Food poisoning?" Jennifer Flanagan asked.

"No, either it was self-administered or he was given a dish with enough of the drug to kill him. That's why we're here this afternoon."

Dave's face turned pale. "I'm in shock," he said, barely audible. "Well, then, you can begin with me. I've tried cleaning up my office a bit. It's just through there." He motioned to an open door.

They walked into his office, a smaller version of the chaos in the main room. "We put two chairs behind the desk," Dave said, "and one in front for the interviewee. I guess that's me today."

Verlaque and Paulik sat down behind the desk, Paulik opening his notebook. "How long did you know Cole Hainsby?" he asked.

"Two years," Dave answered. "I met him the week we arrived."

"What were your impressions of him?"

"I figured you'd ask me that," Dave replied, "but I'm still not sure how to answer. He was a mess." Dave made a sweeping motion with his right hand around the tiny office. "Much like this. *Il était un bordel!*"

"Can you clarify?"

"Cole was a train wreck waiting to happen. I had the impression he was always in trouble, or running from trouble. What exactly it was, I'm not sure. Too much work? Not enough? He couldn't sit still, nor could he pay attention to a conversation for very long."

"What did he do for a living?"

"He ran an upscale tour company," Reverend Dave said.

"Did he run the business alone?" Paulik asked, thinking he had detected a bit of envy in the voice of the reverend.

"No, he had a partner. A local kid named Damien Petit," Dave replied. "Nice young man."

"What do you know of him?" Verlaque asked.

"Damien? Not much. I've only met him once or twice, but I can tell just from those meetings that he's a good sort."

"And Mme Hainsby?" Verlaque asked, not putting too much faith in Dave Flanagan's character assessment of Damien Petit if it was based on only one or two quick meetings.

"Oh, I know her, yes." Dave paused, biting his lower lip. "It's not for me to say . . ."

"Please continue," Paulik prompted him.

"I'm not sure their marriage was a happy one," Dave said. "At least, Debra isn't—wasn't—happy. That was pretty clear to all of us here at the church."

"Did he ever confide in you about it?" Verlaque asked.

"Like a confession? We don't do those here." He smiled. "But I know what you mean. No, like I said, he couldn't sit still long enough . . ."

"Thank you," Verlaque said, leaning back in the chair. "One last thing. I saw you leave the ceremony during the candlelit song. Why is that?"

"Oh, yes," Dave answered, his face neutral. "I had my phone on vibration mode. My mother . . . she's quite ill . . . so I asked my brother in San Diego to call me if her condition worsened. Unfortunately he did call me, in the middle of 'O Christmas Tree,' so I snuck away to take his call."

"Was everything okay?"

Dave waved his hand. "It was nothing serious," he said. "My brother had no way of knowing that I'd be in the middle of our biggest service of the year."

Verlaque noted that Jennifer Flanagan had brushed her hair and applied a bit of red lipstick for their meeting. Like Marine, she wore no other makeup. "How are you feeling, Mme Flanagan?" he asked.

"Bruised," she answered in French.

Verlaque nodded. He liked her.

"Did you know M Hainsby well?" Paulik asked.

"Not really," she answered. "Truth be told, I tried to avoid him."

Paulik raised an eyebrow, and she continued, "It seemed to me that he was the kind of person who invited bad luck."

"Did he ever seem worried?"

Jennifer squinted, as if thinking. She then nodded. "Yes, I'd say he was worried . . . but . . . didn't want to show it."

Paulik tilted his head slightly, egging her on.

"You see, there were certain signs," she said. "Like when he spoke, he'd laugh at things that weren't really funny, and he'd be wringing his hands at the same time. My guess, if I may say this, is that he was worried about money. Many men are, aren't they? Cole would always make it clear to everyone that they lived in Saint-Marc-Jaumegarde. It came up every time you spoke to him. So that made me think that he was pretending to have a lot of money."

Verlaque crossed his legs, impressed with Mme Flanagan. He hated Saint-Marc-Jaumegarde. For lack of a better word, he found it, and the people who lived there, bling. The houses weren't any grander than those along the Route Cézanne, between Aix and Le Tholonet, but those who lived on Cézanne's favorite road were of a different class. They either came from old money, so purposely drove old cars and wore threadbare suits, or had so much money that they had long ago abandoned bragging about it.

Verlaque asked, "Are you close to his wife?"

She shook her head back and forth. "No." She straightened her back and went on, "You see, as the minister's wife, I'm friendly with everyone, especially since some of the expats still don't speak French. But I'm not good friends with any of them, if that makes sense. I'm busy enough: with my own family and friends, my baking, and I'm keeping up with my French studies. I'm taking a graduate class at the university on existential literature."

"In French?" Verlaque said. "That's impressive."

She smiled and folded her hands in her lap, twisting her wedding band.

"Thank you for speaking to us," Verlaque said. "Would you mind sending in Mlle Dubois?"

"Not at all," Jennifer said, getting up from her chair and leaving quietly.

A minute later France Dubois knocked lightly on the door. "Come in," Paulik said, leaning forward with his forearms on the desk.

"*Asseyez-vous*," Verlaque said, gesturing to the empty chair before them. France slid down into it. She patted down the rough wool of her skirt and then pushed it toward her knees, as if it were too short, but it was an unfashionable length that was neither short nor long. She had none of Jennifer Flanagan's poise or confidence, but Verlaque liked her big brown eyes, which looked at him steadily, almost without blinking. He thought he'd begin this meeting the same way, asking her how she was doing.

"I'm all right," France replied, her voice cracking slightly. "A little tired is all."

He introduced Bruno Paulik, who reached across the desk and shook the young woman's hand. "How long have you worked here?" Verlaque asked.

"Six years," France said. Verlaque tried to guess her age. "I did two internships, one in Paris and one here in Aix, and then had a series of semi-permanent jobs for six years, until I was lucky enough to find this permanent position."

Verlaque nodded. Mlle Dubois's career path

sounded very typical for someone of her generation. So she must be around thirty-five. "Are you an Aixoise?"

She smiled, slightly, for the first time. "I was born here."

"Neither of us are real Aixois," Paulik said, smiling. He pointed to Verlaque and said, "He's Parisian, and I'm from the Luberon."

"Oh, the Luberon is so lovely," France said. She hesitated and then added, "But I suppose it's changed a lot since you lived there."

Paulik held up his hands in mock helplessness.

"Bloody Parisians!" Verlaque said, clenching his fist in what he hoped what a good imitation of an angry farmer. The three laughed.

"What happened last night was very upsetting," Paulik began, "and any information you could give us about Cole Hainsby would be very helpful."

Verlaque nodded in seriousness, and wondered to himself why they both seemed to be treating Mlle Dubois with kid gloves. For all they knew, she could be a shark.

"Did you think his death . . . suspicious?" she asked.

"Cole Hainsby died from poisoning. He consumed more than eight tablets of Doliprane, which, as you saw, proved to be fatal."

France's cheeks turned red and she brought her hands up to her face. She took some deep breaths and asked, "Someone killed him?"

Verlaque asked, "Did you know M Hainsby?"

"I didn't know him. We spoke on the phone a few times, that's all. And then I met him for the first time on Saturday evening. We had a meeting to make last-minute preparations for the carol sing."

"Was he well liked?" Paulik asked.

"By whom? The people here at the APCA? I never heard anyone complain about him. He wasn't a mean person or anything like that."

"And his business partner?" Paulik asked. "His name is Damien Petit."

France's eyes widened and she pulled at her skirt. "Um, I've never met him."

Verlaque said, "But you know of him, it seems."

"Well, not exactly," she replied. "But I sat next to them last week, at Café Mazarin."

"What day was that?" Paulik asked, flipping back a few pages in his notebook.

"Friday lunch."

"I was there, too," Verlaque said.

"I know," France said in a firm voice. "I saw you."

"Oh . . . of course you did." He turned to Paulik and explained, "I was there with an old friend, who's married to Margaux Perrot. She was with us. I imagine we turned a few heads."

France continued, making it clear that she wasn't interested in film stars, or that perhaps she was tiring of the questions, "They sat next to me, but Cole didn't know who I was. I recognized his voice, and they called each other by their first names, so I figured it out pretty quickly."

"Did you happen to hear what they were talking about?" Verlaque asked. "Those tables at the Mazarin are jammed so close together," he added, hoping he sounded nonchalant.

France nodded. "Damien was upset," she said. "Cole made a business decision without consulting Damien. It had to do with money, I think."

Paulik wrote down the information, and neither man spoke. When it was clear that France had nothing more to add, Verlaque asked, "And Mme Hainsby. Do you know her?"

"Not well," France said. "I only met her for the first time on Saturday night as well. She doesn't volunteer here. I think she's a secretary at the bilingual school."

"Oh, the one in Lambesc?"

"The Four Seasons," France said. She looked like she was about to add something, then stopped.

"What is it, Mlle Dubois?"

"Nothing. I just realized I have a telephone call to make. A lot of expats call us when they arrive in Aix, asking about schools."

"And you suggest the Four Seasons?" Verlaque said.

"Yes. The children don't usually speak French, and most families only stay for a year or two."

"A year or two? It would be hard to make friends," Verlaque said.

"Yes, it would be hard to make friends," she said, with, Verlaque later thought, a bit of sadness in her voice.

"I feel like an old fool," Verlaque said, taking off his brogues and setting them under the coffee table. "There's something about this afternoon's meetings that bothered me."

"What was it?" Marine asked, walking into the living room carrying two glasses of white wine.

"We spoke to two women, both of them very different. One is confident and outgoing, the other shy, and yet both are very intelligent."

Marine laughed. "And that's a problem, Antoine?"

He took a sip and shook his head. "What I mean is, they are both observant and seem to be far too intelligent to be doing what they're doing. Jennifer Flanagan studied French literature but now she bakes, and why in the world has France Dubois worked at that church for all these years? She is only a bilingual secretary."

"For one thing," Marine said, setting down her glass and talking a handful of salted almonds, "expats, especially those who move here for their husbands' work, have to make due with whatever they find in France. They're away from their families and friends, and often have had to give up good jobs to accompany their *husband* over here." She tossed the nuts into her mouth and held up her hand, signaling she wasn't finished. After she swallowed she said, "As for France Dubois, does she have a CDI?"

"Yes," Verlaque said, feeling like he was being scolded. "She has a permanent contract."

"You know how hard those are to come by in France, Antoine," Marine said. "Perhaps she's tried to find another job, but it's slim pickings in Aix. And she's not the type to make contacts, or use those contacts, to work her way up the ladder."

"Are you?"

"Hell yes!" Marine said, reaching for her wineglass. "You and I both are."

"I suppose you're right."

"We wouldn't hurt anyone, or misuse that ability to, for lack of a better word, schmooze. But some people aren't capable of it. Like France Dubois."

"I saw you talking to her at the dinner," Verlaque said.

"I like her," Marine said. "There's more to her than meets the eye."

"That's what I've been trying to explain. France seemed nervous, like she kept hesitating, as if she were holding something back."

"You always think that of people." Marine got up and kissed him. "I have to get our meal ready. Now, if you follow me into the kitchen with our wineglasses, I'll tell you what I found out at the dinner."

Verlaque did as he was told, frustrated that his evening was turning into one much like his afternoon.

"I spent a while last night chatting with Claudie Pirone," Marine said as she faced the stove, stirring something in a pot. Verlaque peeked and saw green lentils. He looked at Marine.

"No meat tonight," she said. "I didn't make it to the butcher's. Oh, there's bacon in the fridge. I can add that."

Verlaque made a praying gesture and looked up at the ceiling.

Marine grinned as she got the bacon. "To continue, Claudie isn't Claudie Pirone anymore, she's Claudie McGregor."

Verlaque took a sip of wine. "She's an old high school friend, I take it."

"She's the older sister of a girl I went to school with, yes. There were six."

"Six children?"

"Six daughters," Marine replied as she sliced the bacon and dropped it into a hot frying pan.

"Wow. And now it sounds like she's married to a Scotsman . . ."

"Yes, but they live here. His name is Jim."

Into another pot, in which water slowly boiled, Marine dropped a dozen tiny Ratte potatoes, some of them no bigger than a walnut. Verlaque looked on, smiling, feeling extremely lucky.

"Claudie and Jim are members of the APCA?" he asked.

"Yes. Claudie made it clear to me that Jim is the religious one, not her. Anyway, she's still as bossy as she used to be when we were kids. She confided that she and Jim were both quite put out that the Hainsbys were the emcees yesterday. Claudie and Jim had been doing it since it started six years ago."

Verlaque guffawed at the pettiness.

"I know, I know," Marine said. "You see why I never liked Claudie." Marine drained the lentils into a colander, throwing out the clove-studded onion and bouquet garni that had been cooking along with the lentils. She poured the lentils back into the pot and added the cooked bacon.

"Smells lovely," Verlaque said.

"Mmm, it's the cloves." She turned to face Verlaque, leaning against the counter. "Claudie told me that something strange happened on Saturday night between the Hainsbys. Did anyone tell you about it?"

"No. I heard about that meeting, but no details."

"Cole Hainsby broke something, and his wife ran out of the room crying," Marine said. "Claudie seemed tickled while telling me."

"Why didn't anyone tell us about that?"

"They might think it not their business," Marine said, turning around to prick one of the potatoes with a sharp knife. "What goes on between couples is private."

"They might have been each hoping that someone else would have told us," Verlaque said. "Not wanting to be the one to gossip. I see what you're saying."

"It seems odd that Mme Hainsby would cry over a broken glass or dish, doesn't it?" Marine lifted the pot of potatoes, walked over to the sink, and drained them. "Dinner's ready." She took two plates out of a cupboard and arranged big pieces of washed butter lettuce on the plates, spooning the lentils on top. She carefully set a few potatoes on the side of each plate. "How about a red Burgundy?"

Verlaque leaned down and opened their small wine fridge, hoping to find one. He was too tired to walk down the stairs to their basement cellar. He pulled one out, recognizing the vintner's name. "It's a Grand Cru," he said, handing it to Marine as he stood back up.

"We'll have to suffer through it," she answered, laughing.

CHAPTER TWELVE

The next morning Bruno Paulik knocked and opened Verlaque's office door, sticking his bald head in through the gap. "I just got a text message. Hainsby's business partner, Damien Petit, is downstairs," he said. "You're welcome to join." Verlaque got up and they headed downstairs, walking through the building's vast courtyard, which was watched over by a seventeenth-century statue of the Comte de Mirabeau. "Petit's around the corner," Paulik said. "In room three."

He nodded, knowing the room, for he had furnished it, along with the building's other four small rooms used for interrogation. Verlaque had replaced the old wooden tables and chairs, which looked like they had been donated by a high school, with contemporary white tables and transparent chairs designed by Philippe Starck. He craved another coffee.

Paulik opened the door and let Verlaque go through, following behind him. The officer, a woman in her late twenties whom Verlaque vaguely recognized, nodded and left the room. Damien Petit jumped up.

Verlaque crossed the room and extended his hand. "I'm Antoine Verlaque, the examining magistrate, and this is our commissioner, Bruno Paulik."

Petit mumbled his name and shook their hands. He was sweating.

"Please, sit down," Verlaque said, gesturing to the chair that Petit had just vacated. He and Paulik sat down opposite.

"Is it true?" Petit quickly asked. "That Cole is dead? I had a garbled message on my cell phone early this morning, and then the police—I mean, you—called."

Verlaque nodded. "He fell ill at dinner last night, in the cathedral."

Petit moaned and tilted his head back, looking at the ceiling.

"Who called you?" Paulik asked, taking out a pen and a small notebook from his jacket pocket.

Petit looked surprised. "Dave Flanagan from the Anglo church. Am I being interrogated? Didn't Cole have a heart attack?"

"M Hainsby died of an overdose," Verlaque said. "We suspect poisoning."

"What?" Petit gripped the edge of the table with his fingertips. "Who would do this? Could Cole have taken some pills?"

"We don't know," Paulik replied. "But most people don't choose suicide in a room full of people. When you last saw M Hainsby did he seem edgy? Worried?"

"Cole was always edgy and worried." Petit thought for a moment and added, "Except when he *should* have been feeling worried. Then

144

he was carefree, without a worry in the world."

"I assume you'll explain at some point what that means," Paulik said drily. "When did you last see him?"

"We had lunch together, at the Café Mazarin, last Friday."

"Downstairs or upstairs?" Verlaque asked, knowing he had been there the same day.

"Upstairs." If Petit thought the question strange, he didn't let on.

Verlaque tried to remember the other diners that day, but couldn't.

"How's business?" Paulik asked.

Petit winced. "Not great, especially since the financial crisis in 2008. Our trips have been halved."

"Was M Hainsby worried?" Verlaque asked. "Or was that what you were referring to when you said he should have been worried more than he was at times."

"Yes," Petit replied. "Cole was an optimist, and always seemed to believe that business would bounce back. And strangely enough, it usually did. Up until about a year ago. Since then we've been in a real slump."

"During the investigation, we'll need to look at your financial records," Verlaque said. "I hope you'll cooperate."

"Yes . . . of course," Petit said, his voice shaking slightly.

"Did M Hainsby have any enemies?" Paulik asked.

Petit shook his head back and forth, avoiding eye contact.

"Do you have any idea who would want to kill him?"

Petit rubbed his hands together. They trembled. "No."

"Are you all right?" Verlaque asked.

"The trembling hands?" Petit asked. "I get it often."

"How was his marriage? Did he confide in you?"

"We were business partners, but not friends, if that makes sense," Petit said. "I could see that he frustrated Debra, his wife. I like her. It was sometimes Debra's ideas that got our business back on track. But it didn't seem to me that the marriage was in great danger. They both doted on their two kids. What do I know? I've never been married. My parents bickered, too. But they stayed together for us three kids and made it work. Now they're quite close."

Paulik looked at the young man's hands. "We'll let you go now, M Petit. Please stay close to home so we can contact you again. You didn't go to the service last night. Why not?"

Petit shrugged. "Why would I go? I'm an atheist and I don't particularly care for Christmas, or that church crowd."

"What did you do?"

"I was at home, if you're asking me for an alibi," Petit replied. "But I was alone."

"Did anyone call your landline?"

"No. I made myself a *croque monsieur* for dinner, then watched television."

"What was on?" Paulik asked.

"I don't know," Petit said, wincing. "I began by watching the news, but I must have quickly fallen asleep. I woke up on the sofa around midnight, turned the television off, and crawled into bed. I had biked to Arles and back that day."

Verlaque tried not to show his displeasure. Why would anyone be masochistic enough to choose to ride a bike between those two cities? He looked at Petit, whose hands still trembled as he lifted up his water glass and took a sip. Petit had been honest about one thing, though— the church. Because the more Verlaque thought about that day, however joyful he thought it had been and however enthralled with the ceremony they all seemed to be, there was now something disturbing about that "church crowd." He thought of the gossiping: his own mother-in-law; Marine's high school acquaintance. Damien Petit, even though he might be holding something back, was at least honest about religion.

CHAPTER THIRTEEN

"I thought we could kill a few birds at once," Paulik told Verlaque as they cut through the produce market on the Place Richelme. "When I called the APCA they told me that France Dubois is at the Sister City food fair around the corner."

"Let's try to speak to her and some of the people who supplied dinner at the church," Verlaque suggested. He loosened his scarf; it was warmer than when he had left the flat that morning. "Has anyone else reported being ill?"

"No. Officer Flamant is keeping tabs on that; no one from the church has been to the emergency room with food ailments."

"That's a relief," Verlaque said. "It means that the killer was careful, at least. But we have our work cut out for us, as Hainsby ate so many different things that night. We all did."

Paulik said, "I've assigned three officers to call Sunday's dinner guests this afternoon and begin arranging interviews. I'm glad you had the presence of mind to get everyone's name and contact information." They walked past the Hôtel de Ville and passed under the arch of the medieval clock tower, aware that their backs were now in a few tourists' photographs, and turned left onto the Place des Cardeurs. A sea of white tents spread out before them. Paulik said, "When I called the APCA they told me that only Mlle Dubois has a list of the Sister City participants who donated food Sunday night."

"That doesn't surprise me," Verlaque said. "I think in small organizations like theirs it's always one person who has the master list in their head."

"Let's find her, then."

They walked slowly, their hands in their winter coats, watching crowds gather around certain stands. A queue had formed at the Philadelphia stand and both men slowed, looking for France Dubois but also taking in the smell of the fried steak and onions. Verlaque saw Paulik glance at his watch and he grinned. It was indeed lunchtime. "I'd suggest we eat," Verlaque said. "But I don't want to miss seeing Mlle Dubois."

"I agree," replied Paulik. He stopped walking and gently pulled Verlaque aside, so that they stood behind a raised bar table where a group of four Aixois happily ate lunch. "That's her," he said.

Verlaque looked across the crowd to where Paulik's head was turned. Standing opposite, with her back to a stand selling Provençal soaps and lavender sachets, was France Dubois. She had her hands in her pockets, her spine rigid, her face fixed on the Philadelphia stand. Verlaque followed her gaze; she seemed to be focused on the American man frying steaks. "Yes," Verlaque said. "I'd love to know what she's thinking."

"I'd say they aren't friendly thoughts," Paulik replied. "Let's go have a chat."

"Mlle Dubois," Verlaque said, his hand outstretched, once they had zigzagged through the crowd.

She looked at him, he would later tell Marine, with a vague annoyance. She shook their hands, and when Verlaque asked where they could talk, she began walking, saying nothing, in the direction of the information tent.

Once inside the tent the commotion and noise of the fair fell away. She had chosen well; since it was after noon, most of the visitors were outside getting something to eat. They stood off to one side beside a stack of colorful brochures about Tunisia.

"Sorry to bother," Verlaque began, "but we have more questions about Sunday evening, specifically about the dinner."

"Really?" France asked.

Verlaque said, "We understand that you arranged the dinner."

"Yes, I did. I came here"—she motioned outside the tent—"last week, asking the Sister City guests to participate. They all obliged. Some of them have been helping out with the carol sing since it began."

"Were you physically there, in the dining hall, when they brought their food on Sunday?"

"Yes, of course," France answered. "I had to

150

open the back door for them. There's a green door that gives onto the Place de l'Archevêché."

"I know it well," said Verlaque.

Paulik asked, "And you stayed while they set up the dinner?"

France looked directly into his eyes. "I was back and forth. You see, the service had begun, and I so wanted to sing."

"That's understandable," said Verlaque. He knew he could be frank with her. She was a formidable person, of that he was more and more sure.

"I was discreet," she went on. "I had an aisle seat, so it was easy to slip back and forth between the church and the dining hall." Verlaque nodded. He couldn't imagine anyone more discreet than Mlle Dubois.

"Did you see anything unusual?"

"No, nothing out of the ordinary, although it was all rather chaotic, as these things tend to be."

"Was anyone else around?" Paulik asked. "Other than you and the Sister City folks?"

She thought for a moment before answering. "Reverend Dave came in. He was talking on his cell phone."

"That's odd, don't you think?" Verlaque said. He had thought it strange that Flanagan would leave during the service, and wanted to hear her opinion.

She nodded. "He explained to me why, after

he hung up. His elderly mother, who lives in California, is unwell, so he took the call, even though the service was still going on." Verlaque wondered whether Dave had offered that information voluntarily, or if Mlle Dubois had outright asked him. Or it might have been a combination of the two, Mlle Dubois giving Dave one of her piercing looks of disapproval, and he in turn blurting out the explanation for the call.

"And when they were serving the dinner?" Paulik asked. "Did anything seem out of the ordinary?"

"No, nothing at all," she answered. "There was a constant queue, but our Sister City guests were calm and gracious while serving."

Verlaque and Paulik exchanged looks. It was an impossible task: Any one of the people serving could have slipped the crushed Doliprane into Cole Hainsby's food. With the crowd and the commotion, no one would have seen. Except, perhaps, someone standing next to the murderer. Verlaque said, "Thank you very much, Mlle Dubois."

"You've been a help," Paulik said, shaking her hand.

She said good-bye, put her hands into her coat pockets, and left the tent.

"Needle in a haystack," Paulik said as they walked through the fair.

"Yes, and we've missed lunch," Verlaque said. He turned to look at the Bath stand, where two elderly ladies sat, both knitting. "They have some desserts left," he said, motioning to their counter.

"Better than nothing."

They walked over and both women looked up. The dark-haired one, Verlaque noted, was able to keep knitting while she spoke. "May I help you?" she asked.

"Welcome to Bath," her colleague quickly said, having set down her knitting. She smiled broadly.

"Lovely city," Verlaque said in English. "That crescent of Georgian buildings—"

"The *Royal* Crescent," the dark-haired woman said.

Verlaque smiled. "Right." He got out his identification card and showed it to the women. He then introduced Bruno Paulik, explaining to Paulik that he'd speak in English and to ask if he had trouble understanding. Paulik gave him a thumbs-up.

The dark-haired woman put a long, thin hand to her chest. "Is anything wrong?"

"We have some questions regarding Sunday evening's dinner at the cathedral," Verlaque replied, pronouncing his words slowly and carefully for Paulik's benefit.

"That poor man—" the white-haired one said. "Oh, do excuse us. I'm Sally Bennett." She offered her hand.

"Eunice Sumner-Smith," the other one said in turn, offering a limp but thinly elegant hand to the two men.

"M Hainsby died of poisoning," Verlaque said bluntly. "It was administered into something he ate that night."

"My word!" Mme Bennett exclaimed. She looked at Mme Sumner-Smith, who had finally set down her knitting and looked equally shocked.

"The food," Mme Bennett said. She leaned in toward the men and lowered her voice. "You must think the poison came from our food."

"From that dinner, yes," Verlaque said. "But not necessarily yours. We'd just like to know if you can help us in any way—"

"We don't actually bake the food ourselves, you understand," Mme Sumner-Smith explained. "It's sent to us from England. It's fresh, mind you."

Verlaque glanced at Paulik, who rubbed his eyes with the tips of his fingers. The commissioner had clearly understood the English. And, yes, what a needle in a haystack. They'd have to have someone check on the facilities in England. Why would anyone in the UK want to poison someone they didn't know? Unless they were mentally unstable. He looked now to the two old women, neither of whom he could imagine putting crushed acetaminophen into an Eccles cake.

And what would be their motivation? Or that of anyone else at the Sister City fair? How would they have known Cole Hainsby? He then realized he was wasting their time, and missing lunch.

"No one touched your desserts," Verlaque said, "before the dinner on Sunday?"

"Absolutely not," Mme Sumner-Smith answered.

"Well, there were two boys from the church who came to help us carry things over," Mme Bennett offered. "But they were just teenagers, and very polite, weren't they, Eunice? Mlle Dubois sent them. It was too much for Eunice and myself to carry, you see . . ."

"Of course," Verlaque said.

"But we walked beside them," Eunice Sumner-Smith added, in case the two men thought them guilty of carelessness.

"Thank you for your cooperation," Verlaque said. He glanced over at their desserts, the plastic wrap for the trip from England having been removed, as they now sat on antique porcelain blue-and-white plates, much like the ones his grandmother had loved.

"Would you like a dessert?" Mme Bennett asked, her voice rising in excitement.

"Thank you so much," Verlaque said. "One of those desserts looks like flapjacks. My grandmother used to bake them."

"A French woman who makes flapjacks?" Mme Bennett asked. "How lovely."

"She was English," Verlaque said. "She met my grandfather in Paris just before the war."

"That's why your English is perfect," Mme Sumner-Smith said, pursing her lips by way of a smile.

Verlaque smiled, even though he wasn't certain he had just been given a compliment. But he was happy that his English skills had been upgraded from Reverend Dave's "almost perfect" to this woman's "perfect." He looked over at Paulik, who was studying the desserts. Yes, Bruno had understood everything.

CHAPTER FOURTEEN

After they had each eaten two flapjacks and two Eccles cakes, washed down with some tea that Mlle Bennett had insisted upon, they crossed the path between the stands and stopped at the Americans. The steak fryer was now cleaning his grill. A woman, tall and slim with light brown curly hair, put away bags of sandwich buns and condiments. They looked to be close in age; he was a little shorter and wider with the same coloring.

The man held up his hands and shrugged. "Sorry, we're closed for the afternoon. *Fermé.*"

"That's okay," Verlaque replied in English. "We're here to ask a few questions about Sunday evening." The woman set down a crate she had been carrying and came to stand beside her partner. Verlaque and Paulik showed their identification and introduced themselves.

"Jason Miller," the man said, shaking Verlaque's hand. "This is my sister, Kendra." Verlaque estimated the Millers to both be in their early to midthirties.

"Hello," Kendra Miller said. "I'm sure glad you speak English. We've been using our junior high school French all week and are exhausted."

"That guy died, didn't he?" Jason said. "Sunday night."

Verlaque looked at him, trying to decide if he wore a look of compassion or fear. "Yes," he replied. "Of poisoning."

Both Millers gasped.

"It wasn't a heart attack?" Kendra asked. "That's what we both thought." She looked to her brother for confirmation, and he nodded.

"No," Verlaque answered. "Something he ate had been tampered with. Did anyone other than yourselves touch your food?"

The Millers shook their heads. "Just us, I can assure you," Kendra said. "We couldn't make our steak sandwiches since we didn't have the grill, so Jason made coleslaw and I made Irish potato candy."

Verlaque's look of confusion made her smile. "Sorry," she said, her shoulders falling in relaxation. "Coleslaw is cabbage salad, kind of an Irish ancestral thing. And the Irish potato candies are made with coconut, icing sugar, vanilla, and cream cheese. I roll them in cinnamon and they kind of look like little brown potatoes."

"I see," he replied. He held up a finger, signaling a pause, and translated for Paulik, who in turn politely nodded, trying to imagine such a dessert. Verlaque was quite sure he hadn't eaten either of those things on Sunday evening, but he vaguely remembered Marine talking about coconut.

"Did you see anything out of the ordinary?"

"No," Jason replied, looking to his sister for confirmation.

"Nothing," Kendra said.

"Is this your first time here?"

"We've come the past three years," Jason said.

"And everyone gets along?"

"Everyone?" Jason repeated.

Verlaque thought he saw Kendra flinch. "You mean between the sister cities?" she asked. "Of course we do."

"No rivalries?" Verlaque asked.

"No, we come to make a bit of money, that's for sure," Jason said. "But we also participate for the fun. It's a beautiful city, Aix, and we're proud of this collaboration."

Kendra nodded in agreement.

"Do you know the church people well?" Verlaque asked. "I'm sorry I have to ask these questions, but the dead man was involved in the Protestant church here in Aix."

"No, we only met France Dubois," Kendra said. "She arranges the carol sing dinner every year."

"I spoke with the reverend," Jason offered. "But it was just chitchat."

"Do you remember what Cole Hainsby looked like?" Verlaque asked. Paulik understood his question, as he then produced a small color photograph of Hainsby that the APCA had provided.

Jason shook his head. "I didn't know him."

159

"Do you remember serving him at the dinner?"

"No," Jason said.

"I don't either," Kendra added. "It was really busy."

"Yes, it was," Verlaque said.

"Feel like speaking French for a change?" Verlaque asked as they walked away from the Philadelphia stand.

Paulik laughed. "Thanks, I could use a break," he said. "The Tunisian must speak French."

"That's his stand over there," Verlaque said as he tilted his head to the right. The Carthage stand was a riot of color, every square inch covered in patterned or striped cloth and rugs. Five or six woolen rugs covered the concrete floor, and more hung from the walls, alongside tablecloths and bedspreads. Two tables held kitchen utensils made from olive wood and stacks of colorful earthenware bowls. In the middle was an armchair that had been upholstered in the same wool and zigzag pattern used on one of the rugs.

"Hélène would have a field day here," Paulik mumbled as they got close to the stand, their heads turning from side to side to take everything in.

Behind one of the tables stood Mehdi Abdelhak, who was small and trim with oily black hair. He spoke to a client who was trying to decide which olive wood bowl to choose while Verlaque picked up a small earthenware dish covered in a red and white glaze. "Olives," Verlaque said, showing it to Paulik.

Paulik picked up another bowl, slightly smaller, with white and green glaze. "Olive pits," he replied, grinning, giving it to the judge.

"*Bonjour*," Abdelhak said, now standing before them, the client having paid and gone.

Verlaque set the bowls down and shook the Tunisian's hand. "Antoine Verlaque, examining magistrate of Aix," he said. "This is my colleague Bruno Paulik, commissioner. Do you speak French?"

"*Bien sûr*," the Tunisian replied. "Mehdi Abdelhak. Boutique owner in Carthage."

Verlaque smiled, sensing that Abdelhak was slightly teasing him. "We'd like to ask a few questions about Sunday evening's dinner at the cathedral," he began. "A man fell ill while there, and died. Did you know him? His name was Cole Hainsby."

Paulik held up Hainsby's photograph.

"So sad," Abdelhak replied. "I remember him, though."

"You do?"

Abdelhak nodded. "He liked to eat everything. Everything."

Needle in a haystack indeed, thought Verlaque. Seeing the judge's expression, Abdelhak asked, "How did he die?"

"M Hainsby was poisoned," Verlaque replied. "The poison was added to one, or perhaps several, dishes."

Abdelhak held his hand to his chest.

"We don't know which dish," Verlaque continued, "but will soon." He hoped Dr. Cohen could indeed identify the poisoned food.

"I can tell you that the dead man ate my eggplant salad twice, and had three pieces of baklava. Perhaps more. Was anyone else ill that evening?"

"No, thankfully."

"Then it was only *his* food—"

"Yes," Paulik answered. "It would seem that M Hainsby was intentionally poisoned."

"But who would do such a thing?"

Verlaque looked at the neat, well-dressed man, who was the first person to ask what he regarded as natural questions to an event such as this one.

"I'm sorry," Abdelhak said. "I'm curious. And I'm saddened by this." He once again put his right hand to his heart and gently pressed down.

"Did you see anything out of the ordinary?"

"No, nothing at all. It was the same ceremony, same dinner, as last year."

"You went to the ceremony, too?" Verlaque asked. "I did as well. Did you see anyone else there from the sister cities?"

"Yes, the German couple," Abdelhak answered. "No one else. But as you saw, the church was full."

"And when did you bring in your food?" Paulik asked.

"Mlle Dubois arranged to meet us at the green door in the square just before the ceremony. I was there early, and so were the Germans. The others must have come after the ceremony, or perhaps earlier. She gave us all her cell phone number."

"And when you brought the food in," Verlaque asked, "was anyone else there?"

Abdelhak crossed his arms and looked down. "Yes," he replied after a few seconds. "Mlle Dubois, of course, the American reverend, and the old priest. That's it, I think. No, wait. There was a thin elderly woman wearing glasses; they kept calling her 'Doctor.' She was very bossy."

"Dr. Bonnet?"

"I think so. Yes, *bonnet,* like 'hat.' That was it."

Paulik put his hand to his mouth, pretending to stifle a yawn. He rubbed his cheeks in an attempt to hide the creases from his smile.

"Thank you," Verlaque said, trying to get the image of his mother-in-law out of his head. "If you think of any other details, please call us." He handed the Tunisian his business card. "In the meantime, I'd like to buy these bowls."

"And me, a small rug," Paulik said.

Verlaque looked at the commissioner, surprised.

"For Léa's room. The tile floor is cold in the winter," he explained.

"We'll speak to the Germans and the Italians

later," Verlaque said as they walked away. "They seem to have cleaned up and gone for the afternoon anyway." Verlaque now carried a small plastic bag containing the two bowls wrapped in newspaper. Paulik had the rolled-up rug under his arm, a rug that had grown from small to medium by the time he made his final decision. "Mme Hainsby is due at the Palais de Justice in an hour," Verlaque continued, looking at his watch. "Do you mind if I speak to her on my own? I'll explain later."

"That's fine," Paulik said. "I'll see if the officers speaking to the cathedral staff and choir singers have discovered anything interesting. I've also asked Flamant and Schoelcher to dig up the backgrounds of the church employees, Damien Petit, and the Hainsbys."

"It's just occurred to me," Verlaque said, slowing down his pace in order to look at Paulik and to gather his thoughts. "If only Cole Hainsby was poisoned, the murderer must have been someone standing behind those serving tables at the dinner. Someone who was meant to be there. When they saw Hainsby, presto. They added the crushed acetaminophen. Otherwise it would have been too dangerous; the dish, had it been poisoned earlier in the evening, could have been given to anyone."

"Or it could have been someone standing beside Hainsby in the queue," Paulik suggested.

"I know what a frenzy those buffet dinners can be." As they walked back to the Palais de Justice Paulik told the judge about the various buffet dinners he had been to recently, most of them for weddings or baptisms of cousins and their children. Verlaque smiled as he listened, glad that buffet dinners were something he knew nothing about.

Verlaque showed Debra Hainsby to a chair opposite his glass-topped desk. He hoped his stomach didn't growl. On their way up the stairs inside the Palais de Justice, Verlaque and Paulik had each bought a chocolate bar from the second-floor vending machine. Verlaque had passed by the small kitchen behind Mme Girard's desk, hoping to find an apple or orange in the fruit bowl, but it was empty.

"How are you doing?" he asked in English.

"Still shaken up," Mme Hainsby replied. "But a bit better now that my sister and brother-in-law have arrived from California. Do you mind if we continue in English? My French is good but I'm feeling so tired . . ."

"Certainly. I'm afraid I have some bad news for you."

"What could be worse than my husband dying?"

"M Hainsby was poisoned. Or the food that he ate was poisoned."

Debra Hainsby looked at him, wide-eyed. "That's ridiculous. Was the food that off? And why did no one else get food poisoning?"

"No, someone put poison in his food. Enough crushed acetaminophen to kill."

She put a hand to her mouth and her eyes filled with tears. Verlaque slowly nudged a box of tissues toward her on the desk. "I'm sorry," he said. She let out a loud sob, her head moving up and down as she held a tissue to her face. Verlaque looked out his office window at the clear blue winter sky and flinched when he saw a seagull fly past. He sometimes forgot how close Aix was to Marseille and the sea. He looked back at Mme Hainsby as she dried her eyes. "Will you go back to the States?" he asked. He had more pressing questions, but he wanted her to calm down a little bit first.

Mme Hainsby shook her head. "No, I don't think so. We like it here, and I have a job."

Verlaque nodded, knowing where she worked.

She went on, catching her breath, "We've been here for ten years. We love it, you know; the great food, the markets, the slower way of life. When my sister visits all she talks about are their big four-by-fours, their credit card debt, and how worried they are about hospital bills and health insurance."

"I can't imagine having to pay to go to the hospital," Verlaque said, honestly. "You told me something on Sunday evening. A sort of confession."

"Oh, did I? I can't remember anything clearly from that night . . ."

"You said that you hadn't been a good wife."

Mme Hainsby pulled at the end of her sweater in what seemed an affected way. "Did I," she said, neither a statement nor a question.

"Yes."

"I meant it in a general sense."

"It's an odd thing to say when your husband's just died, to someone you don't know," Verlaque said. "It very much sounded like a confession."

"That I don't doubt," she replied. "We had just been arguing. That's why I said it."

Verlaque opened a file folder and took out the advertisement he had clipped from *La Provence*. "I assumed you were referring to this man," he said, pointing to Alain Sorba. "To your love affair with him." He didn't have much doubt that Florence Bonnet was right in her observations.

Mme Hainsby brought her hand to her chest, much like Mehdi Abdelhak had done, confirming what Marine's mother had suggested. "So that's what some of the teachers were laughing about," she quietly said, choking on the last few words. She stopped, gathered herself together, and continued, "I saw them last week, gathered around that newspaper in the faculty room. When I came in they stopped laughing and quickly put it away."

"Were they jumping to conclusions?"

She paused and then looked straight into his eyes. "No. I warned Alain that people at the school knew about us."

"*Bon*," Verlaque said, putting the clipping back in the folder. "I'm afraid I have to ask you this: Would M Sorba be capable of poisoning your husband? Or would you?"

"Never. To your first and second questions."

"How are you so sure? About M Sorba, I mean."

"Alain? Why would he want to hurt Cole?"

"To get him out of the way? Because M Sorba wants to marry you? Because he's jealous that Cole was married to you and not him? Should I go on?"

"No, no," she answered.

"How serious is it between you and M Sorba?"

"We've been . . . seeing each other . . . for almost six months." She held her head down.

"Is he married?"

"Yes," she said quietly. "But his wife lives in Marseille."

Verlaque pursed his lips. What did she mean by that comment? Marseille was hardly far, a twenty-minute drive. The seagull had just reminded him of that fact. "There was a meeting on Saturday night at the Protestant church," he said. "Your husband broke something and you ran out of the room crying. Why?"

"Can't a woman get emotional sometimes?"

"Crying over a broken glass or plate?"

"I was frustrated with Cole that evening," she said. "I was so confused—"

Verlaque asked, "Were you going to leave him?"

"I told myself I'd wait until after Christmas before telling him."

Verlaque nodded. He felt so tired; he wanted only to be at home, alone with Marine, looking at her bright green eyes. Making a silly joke and seeing her laugh.

CHAPTER FIFTEEN

"I was sitting in my office this afternoon, thinking only of being alone with you," Verlaque said as he held Marine in his arms. He caressed her thick wavy hair and smelled the back of her neck. Again, roses.

Marine pulled away and looked at him. She put a hand to his cheek and gently rubbed it, running her fingers along his usual three-day beard. Tomorrow morning he would trim it after showering. "I think of you, too, during the day," she said. "There's nothing nicer to come home to. My partner." She stopped caressing his cheek and said, "But tonight we won't be alone."

Verlaque let his arms drop quickly to his sides in what he hoped was sufficiently dramatic fashion. *"Pardon?"*

"You invited your old school friend and the movie star."

He slapped his forehead, this time with no calculated drama. "I forgot. It's because it's midweek; we usually entertain on the weekends."

"Right, but I remember you telling me they were going somewhere this weekend."

Verlaque laughed. "Yes, but I can't remember where. Megève? St. Moritz?"

"If you'll set the table," Marine said, "I'll finish up in the kitchen."

"What are we eating?"

"A sort of quick cassoulet. A friend gave me the recipe."

"You're serving sausage and beans to a film star?" Verlaque asked. "I love it." He decided not to tell Marine about Bruno's cousin Yvan. "I'll pick some reds from the cellar. What's the first course?" He suddenly remembered that he had eaten only a few desserts for lunch. With tea.

"The usual suspects. Sliced salami, nuts, olives. I didn't have time for anything else."

"Oh, I almost forgot!" Verlaque said. He went to the front hall and picked up the plastic bag off the Empire-era console, one of the few pieces of furniture he had taken from his grandparents' home in Paris. He gave the walnut console a quick glance, taking in its thin legs trimmed at the top with gold leaves. So elegant, like Emmeline, like Marine. He went back into the kitchen. "This is for you. From the Tunisian stand at the fair."

Marine set down a head of frisée lettuce and opened the bag, gently removing the newspaper. "They're beautiful. Thank you," she said, turning each bowl around in her hands. "What a pretty pattern. Perfect for olives."

Verlaque looked at her feet.

"What is it?" Marine asked.

"Would you like a little rug right there? In front of the sink?"

"No," Marine replied firmly. "It would only get dirty."

"Think about it. I'll go down to the wine cellar and when I come back up I'll tell you about Debra Hainsby," Verlaque said as he walked toward the front door.

Marine turned back to face the sink and smiled, listening to her husband whistle while he skipped down the stairs. She washed the lettuce, put it in the spinner, spun it, then set it aside. In a large ceramic salad bowl she made the dressing, beginning with some finely chopped shallots and a tablespoon of mustard. She added a good amount of walnut vinegar and then slowly poured in the dark green olive oil from Les Baux, stirring quickly until a thick dark yellow sauce formed. She breathed in the smell—a mixture of pungent mustard and onions, walnuts, old wine, and olives, not one ingredient overpowering the other. She closed her eyes, thankful that her mother had at least taught her to make a proper salad dressing. Everything else she had learned from books, from Antoine, or from watching friends cook.

"Ready!" Verlaque said, back in the kitchen holding two bottles. "I picked two local reds. Thought we'd introduce our Parisians to some great wines from Aix. One of them is Hélène's 2003 Syrah."

"The year of the heat wave!" Marine said. "How strong is it?"

Verlaque looked at the bottle's label. "Fifteen percent." Before Marine could object he added, "The beans will soak up all the alcohol."

Marine looked at the clock on the wall. "They'll be here soon," she said. "Tell me about your day while we set the table."

Verlaque gave the Riedel wineglasses a last-minute wipe with a linen tea towel and told Marine about the English women, making her laugh with his imitation of Mme Sumner-Smith, his back erect, his cheeks sucked in, and his hands folded in front of his chest. He put less performance into his description of the Americans and the Tunisian, but he did tell her about France Dubois staring at Jason Miller. "Lovers' quarrel?" Marine asked.

"With France Dubois?"

"Antoine . . ."

"But the most interesting interview was with Debra Hainsby," Verlaque said. "It started off as you would expect; she was full of questions, and grief. By the end of it she had admitted that she was going to leave her husband."

"Despite what you say, I can't see a wife killing her husband," Marine said, setting down the last dessert spoon. "Sorry."

"Why is that? It's certainly been done in the past."

"The children."

Verlaque was about to reply when the buzzer sounded. He walked over to the intercom, lifted up the receiver, and yelled into it, "Fourth and last floor. Sorry, there's no elevator." As he hung up he heard Léo Vidal-Godard mutter, "*Merde.*" He opened the front door slightly and waited, while out of the corner of his eye he could see Marine applying a last-minute coat of lipstick, using one of the glass-fronted kitchen cabinets as a mirror. She quickly took off her apron and gave her husband a thumbs-up, smiling widely. His heart melted.

Margaux Perrot, with her porcelain skin and expensively trained trim body, entertained the others during dinner with stories about filming in Russia in winter with a famous young actor who kept adding vodka to his hot tea and could, miraculously, still remember his lines. And yet Margaux seemed entirely unaffected by her fame. Her questions about their lives, and Aix, were natural and sincere. She asked Marine what kind of sausages she had used, and it reminded Verlaque of a heroine in an English novel from the turn of the century that Emmeline had loved. Was her name Lucy? Yes, he thought so. Lucy, who, despite her wealth and well-bred family, couldn't help but follow the kitchen staff around, demanding how the pudding was made. He smiled because, as if on cue, Margaux's next question was about the dessert. He turned to Léo and asked if he'd like a cigar.

"I'd love one!" Léo replied.

"Not around me," Margaux quickly said. "Sorry, I don't like the smell and they remind me of my first husband."

"Let's go for a stroll," Léo suggested. "It's not very cold out tonight."

"Let's," Verlaque agreed. "Aix is at its best at night, anyway."

"I'll put on some tea," Marine said. Verlaque looked at her, surprised. She usually had a digestif with him after a big meal like the one they had just eaten. But he supposed that Margaux wouldn't be drinking one, and so Marine was being a good host. And he'd have to be a good host and walk around Aix, when he wanted nothing more than to smoke sitting in his armchair with a book of poetry on his lap. He got up from the dining room table and went into the living room, taking two Bolivar cigars out of his humidor, and slipping a cigar cutter and lighter into his jacket pocket.

Léo stood in the doorway, his winter coat already on, while Marine and Margaux settled themselves into the living room, Margaux Perrot sitting in Verlaque's favorite chair. Verlaque put on his coat and they went down the four flights of stairs out into the Aix night, the cobblestone streets lit by lamps shedding a golden light. They walked through the Place de l'Archevêché and Léo stopped to read a wall plaque above a fountain. "Who's this guy?" he asked, looking at the bust, in bas-relief and side profile, of a heavily mustached man from the previous century.

"His pen name was Marcel Provence," Verlaque said as he cut his cigar and lit it. "He died in the early 1950s and has been largely forgotten, which is too bad as he saved Cézanne's studio from being demolished by buying it with his own money. He also wrote an exhaustive survey of every home on the Cours Mirabeau. Marine managed to find me a copy in a used-book store. I can't imagine what she paid as they're highly sought after." He looked over and saw that Léo was losing interest and fumbling with lighting his cigar, so he suggested they get a digestif at the bar around the corner. "I think they have an outdoor heater on their terrace," he added, seeing that Léo looked cold. They continued walking, passing the cathedral, its medieval stone saints lit up for the evening, and stopped at a small bar that almost shared the north wall of the great church. "Let's grab that table under the heater," Verlaque said. "I was hoping it would be free."

Verlaque knew the woman who was always behind the bar only by sight and quite liked her. She was short and stocky with bright eyes and a wide smile. He had only ever seen her wear T-shirts and jeans. His favorite T-shirt was a black one that read "Castro" across the front; he once asked her about it and she explained that it wasn't for Fidel Castro but for a neighborhood in San Francisco. But it was another bartender who came outside to get their order tonight. This one, also a woman, wore a T-shirt even though it was a late December evening, showing no sign of being cold. "What do you suggest to keep us warm?" Verlaque asked.

"Well, not many of our customers smoke cigars," she said, "except for those cheap ones dipped in rum, so I'm not sure." Verlaque smiled, thankful that there were old-time bars like this one, where men who had worked hard all their lives on the railways or cleaning city streets could be comfortable. No tourists and no students.

Verlaque said, *"Donc, deux poires, s'il vous plaît."* He looked at Léo, who smiled in approval. She left, and as she went inside to get their pear *eau de vie*, Verlaque could see the bar's interior through a window. At the end of the bar stood the other barmaid, the one he usually saw, wearing the Castro T-shirt again; she was speaking with a tall, wide-backed customer who was facing away from them. Verlaque could hear Léo talking, but he was more interested in what he was seeing, as the barmaid was now arguing with her customer. The customer turned his face

177

and Verlaque saw that it was Père Fernand, from the cathedral.

Realizing that he was being rude, Verlaque turned to listen to Léo, who was talking about a business venture in North Africa. "Quarries," Verlaque heard. The large number of trucks and bulldozers that needed to be purchased, and how expensive they were. Verlaque took a sip of the *eau de vie* that had just been set down on their table and tried to pay more attention to Léo, but found watching the scene inside the bar much more interesting.

Marine tried not to yawn; she had seen that it was 11:00 on the stove's clock when she was making tea. That meant that it was almost midnight now. She knew now how long it took to smoke certain cigars; she had seen the Bolivars Antoine had selected and she thought an hour and a half. "Have you seen any good expos lately?" Marine asked, using the go-to question raised at almost every Parisian dinner party.

Margaux sat back and sighed. "The Pierre Soulages exhibition at the Pompidou was sublime," she said. "I went twice."

"Oh, we were invited to the opening," Marine said. "Antoine lent them a painting for the show. We just got it back."

Margaux sat up straight. "Are you serious?"

"Yes, would you like to see it?"

"Of course!"

Marine got up, thankful that the cleaning woman had been at the apartment all afternoon, as the painting was in their bedroom. "Follow me," she said. They walked down the hallway to the bedroom, Margaux making pleasant remarks about the framed photographs that lined the hall's walls, mostly purchases made by Marine; a few were by her friend Sylvie, from a time when Marine could still afford Sylvie's work.

"There it is," Margaux said when they walked into the bedroom. She stood in front of the enormous painting, its black paint thick and shiny like oil even in the dimly lit bedroom. "They're not sad, despite the fact that there's only one color," Margaux said.

"I agree."

Margaux walked backward, still looking at the painting, and then sat down on the edge of the bed. Marine was surprised at her boldness; she had always thought that beds were intimate places, even when she was young. Her bedroom had always been a sanctuary. She continued looking at the painting when she heard what she thought was a quiet weeping. She turned around to see Margaux Perrot—grande dame of the red carpet—sitting on Marine's bed, her head in her hands, crying. Marine sat down beside her. "May I help in any way?" Marine asked.

Margaux got a tissue out of her sweater pocket

and blew her nose. "Thank you. You've been very kind this evening. It's moving here, I think. I miss Paris. And it's Léo, too. I know he's worried about his business but he won't confide in me. So my husband is keeping secrets from me, and here I am, away from Paris, where other, *younger,* actresses are going to snap up all the good roles before I can get back." She dried her eyes and smiled.

"I'm sure your agent is looking out for you," Marine said. She guessed that Margaux was approaching forty, and that part of her blues had to do with the lack of women's roles at that age and older. At least that's what she'd read. "You're not the only actress who lives in Provence, either."

"You're right. I'm just feeling cut off."

"I understand."

"Do you think you could speak to Antoine about Léo?" Margaux asked. "I know that Léo was very worried about money, and now all of a sudden he's walking around the house whistling, as if he didn't have a care in the world." She blew her nose, rather loudly for a film star, thought Marine.

"Don't worry," Marine said. "Don't forget that Léo's in the construction business, which I've always understood as a business that can go from disaster to triumph overnight. But I'll see if Antoine can have a chat with him the next time they're together." Marine didn't think that her husband would want to have anything to do with this idea; he hadn't seen Léo in decades; they didn't have anything in common except a shared past as undergraduates. And why couldn't Margaux ask Léo herself?

Margaux stood up, her face freshened by a quick pinch to each cheek, and ran her hands through her hair to fluff it a bit. "Gorgeous painting," she said. She turned on her fashionable very high heels and walked out of the bedroom without, Marine mused, thanking her.

CHAPTER SIXTEEN

"We need to get Debra Hainsby back for questioning as soon as possible," Verlaque told Paulik as they walked toward the Place des Cardeurs. "At the church dinner on Sunday, Florence Bonnet told me something that I'd forgotten about until last night. Debra fed Cole something, I can't remember what. It might have been a pastry."

Paulik looked at the judge with wide eyes and got out his cell phone. He dialed and gave instructions to someone on the other end as he and Verlaque walked under the clock tower.

Matteo Ricci saw them first. "Here come two cops," he said as he cleaned off a long carving knife.

A woman in her early thirties came to stand beside him. "Don't be paranoid," she said. She began to arrange cheeses and fresh pasta in their display case, sticking little Italian flags, marked with the price per kilo, in each one. She sized the men up as they got closer; the shorter one had a crooked nose and salt-and-pepper longish hair, and the taller one was bald. She added, "They could be mafia." She frowned at the fingerprints on the display case's glass front; she took a sheet of paper towel and window cleaner and began rubbing.

"That's not even funny, Vittoria," Ricci said.

"*Buongiorno*," Verlaque said, resting his hands on their wooden counter. He got out his identification card and Paulik did the same. Ricci looked at Vittoria and rolled his eyes. "Do you speak French?" Verlaque asked in Italian.

"Of course we do," Ricci said. He introduced himself and his girlfriend, Vittoria Romano.

"My French is better than his," Vittoria said, laughing some more. "I took lessons at the Alliance Française in Perugia."

Paulik showed them Cole Hainsby's photo. "I don't know him," Matteo Ricci said.

"I remember him from Sunday evening's dinner," Vittoria said, holding the photograph in her hands. Verlaque saw Ricci give his girlfriend a quick look of annoyance. Vittoria saw it, too, as she now looked at her partner and gestured angrily with her hands. "He was eating all of our mushroom lasagna!"

Verlaque smiled, trying to make Vittoria feel at ease. It was cold outside but she had rolled up her sleeves to arrange the cheeses and clean the case. He saw an elaborate tattoo on her right forearm and tried to read it. It was of two birds flying, carrying a banner in their beaks with someone's name written in an old-fashioned font. What looked like a walnut hovered above the birds; whatever the message was, Verlaque was as lost as he usually was with tattoos. The message usually seemed apparent only to the wearer. Another fad he detested.

"What else did you serve that night?" Paulik asked.

"Cheese," Ricci said, crossing his arms. "Including an expensive truffle Pecorino."

"I hid the Pecorino from him!" Vittoria said, smiling. She took the photograph once more and studied it. "He wasn't the man who collapsed, was he?"

"Yes," Verlaque said. "He died of poisoning."

"In the food?" Ricci asked.

"Yes, but for the moment we don't know which dish."

"Well, it wasn't the Pecorino," Ricci said as he began to load the refrigerator with miniature bottles of Prosecco and Italian sparkling water, signaling that he was finished answering questions.

Verlaque and Paulik thanked the Italians and left. Verlaque turned around to look at their stand, one of the more elaborately decorated ones: flags of Italy and Perugia hung inside and out, as well as posters of Umbria's many glorious sites, and outside stood three white plaster columns that were being used as tables by some Aixois with coffee cups. "The columns are a nice touch," Paulik said. Verlaque peered at him, not sure if it was a joke or not, so he stayed silent.

They wandered to the Tübingen stand a few

tents down. A couple in their fifties or sixties worked quickly at setting up for lunch. "We're not ready yet," the woman said when she saw Verlaque and Paulik. "Could you come back in twenty minutes?" Her French was accented but very good.

The men showed her their badges and her husband appeared quickly at her side. "What's going on?" he asked. His French was more accented, less fluid. He held his hands up and shrugged in case they hadn't understood his French.

"We'd just like to ask you both a few questions about Sunday evening's dinner at the cathedral," Verlaque said. "It's routine."

The German grunted and then held out his hand. "Gerhard Rösch," he said. "This is my wife, Anna."

"That man died, didn't he?" Anna Rösch asked in a quiet voice. "Is that what this is about?"

"Yes," Verlaque answered. "One of the dishes he ate was intentionally poisoned."

"And you think one of us did it?" Gerhard Rösch asked. "What would we possibly—"

Paulik held up his hand, palm facing the Germans. "No, no," he said, lowering his voice. "At this time, it's difficult to ascertain which dish had the poison in it that night. We'd like to know if you noticed anything strange, or out of place, that evening. Especially while setting up for the dinner, or while serving." He took the photo out of his coat packet and held it up. "This is the man who died. He was an American, Cole Hainsby."

Anna Rösch nodded. "He was the emcee at the carol sing. We were there. We went last year, too."

"He was annoying," Gerhard Rösch said.

"Gerhard!" Anna replied, making the sign of the cross.

Gerhard Rösch sighed. "We got to the church early, because of the service." Anna nodded in agreement. Gerhard continued, "That young girl met us at the green door . . ."

"Mlle Dubois," Anna said. "She's a gentle soul. A wounded—"

"Yah, yah, Anna. Let's answer their questions. The cathedral's priest was there, and some of the church people, and our fellow sister cities."

"Who, exactly?" Paulik asked. "Can you remember?"

M Rösch guffawed and began to stir a pot of simmering broth.

"I can try," Anna said. "When we got there, at five o'clock, Mlle Dubois was there, of course, and Père Fernand, from the cathedral. He's very nice. The Americans were there, weren't they, Gerhard?" Her husband nodded. Anna went on, "The English women were there, setting up their stand. . . . The nice gentleman from Carthage came but then quickly left. And that man in the photograph, Cole, he was there. With his wife and some other Americans. They were setting up the chairs and putting paper tablecloths on the tables. Oh, and the Italians, they were there—"

Her husband held up a finger. "Only one?" Anna asked.

"Yah. One." M Rösch noisily set down his wet ladle and began to rummage through a shoe box, pulling out a pen and a scrap piece of paper. "I draw," he said. "Anna misses some things."

"Gerhard has a great visual memory," Anna said, smiling awkwardly.

While Gerhard Rösch drew, Verlaque asked, "Did anyone other than you touch your food, madame?"

"No. Only the two of us."

"And nothing seemed odd?"

Anna shook her head. "It didn't take us long to set up, and we were told we would have time to reheat the food after the service, as the Protestant church was taking care of the aperitif; chips and things."

Gerhard pointed to his drawing. "Round table in middle is aperitif," he said. Verlaque nodded, remembering. "This table next to it is wine." Gerhard laid the drawing down on the counter and pointed with the end of his pen. "The teenagers and some others set up six long tables for guests, ten at each table. At the top of the room is green door and windows out onto the

Place de l'Archevêché. Our dinner table was set up here, in front of the windows."

Anna pointed to the Sister City food table and said something in German.

"Okay," Gerhard said as he began to write on the drawing. They watched as he labeled who was where. "Finished," he said. "On the right, closest to kitchen and at the end of the table, is me and Anna. Then USA. Then Italy. Then Tunisia. Then, closest to green door, the old English ladies."

"Gerhard!" Anna said.

He shrugged his shoulders and smiled slightly at Verlaque and Paulik.

"You said there was only one of the Italians," Verlaque reminded M Rösch.

"Yah, only her," he answered.

"Gerhard's right," Anna said. "The Italian man came after about a half hour. And like I said, the man from Tunisia came and set up but then left. You know," she lowered her voice, "perhaps because he's Muslim. The carol sing may not have been of interest to him."

Paulik glanced at Verlaque, both of them remembering that Mehdi Abdelhak had been to the service and seen the Germans there. "Something else you said, M Rösch," he said. "That Cole Hainsby was annoying."

"He asks questions about Tübingen and doesn't listen to answers."

"What kinds of questions?" Verlaque asked.

"How much does house cost. How many people live there. Do I know anyone in chamber of commerce."

Anna said, "We do know one person in the chamber of—"

Gerhard slapped his hand down. "I tell him nothing!"

"Thank you both for your time," Verlaque said. "May we keep this drawing, M Rösch?"

"Of course."

Paulik thanked them as well and pointed to a small color photograph of two handsome young men, both in their twenties, taped to the side of the refrigerator. "Your sons?"

"Edmund and Clovis," Gerhard said, pointing to the brothers from right to left. "Will be dentists, not cooks like us."

Anna tilted her head down and stared at the countertop.

"They're obviously very smart," Paulik said. "You must be proud."

Now looking up, her gaze solemn and steady, Anna said, "We'd do anything for them."

By the time they left the fair, queues of hungry customers had formed at most of the stalls, especially those selling hot food. As they walked, Paulik listened to messages on his cell phone. "Debra Hainsby is available this afternoon at her house," he said to Verlaque after hanging up. "The school's director, Alain Sorba, might be available on Thursday. He's away on a field trip tomorrow."

"Another one?" Verlaque asked. "They just went skiing. Is it a school or a country club? Do you know what the price of that place is?"

"More than fifteen thousand a year," Paulik answered. "We considered it for Léa, in case she didn't get into the music program at Mignet."

Léa Paulik, an accomplished singer, had just turned twelve. "Of course Léa would get into Mignet. Are you nuts?"

"Stranger things have happened."

Verlaque opened his mouth to protest further but then considered the options for the Pauliks: the integrated music program at Mignet, the city's highly rated public-funded junior high school, where gifted music students split their day between the school and the conservatory, or a mediocre junior high on the north side of town. At least the Four Seasons offered a bilingual education; perhaps he and Marine would do the same in their shoes. At any rate, he couldn't judge, nor did he have to make that kind of decision, as they were child free. "We're not missing lunch today, that's for sure," he finally said as they crossed through the flower market being held in front of the town hall. He looked at his watch; it was half past twelve and he picked up his pace, now very hungry. They stopped as a tourist took a photo of his wife, standing with her back to bouquets of bright yellow fragrant flowers.

"Flowers in winter?" Verlaque asked. "I had no idea."

"Winter jasmine," Paulik said, waiting for the tourist to retake his photo, as he wasn't satisfied with the first.

"It never ceases to amaze me that people choose to come here," Verlaque said, sighing. His stomach growled. "It's just a small town."

Paulik said nothing as he looked around the square: two sides were lined with medieval apartment buildings painted in ocher, orange, or pale rose; the west side held the golden-stone town hall with its elaborately carved wooden doors and pebbled interior courtyard; and the eighteenth-century grain hall stood on the south end, its façade topped by a sculpture of two allegorical figures representing two rivers, the male the Rhône and the female the Durance. Or was it the other way around? Paulik looked up at the female figure's giant foot dangling over the stone enclosure that had supported and protected them for more than three centuries. She was the Durance, as it was famous for its flooding; hence her dangling foot. He thought of childhood excursions into Aix, piled into his parents' car. His sisters would shop for clothes and school supplies; he and his two brothers would go to a rugby game at the stadium just outside Aix. When their Renault station wagon crossed the Durance, they'd yell that they were halfway from the Luberon to Aix. On the way back they'd be too tired to notice the river, usually asleep, one or two of them sprawled out in the back of the wagon, when such things were still legal. For years Paulik and Hélène lived in Pertuis, just to the north of the Durance. They would joke that the river had only two states: completely dried up, with only a dry rock bed visible, or overflowing, water pouring onto its banks. He smiled, remembering a young Hélène, just graduated from enology school, and he a young police cadet. Before Léa, their pride and joy. "Pardon me?" he asked when he realized that Verlaque was speaking.

"I asked if you would come here as a tourist."

"Absolutely," Paulik answered.

Well fed on Fanny's daily special, Verlaque and Paulik walked to the parking garage to pick up Verlaque's car, and ten minutes later they were on the narrow road that swerves and bends toward the hamlet of Saint-Marc-Jaumegarde to the northeast of Aix. Paulik ran his hand along the 1963 Porsche's dashboard and said, "I love this car, but is maintenance a nightmare?"

"No, partly because I don't drive it far or often, and I get it serviced once a year. The clutches and brake pads every fifty thousand kilometers, and I change the tires often; a new set of fronts with every other set of rears."

Paulik looked behind the front seats. "It's hardly a four-seater, is it?"

"No, more like two people and two cases of wine," Verlaque said.

Paulik turned back around and, to Verlaque's relief, stopped asking disparaging questions about his car, which he affectionately referred to as Ferdinand, after Ferdinand Porsche, who started the company in 1931. Verlaque used the remainder of the drive to fill Paulik in on Debra and Cole Hainsby's rocky relationship, including her affair with the director of the Four Seasons bilingual school.

"It's this lane on the right," Paulik said, consulting his cell phone. "There should be a sign on a tree. *Voilà.* LES CHÊNES."

Verlaque slowed the car and began to drive up the steep dirt road that was littered with potholes. He gripped the steering wheel and tensed up every time they drove over one. "Do you mind if we park here and walk up?" he asked, now wishing they had brought a police vehicle. But his parking garage was close to Fanny's, and he hadn't felt like waiting for someone at the Palais de Justice to find them an available car.

"Not at all," Paulik said. He pointed to a vineyard track where they could turn around and park in the right direction for pulling out later.

"This isn't how I imagined it," Verlaque explained as they walked up to the house. "I thought they'd be in one of Saint-Marc's fancy subdivisions."

Paulik said nothing, as he hadn't met the Hainsbys, nor did he care much about where people lived, or which neighborhoods of Aix had cachet or were now unfashionable. Past an ancient, spread-out oak tree they were able to see the house: small and charming, two stories, in stone with white shutters. More ancient oaks surrounded the house, protecting it. "*Les chênes*," Paulik said.

The front door opened and Debra Hainsby stood on its threshold, looking very small and old. Verlaque had no idea if she had loved her husband or what she might be feeling. *Would she be grieving if she had poisoned him?* he wondered. But as they got closer, he thought that this was a woman who certainly looked like she was miserable.

"Mme Hainsby," Verlaque said, shaking her hand. "Thank you for being available to meet with us. This is the police commissioner, Bruno Paulik."

Paulik shook her hand and she mumbled for them to enter. Inside was not what Verlaque had expected, having heard that Cole Hainsby was "annoying," "silly," "reckless," "naïve,"

194

and, especially, "broke." It was like being in the pages of a glossy English magazine. *Country Life*, he recalled, which Emmeline had delivered to their house in Normandy weekly. The walls were painted a pale yellow, sunny without being sickly or vulgar. The curtains were of a thick, good-quality cotton in a floral print. The antiques were polished, and expensive. Table lamps lit the room, and real art—watercolors and oils, mostly landscapes—hung on the walls. One or two of the better ones were lit from above with brass lights. The ceiling was beamed, and the floor a rustic brick.

"English people own it," Debra Hainsby explained. She didn't seem to mind that the examining magistrate had been looking over, and admiring, her house. "We move every year or so, depending on who's got a cheap furnished house for us to rent," she said, motioning for them to sit down. "This is by far the best. The owners are Londoners who used this house for vacations, but they've moved to Hong Kong."

"How are your children doing?" Verlaque asked. He thought he remembered that they had two.

"Devastated," she replied. "They're out for a long walk now, with my sister and brother-in-law. I'm keeping them out of school this week. I'm not going in either, maybe ever." She looked at Verlaque and raised an eyebrow, which he took to mean she was cooling her relationship with Alain Sorba. What happened? Just yesterday she was bragging about him. Or was she just being more careful this time? Acting the wounded widow?

"Given the nature of your husband's death, which is now being treated as a homicide," Verlaque began, "we need to ask you more detailed questions, and look into your finances, and search the house as soon as possible. I wanted to tell you that in person."

"Am I a suspect?" she sputtered, losing her cool for the first time.

"Yes," Verlaque said flatly. "You were seen feeding your husband while in the queue at the dinner."

She looked stunned. "I can't remember a thing about that. And if I did feed Cole something, so what? He was my husband."

"He was poisoned, Mme Hainsby."

"Our marriage wasn't perfect," she said, looking out the window with a puckered brow, as if worried that the children would come in at any minute. She lowered her voice. "Yes, I was having an affair with Alain Sorba. But I did not poison my husband."

"Did M Hainsby tell you about his business?" Paulik asked.

"Rarely," she replied. "I should have asked more, especially about the finances. But I knew from experience that if the business was in trouble, there was no arguing with Cole."

"Did your husband seem worried lately?"

"Yes. But just before the carol sing Cole seemed relieved. He told me he had a solution."

"But you don't know what?"

"No," she answered after hesitating a split second.

"Really?"

She got up and began to pace around the room.

"We will need to look at your husband's life insurance plans," Paulik said. "If you could have them ready by tomorrow, when I'll be back with a few officers to look over your husband's personal possessions."

"That's fine," she said. "One of the policies is with our bank on the Cours Mirabeau, the Crédit Lyonnais. The other is back home, in the States."

Verlaque got up and shook her hand. "Where did you live before coming to France?"

"Michigan. Ann Arbor. It's where we're both from. We met at the university there."

He knew Paulik would contact their American colleagues in Ann Arbor once he got back to the Palais de Justice. Or an officer who spoke English would. But he doubted that their time spent there had anything to do with Cole Hainsby's murder. It was very much something, or someone, to do with Aix-en-Provence, and that service at the cathedral.

CHAPTER SEVENTEEN

Verlaque walked down rue Jean de la Roque thinking of the Hainsby family, and the children out walking over the dry garrigue with their aunt and uncle. Did the elders have words of wisdom? Or did they just walk, and let the children speak if and when they desired? Paulik had hurried on ahead, in a rush to get back to the Palais de Justice for a meeting and then to make the telephone calls to Michigan. The Porsche had made one or two funny sounds—like coughs—as they drove back to Aix, but Paulik hadn't made a comment about it. Perhaps Bruno thought old cars always made noises.

Verlaque walked slowly, looking in shop windows. The Alsatian delicatessen was decorated for a Christmas in Strasbourg, not Aix. Brightly lit stars illuminated the interior, hanging from the ceiling. Through the window he could see a Christmas tree, every branch full of decorations. Red-and-white-checked cloth seemed prominent, as did gingerbread in all sizes and forms. He texted Marine to see if he should buy something for dinner and she replied immediately with a smiley face. He walked in and said hello, shaking hands with the owner, whom he knew from sight. As the owner prepared Verlaque's order of sausage and sauerkraut he looked around, daring to touch some of the ornaments. He texted Marine again, asking if they were going to have a Christmas tree that year. She answered, "*Ouuuuuui!*" He wondered if the Christmas tree would be in town or in their country house and then put the thought out of his mind. He didn't want to let the two residences complicate life.

As he waited he examined some ornaments made from felt that were hanging from the tree. They were *petits bonhommes* with fat stomachs, little outstretched arms and legs, and high pointed felt hats. He took one in his hands and touched the hat, running his thumb and index finger from the top of the little man's head to the point of his hat. He lifted one off the branch—he preferred the ones with green hats—and laid it on the counter. The shop owner wrapped it in a piece of tissue and added it to Verlaque's other purchases, which at the last minute also included a bottle of Riesling. Another client came up to the counter and Verlaque thanked the owner and moved aside, taking the *bonhomme* out of the paper bag, removing the tissue, and putting the little man in his coat pocket. He left the shop, having no idea why he had just done such a thing. Did he not want Marine to see it? Was it to be a surprise for her? Or was he embarrassed by it? In fact, he realized as he walked, he had no idea why he bought it. Was it because it put a smile on his face? Or were there deeper reasons that a therapist would analyze—not enough toys or affection at home? Their mother hadn't bought many toys for Verlaque or his brother, for fear they'd be spoiled. But she had no problem spending the Verlaque family money on herself, wearing the latest haute couture or redecorating their 1st arrondissement Parisian home every two or three years. Reaching a hand in his pocket, he touched the pointed hat again, stroking the soft felt, and ran into Père Fernand. Verlaque was relieved to see the priest and think of something else, not his mother, nor the reason why even now he was touching the pointed hat in his pocket.

"*Bonsoir, mon père,*" he said, pulling his right hand out of his pocket and shaking the priest's hand.

"*Bonsoir,*" Père Fernand answered, smiling down at the bag. "You've been buying choucroute?"

"I couldn't help myself." Verlaque realized he hadn't spoken to, or questioned, the priest since Sunday evening's grave event. "Do you have a few minutes?" he asked.

Père Fernand turned and gestured with the back of his hand to the same bar next to the cathedral where Verlaque had taken Léo Vidal-Godard. They walked in, nodded to the two-woman bar staff, and took a table for two against the far wall. One of the women called across to them, and they both ordered half-pints of Leffe.

"Gentlemen," she said, setting down the beers on the Formica-topped table.

"*Merci*, Pierrette," Père Fernand said, reaching for his beer to toast Verlaque.

Verlaque lifted his glass to the priest's and said, "*Santé*," taking a sip of the amber-colored Belgian beer. "You know her?" he asked, once she was back behind the bar. He knew the answer, as he had seen them arguing that night he was with Léo.

"I've been coming here for years. It's good to support local businesses, don't you think?"

Verlaque smiled and drank. "It's a very old-fashioned name for such a modern woman," he said quietly.

"She hates it," Père Fernand said, leaning across the table. "Her friends call her Pierrot but I prefer to maintain an owner-client relationship."

"She owns this bar?" Verlaque asked, looking around the bar that, while small, was sitting on prime Aix real estate.

The priest nodded. "Inherited it from her grandfather. It's a very good thing that Aix still has old bars like these."

"They are quickly disappearing, I'm afraid."

"They needn't," Père Fernand said.

"On Sunday evening," Verlaque said, putting his beer down, "we didn't get a chance to talk after M Hainsby fell ill—"

"And died."

"Yes. Did you notice anything peculiar that evening? Or even during the day?" The priest looked bewildered and Verlaque continued, "You see, Père Fernand, Cole Hainsby was poisoned that evening. Someone put enough crushed acetaminophen in one of the dishes to kill him."

Père Fernand folded his arms across his chest. "Someone murdered him? That's unbelievable, and heartbreaking."

Verlaque nodded and waited for the priest to continue, which he did. "There were so many people in and out of the church and dining hall that day," he said. "I don't know how I can help. I'd say you'd get the most help from the young woman from the APCA. France is her name."

"France Dubois."

"I think that's it," Père Fernand said. "She organized the dinner so was the person who was most present. I kept bumping into her all afternoon."

Verlaque asked, "Anything else? Did you know Cole Hainsby?"

"Never met him in my life, until that afternoon, of course, when he came early with his wife to rehearse a few things before the service began."

"And how was that?"

"How did they do?" the priest asked. "If you ask me, they needn't have repeated every song instruction in French and English. It took far too long, and I believe that almost everyone in the

202

church understands the basics of one of the two languages."

Verlaque smiled. "I agree. But between the Hainsbys?"

"Oh, I understand. How was it between them? Icy."

"Did anyone from the sister cities behave strangely?"

The priest took a sip of beer and set it down, again crossing his arms and leaning back in the chair. "The Tunisian," he said slowly. "I'm probably making a big deal of nothing, and I don't want to sound . . ."

"Racist?"

"Precisely. But about an hour before the service, he was in the cathedral, taking photographs. I came up to him from behind, so I may have startled him. He jumped, and held on to his camera as if I would steal it. I had only wanted to tell him that we needed to clear the church as the service would soon be starting."

"What was he taking pictures of?" Verlaque asked.

"The chapel of Saint-Roch."

CHAPTER EIGHTEEN

At 9:00 a.m. the next day, Antoine Verlaque was already seated at his desk, looking at the telephone, willing it to ring. He felt like nothing had been uncovered in the Cole Hainsby case. Marine had gone to bed early; she was unusually tired, and he hoped it was just the winter blues and the upcoming holidays. She was planning various dinner parties that they would host, and an elaborate Christmas Eve dinner. He kept finding scraps of paper scattered around the apartment, with menus or grocery lists scrawled on them.

Someone knocked on the door, and Verlaque thought he recognized the three steady knocks of Bruno Paulik. "*Entrez*," he said.

Paulik slipped through the door and closed it behind him. He carried a file in his left hand, and with his right he shook the judge's hand. He held up the file and said, "There's gold in here."

"*Ah, bon?*" Verlaque asked, sitting back down and motioning for the commissioner to sit across from him. "Have you come to save me from eternal boredom? Is there something in that file that proves that Debra Hainsby, or Alain Sorba, killed Cole Hainsby?"

Paulik pulled his chair closer to the desk and laid the file down on the glass-topped surface.

"It's exciting news, yes, but it has nothing to do with the wife or her lover."

"Or the cook or the thief?"

"*Pardon?*"

"Sorry," Verlaque said. "It was an English film from the 1980s that I really liked. Go on."

A slightly irritated Paulik opened the file and said, "This file contains a report of a car accident. It was six years ago, on that *route départemental* north of Aix, after Célony and before the big roundabout toward Éguilles."

"Where the antique stores are?"

"Exactly, and the rows of plane trees on either side of the road," Paulik said. "It was a head-on collision between a Twingo and a bigger car . . ." He looked down the first page, read, and said, "A Volvo station wagon."

"Did the people in the Twingo make it?" Verlaque asked, relieved that Marine had long ago sold her Twingo, a car so small and cheaply made it always made him nervous.

"No," Paulik said. "Husband and wife, declared dead at the scene. No other passengers."

"And the people in the Volvo walked away?"

"Yes," Paulik said. "The driver of the Volvo was at fault. He was trying to pass a little Citroën and hit the Twingo, which was coming south from Éguilles . . ."

"Why is this gold, Bruno? Was the Volvo driver Cole Hainsby?"

Paulik nodded.

"And the Twingo driver and passenger? Where do they fit in? Who were they?"

"Pascal and Myriam Dubois."

"France's parents?"

"*Si, señor*," Paulik replied, folding his arms and sitting back.

Verlaque ran his hands through his graying hair. "The poor girl," he finally said. "So that's where her sadness comes from. And why I thought she was holding something back . . ."

"Do you think it's enough of a motive?"

Verlaque considered the question. "Could you hate someone enough for killing your parents to seek revenge? Probably. But why wait six years to do it?"

"Building up your nerve?"

"And France Dubois was everywhere on Sunday," Verlaque cut in. "Her name keeps coming up."

"It would be easy to crush a handful of Doliprane and put it in someone's food. I'm surprised that method isn't used more often."

"The dinner on Sunday was the perfect occasion," Verlaque said. "Perhaps France rarely saw Cole Hainsby. At the cathedral she'd be with him all day."

"Do you think she got the job at the APCA because of him?" Paulik asked. "An American church in the center of Aix . . ."

"And what in the world was she doing at that fair yesterday? Staring down the guy from Philadelphia?"

"She might hate all American men now," Paulik suggested. "He and M Hainsby are kind of the same age."

"Don't tell me you think France Dubois is going to go on some kind of killing spree, Bruno. Poisoning all the American men between the ages of thirty and fifty."

Paulik shrugged.

Verlaque picked up a pen. "We don't have anything else, do we? Our two principle suspects are now women. The unhappy wife, and the wallflower. I'd much rather it point to someone like Alain Sorba."

"Because he has a Corsican name?"

"No, because he charges unsuspecting expats fifteen thousand a year for his posh school, when our public ones are free and rated better."

The address they'd been given was 18 rue Cardinale. France Dubois had called in sick that day—a cold, Reverend Dave had reported. "She usually gets them around this time of year," he had said. "I hope it's nothing serious you want her for."

"No, no," Verlaque lied. "Just more boring routine questions."

Paulik looked up at the street numbers as they

walked while Verlaque looked ahead at Saint-
Jean-de-Malte, hoping they didn't run into
Florence Bonnet or her sidekick, Philomène
Joubert. "*Voilà*," Paulik said, stopping to read the
brass name plate at number 18.

"Joubert," Verlaque said, sighing. "Second
floor."

"You know them?"

"A crony of Marine's mother," Verlaque
answered.

Paulik laughed, sensing perfectly well what
kind of woman Mme Joubert must be. "F Dubois,"
he said. "First floor." He rang the buzzer beside
her name.

Verlaque tilted his head up to inspect the classic
four-story building. The ground floors in Aix
usually held offices or shops. This one housed
an apartment; the owner's name was engraved
on the plaque. He now remembered the garden
in the back; Marine's old apartment, one street
north, had a view of it. The garden was big, with
a fountain and mature trees. France's apartment
had the tallest windows in the building, so the
ceiling must be high. Then the Joubert second-
floor apartment, always desirable, he thought,
as the ceilings would still be a good height, but
the apartment was that much higher up—quieter,
with better views. Another name he didn't
recognize on the third floor, and then two names
on the least-expensive fourth floor, with its

usual slanting low ceiling that leaked. Probably a young couple, thought Verlaque, or even two students.

"*Oui?*" France Dubois's voice sounded over the scratchy intercom.

"Antoine Verlaque," Verlaque said. "I'm sorry to bother you. I'm here with the commissioner. May we come up?"

"Of course." The buzzer sounded and the heavy red door opened with a thud.

The entryway looked much like other seventeenth- or eighteenth-century foyers in Aix, including his own: a black-and-white-checkered marble floor; an old wooden chair in the corner that somebody no longer wanted in their apartment; pale blue walls, the paint chipping in many places; and, where the top of the wall met the ceiling, *gypseries*, white plaster moldings common in Provence. They walked up the red tiled stairs to the first floor, where France was waiting for them, standing in her doorway, a woolen shawl wrapped around her tiny shoulders. She blew her nose and stepped aside so that they could enter.

"Would you like some tea?" she asked, closing the door.

Both men refused, and asked how she was feeling. "Better than this morning," she said. "But these old apartments never warm up."

Verlaque quickly looked around as he took a

seat opposite her. Paulik sat in another armchair to his right, and France sat on the sofa. The room had once been elegant, but the *tomettes* on the floor needed polishing and the walls repainting. The two large windows that he had admired from the outside didn't let in as much light as he would have thought. Another look revealed why; they were dirty and dusty. But while the apartment needed some cleaning and upkeep, it was homey and tastefully decorated. An enormous framed print of a Picasso exhibition in the Côte d'Azur hung above the sofa and brightened the room. Some interesting throw pillows and a few vintage lamps and vases added a quirkiness and color that he enjoyed.

Verlaque leaned forward with his elbows on his knees. France looked at him, and her eyes watered. He couldn't tell if it was from her illness or from sadness. "You know, don't you?" she asked, sniffling.

"What about?" Verlaque said.

"The car accident."

Verlaque looked at Paulik, who nodded. "Yes," Paulik said. "Six years ago on the *route de Célony*. Cole Hainsby was driving the car that killed your parents."

She dabbed her eyes with a fresh tissue and said, "I think of it every day."

"I can imagine," Verlaque said. "Is that why you took the job at the APCA?"

She shook her head. "You probably won't believe me when I tell you that getting the job there was a coincidence. When I heard about . . . the accident . . . I was living in Paris. I immediately quit my job and came back to Aix to live."

"Wasn't that difficult?" Verlaque asked. "The memories?"

"The memories were all I had, Judge." She straightened her posture, a move that touched Verlaque. "I had a degree in English," she said. "There weren't many jobs in Aix. I was so lucky to get the job at the Anglo church. At first it was part time, but I didn't need the money, because my parents left me . . ." She choked and stopped speaking, catching her breath.

"Please, take your time," Paulik said.

"They left me money," she went on. "I bought this place very quickly, too quickly, perhaps, as it still needs a lot of work, and I just don't have the energy on my own." She sighed. "When I took the job, I didn't know that the man who was responsible for my parents' deaths was involved in that church."

"Until very recently," Verlaque suggested.

"Yes. Because of the carol sing, it was the first time I met him. He of course had no idea who I was. I'm not even sure if he remembered the name Dubois."

"Did you wish him dead?" Verlaque asked.

"Of course," she answered flatly. "Many times

over. But that was six years ago. Last week, when I sat beside him at the café, I could barely hold my fork. But when I finally met him, I felt nothing. Even that bothered me; that I didn't feel anything. Don't you think?"

Verlaque thought about his own ambivalence when his mother died, and nodded.

France said, "I didn't kill him. I know that's why you're here."

"Did you watch him at the dinner?" Verlaque asked.

"How could I not?" she said. "It was like a train wreck. I despised him, yet I couldn't keep my eyes off him."

"Did you notice anything odd?" Paulik asked. "Did anyone mess about with the food, especially on M Hainsby's plate?"

"M Hainsby was moving around so much, it's hard to say. I saw him go up to the food table at least three times, the last time with Père Fernand. Oh, and once with Alain Sorba, who owns the Four Seasons bilingual school."

"He's the director of the school, I believe," Verlaque said.

"He owns it as well," France confirmed.

"And during the dinner's setup?" Paulik pressed on. "Did everything happen in a calm and orderly manner?"

"It was chaotic, but so was last year," she said. "So I'm not sure how to answer that. I was worried that M Abdelhak from Carthage was late, but Père Fernand found him in the church and showed him to the dining hall. There were the usual last-minute crises, as there always seem to be, but on the whole it was nothing I couldn't handle."

"The American from Philadelphia," Paulik began. "We saw you watching him."

She flinched but then waved her hand through the air. "Oh, him," she said. "He'd complained about his stand at the fair so I was watching him work, to see if his claims were valid. He said he didn't have enough space, or electricity."

Verlaque rubbed his hands along his thighs, thankful that he had chosen to wear woolen pants that morning. Her apartment really was very cold. Paulik took it as a sign for them to leave. "*Merci beaucoup, mademoiselle*," Paulik said, getting up and shaking her hand. "Get well soon."

"*Merci*," France Dubois said, her voice now quiet, as it had been when they had first arrived.

Verlaque said, "We'll see ourselves out." He took one last look at the Picasso print. It was a view from a window, onto the Mediterranean, the type of scene made famous by Picasso's friend and rival Matisse. There were colorful pigeons sitting on the windowsill and balcony, not going anywhere, pleased to be there; *did Picasso's father have some kind of connection with pigeons?* Verlaque tried to remember; he'd check when he got home. The sea was a dark blue with white caps, and a bit of rocky peninsula jutted out into the water, framed by swaying palms. The predominant colors inside Picasso's seaside room were orange and yellow; outside, blue and green. Warm and cold. Verlaque looked back at Mlle Dubois, who was now sitting in the armchair Paulik had used, staring straight ahead at the pigeons and the palms and the Mediterranean.

Mme Girard put her hand up, commanding them to stop, when they got back to the Palais de Justice after lunch. "Officer Flamant has called twice," she said. "He'd like you to go downstairs to his office."

"Thank you," Verlaque said, smiling. She sighed and turned back to her computer screen, and out of the corner of his eye he could see the green background of a solitaire game. He wondered how old she really was, and why she still worked when he knew her husband was wealthy. "Shall we?" he said to Paulik, and they turned back the way they had come.

As they descended the wide stone staircase Paulik said, "Mlle Dubois doesn't seem like a killer."

Verlaque observed that the stairway's walls, like those at France Dubois's, were pale blue and needed painting. "No, I agree. Even with crushed Doliprane, however easy that would seem."

"Does anyone of the group seem like a murderer? I mean, half of them are church people, and the other half are visiting from Italy or Germany or wherever, and are generously cooking dinner for everyone. It just doesn't make sense." He held the door open for Verlaque when they got to the first floor.

"The fact that they go to church doesn't make them automatically innocent," Verlaque said as they set off down one of the many mazelike hallways of the Palais de Justice.

"I know," Paulik said. "I'm just thinking out loud." He looked at Verlaque and asked, "Do you often go to church?"

"Pardon me?" Verlaque asked. "Oh. You mean because I was at that Christmas service?"

"Yeah."

"No, that was the first time in years I've been to any kind of religious service, except for weddings and funerals. Marine wanted to go . . . you know, with her mother's choir and all . . ."

"Right. Right."

Verlaque looked at Paulik. "Do you and Hélène?"

"Nope," Paulik answered. "We didn't even baptize Léa. Hélène's parents wouldn't speak to us for weeks."

"I take it your parents weren't equally upset by the nonbaptism?"

Paulik laughed. "No. They were farmers and

Communists. The church didn't play a big role at our place."

Flamant was staring at his computer screen when they got to his desk. "You called?" Paulik asked.

Flamant jumped up. "Scram," he said to a young cadet who was working beside him, yawning and filling out a form. The young man ran off and Paulik filled Flamant in on their visit to France Dubois.

"I've dug up some stuff on the deceased, Cole Hainsby," Flamant said, fanning out a computer printout for them to look at. "Most of the info I was able to find over the internet, and someone at the Ann Arbor police precinct speaks pretty good French."

"Seriously?" Verlaque asked.

"Well," Flamant said, "better than my English. He was a French major before becoming a police officer. In fact, he went to the same university as the Hainsbys . . . University of Michigan."

"That's where they met, right?" Paulik asked.

"Yes, they graduated the same year," Flamant said. "Cole was a history major, and his wife, theater." He showed them a photocopied photograph. "I found this on the university's website from their graduating year. It looks like Debra . . . her last name was Collins then . . . won a prize for a play." He looked closely at the photograph's fine print and read them the play's title, which neither man could understand in Flamant's butchered English.

"Oh!" Verlaque said. *"Un Tramway*. It's a Tennessee Williams play." He tried translating *A Streetcar Named Desire* into French, but knew he didn't have it quite right.

"To continue," Flamant said, making Paulik grin, "they stayed in Ann Arbor for two years after university, then moved to Italy."

"This is getting more and more interesting," Verlaque said.

"Not Perugia," Flamant said. "Alba."

"In Piedmont? Where the white truffles come from?" Paulik asked.

Flamant nodded and showed him one of the papers. "They weren't there long," he said. "Eight months. Cole ran a tour company for Yanks . . . I mean Americans. Then they went back to the US. Three years in Michigan, where M Hainsby worked in a bicycle shop, and then here, to Aix."

"And his tour company here?" Verlaque asked.

"That will take more time, nosing around on the internet," Flamant said. "I did find their website. People who took the tour gave good reviews, four or five stars. Only one person didn't seem to like it; a Frenchie. He gave one star."

"Call the disgruntled customer. You'll be able to speak in French," Verlaque said. "Does it have their name listed?"

Flamant looked down at the paper. "Cédric Farou. From Lyon."

"But it probably doesn't have his phone number there."

Flamant smiled. "That'll be easy to find."

"And Mme Hainsby's job?" Paulik asked. "At the bilingual school."

"All I found was their website. They have a swimming pool and tennis courts!" He whistled. "But I can't find anything on the school's finances, or the director. I'm usually pretty good at hacking . . . I mean digging . . . but all roads were blocked. I'll try again."

"The Sister City participants?" Verlaque asked. "None of them are, by chance, ex-criminals out on parole?"

"No such luck," Flamant said. "One of the women from England worked as a nurse, though."

Verlaque and Paulik looked at each other, perplexed. Flamant said, "The poison."

"It was acetaminophen," Verlaque said. "A kid could have done it."

"I just thought that perhaps a nurse would have the nerve," Flamant explained.

"*Pas mal*," Paulik said.

"No, not the English grannies. And the other participants?" Verlaque asked.

"Nothing so far, but I've just started. I only had time to research Bath and Tübingen."

"You've done a great job," Verlaque said. "Thanks."

"We'll leave you to it," Paulik said. "Make sure to stretch after all that computer time." He could stand only thirty minutes at most on computers before his back started complaining.

Flamant said, "One last thing. Once I saw the swimming pool at the Four Seasons school I looked up the tuition costs, which aren't so easy to find on the website—"

Verlaque laughed. "I don't doubt it."

"I ended up phoning and asking the secretary. And what I'm wondering," Flamant said, "is if Mme Hainsby was just a secretary, and Cole Hainsby's business partner told you they weren't making much money, then how could they afford to send their two kids to that school?"

CHAPTER NINETEEN

It had been easy to find the Four Seasons bilingual school. Verlaque began seeing signs for the school on the road heading into Lambesc from Saint-Cannat, and he soon found himself on a *départemental* road north of the town numbered 66. He laughed and sang to himself "Route 66"—his grandparents had played it often, in Paris, at parties—all the way up to the school's gates. He drove in and managed to squeeze his car into the very last parking spot, half on grass and half on gravel.

The school was in a low, long building, one of its walls still dressed in rough fieldstone, giving away its origins: it would have been a farmer's house, or a rural outbuilding, or a sheepfold. The windows and doors were new and cheap, replaced ten to fifteen years ago, he guessed. There were no signs of Flamant's cherished swimming pool and tennis courts; they were probably on the other side of the building, the south side. So far the north side, with its dusty parking lot, did not give a good impression. He got out of his car, locked the door, and headed for a glass door marked with a slightly crooked sign that read OFFICES/BUREAUX.

"May I help you?" a middle-aged woman with

a thick Provençal accent asked him when he walked in. She sat behind a desk in an office so small he had almost walked right by her.

"Yes, thank you," he said. "I have an appointment with M Sorba. Antoine Verlaque, examining magistrate."

She looked at him but said nothing. She picked up the telephone and told whoever answered—Verlaque assumed it was Sorba—that his visitor had arrived. She hung up and said, "He'll be right here."

Verlaque again thanked her and stood in the small hallway, waiting. She hadn't offered him a chair, or told him where he could wait. He wondered what expats thought of her when they arrived, far from their old lives and worried about their children, and if they even understood her thick Midi accent. She was one of the most unwelcoming people he had ever met, and he was a civil servant. The women in the passport office in Aix had more personality, and they were notoriously rude. He tried to amuse himself in the narrow hallway by looking at photographs that had been taped to the wall; students, happy and smiling, at events and on trips. He scanned the wall looking for a shot of kids in class, with books. He found only one.

"M Verlaque?" a young woman called out in French, but with an Anglo accent.

"Verlaque. Yes."

She approached him and offered her hand. "I'm Colleen Fairchild. Please follow me."

He greeted the woman, who looked to be in her late twenties and was wearing a remarkably short skirt. He heard a huff from the other secretary. He followed her to the first floor, deliberately looking at his feet.

They entered a room with a low, wood-beamed ceiling and she offered him a seat in a black leather chair. "M Sorba will be right with you," she said, sitting down behind a white modern desk.

"You're his secretary?" Verlaque asked, crossing his legs.

"Only temporarily. M Sorba's assistant is on leave. She—"

A wooden door opened beside her desk and a big, barrel-chested man strode out. "Thank you, Colleen," he said, cutting her off. "Alain Sorba. Please, come into my office." Verlaque turned to thank Mlle Fairchild and saw her watching Sorba, blushing.

Verlaque followed Sorba and was ushered into another leather chair, also black. The office had a window that faced south, and he saw the infamous swimming pool. Sorba noticed Verlaque looking and said, "It's heated in the summer."

"You do summer school?" Verlaque asked.

"It's a big business for us," Sorba replied. "Mostly Parisians sending their kids down from

Neuilly or Versailles to learn English. The kids love it. But I assume you're not here to talk about school. Unless you have kids . . ." He smiled and pushed a colored pamphlet along his desk toward Verlaque.

"No kids," Verlaque replied, returning the smile. He studied Sorba and tried to see the female attraction to him. He was big, and seemed to keep himself in shape for someone approaching fifty, and had a wide smile. "You're right, I'm not here to talk about school, but about Cole and Debra Hainsby."

"Terrible, terrible."

"You were there Sunday evening," Verlaque said.

"Yes, so many of our students and their families go to that carol service," Sorba replied. "I go every year, as do most of my teachers and staff."

"Do your teachers and staff know about your affair with Debra Hainsby?" Sorba looked toward the door, as if the young Mlle Fairchild could hear them. "Mme Hainsby told me," Verlaque said.

"That's over," Sorba said, his weight on his thick arms that were resting on the edge of his desk, his head slightly tilted and with a furrowed brow, as if he were in penance.

"It's over now that her husband is dead?"

"Before that. Listen, Judge, I don't know why you're here, but I don't appreciate your questions." Sorba got up and gestured toward the door. Verlaque imagined Colleen Fairchild on the other side, trying to listen.

"Cole Hainsby was poisoned," Verlaque said, getting to his feet, "as I'm sure you know. And we will find out by whom."

"I hope you do," Sorba said, picking up the phone.

Mlle Fairchild jumped up when Verlaque emerged. "I'll see myself out," he said. He walked quickly and purposefully down the narrow winding stairs, and instead of turning left, to the parking lot entrance, he turned right and walked outside onto the terrace. The covered swimming pool was off to his right, and in front of him were three tennis courts. Beside them were about ten small white portable buildings with dusty paths connecting them. He imagined they were classrooms, as the building he had just left would be too small to house the offices, the cafeteria, and other necessary rooms.

He began walking toward the portables when the doors to each suddenly opened and children of various ages—around twelve to about eighteen, he guessed—charged out, running in all directions. A teacher walked out of the nearest one and lit a cigarette.

Verlaque smiled as he approached her. "Break time?" he asked.

"Ten minutes," she replied, looking at her

watch. She had an accent when she spoke French, but he couldn't tell if she was American or British. "Are you a parent?" she asked. "We haven't met."

Verlaque extended his hand. "Antoine Bonnet," he said. She introduced herself as a math teacher, but he didn't catch her name. He went on, "I'm getting transferred from Paris and looking around the school for my kids. My wife taught English in Paris and might apply for a job here."

The teacher—in her midforties, he guessed, nice looking, with large blue eyes but badly dyed blond hair—laughed. "I wouldn't advise it."

"For my kids or my wife?"

She looked around her and lowered her voice. "Oh, the kids love it here. They're lucky to have us. We're good teachers and we love them. But I wouldn't recommend teaching here, especially if your wife is French and has passed the CAPES for teaching in France."

"She's from London," Verlaque said. "So, no."

"I didn't, either, sadly," she said. "When my husband and I first got here from Glasgow, I kept saying I would sit the exams, but when I got the job here, at a private school, I was over the moon. I could teach without doing the dreaded CAPES . . ."

"But you don't like it here?"

"Like I said, the kids are great," she said. "They are international, and most have smart, caring parents who've been sent here for a year or two for work. Most of the kids don't speak French when they arrive, so it's a logical solution for parents to send them here, and the companies pay the tuition."

"Ah, I see."

"But it's run as a business," she continued, taking a long drag on her cigarette. "For example, this ten-minute break? We get paid hourly but don't get paid for the ten minutes between classes. So I stopped speaking to the students between classes, and stopped prepping between classes, and now smoke a cigarette or two."

"Ten minutes between how many classes per day?" Verlaque asked.

"Eight or nine," she said. "So the lost salary adds up."

"Yes, it certainly would."

She again looked around the portables and said, "I'm telling you this for your wife's sake, so please keep it between us. We don't get paid for meetings, or for the dozen or so times a year when we're expected to be here all day Saturday for parent-teacher meetings, for *fêtes*, or for sporting events. The teachers' morale is pretty low. But for your kids, it's great. They must speak French, right?"

"Yes, they do," he said. He consoled himself that he wasn't really lying to the Scottish math teacher; if he and Marine did have children, they would certainly speak French. And possibly English. He had never thought about it before. "Well, thank you very much," he said. "Your ten minutes is almost up." He smiled a wide smile, knowing it could match M Sorba's.

"It's barely even time for one cigarette," she said, laughing. "Good luck with the move. You'll love Provence!"

He pointed to the bright blue sky and raised his hands in the air, and she laughed. As a Glaswegian she would understand a Parisian's love of the south and its blue skies and warmth. He walked away, continuing around the far end of the building in case Sorba was looking out his office windows. As he passed by the last portable, he heard adult giggles and stopped to look in the window. Two teachers—he assumed they were teachers—were locked in an embrace. Maps hung on the wall, and he saw a globe on a desk. Is that all they did at the Four Seasons? Sleep around with one another? He ducked away and walked quickly and quietly until he got to the parking lot. He was about to open the door of his Porsche when a soccer ball landed at his feet. He picked it up as two teenagers came running up to him.

"Sorry!" one of them said in French. "Lucas kicked it clear over the building!"

"It's no problem," Verlaque said, handing it to them.

"It kind of is," his shorter friend said. "We're not supposed to be in the parking lot during break."

His friend laughed, twirling the ball in his hands. "Yeah, we might scratch the gangsta's car!"

"Gangsta?" Verlaque said, trying to join in on their joke. He looked around and saw an enormous German-made SUV, black, with tinted windows.

"Is that the director's SUV?" he asked, winking. He knew the car must be Sorba's, having met him and listened to the math teacher complain about low salaries. He took in the license plate number, and the sticker on the rear bumper that advertised a luxury automotive dealership in Marseille.

"Yep," the shorter one answered. "Gangsta Sorba."

They broke down in giggles and his friend poked him in the ribs. "Matthew!" he said in warning. They laughed again.

"But your car is sweet," Matthew continued. Verlaque marveled at their flawless French. Matthew was obviously Anglophone; his friend, Verlaque couldn't tell.

"Yeah, it's gorgeous," his friend added, walking around the Porsche and peering into the window on the driver's side. "But doesn't it break down a lot?"

Verlaque frowned. Had they been taking lessons from Bruno Paulik? "No, it's very reliable," he insisted.

CHAPTER TWENTY

"I met two very funny teenagers at the Four Seasons today," Verlaque said as he chopped leeks. "Everything was a joke to them. They both had some serious acne happening, poor guys. They reminded me of me and Sébastien at that age." He went on to tell Marine about the parking-lot conversation, but left out the comment about his Porsche being temperamental.

Marine laughed at the story. "Did you and Séb have acne?"

"Oh yeah," Verlaque replied, putting the chopped leeks in a frying pan. "Didn't you at that age?"

"Not a one."

Verlaque looked at his wife and she self-consciously put a hand up to her chin. "Until now," she said.

"I hadn't noticed."

"Liar," she said, "but thanks. How did I get pimples at my age?"

"You're still beautiful," he said, knowing it was a poor reply. "Are you stressed? You don't seem it."

"Are you kidding? I'm more relaxed than I've ever been. Thank you for supporting me in my decision to quit teaching." She hugged him and he kissed her. "I suppose in the grand scheme of things a few pimples aren't really important."

"No, they aren't."

"Tell me more about you and Séb as kids," she said. Antoine so rarely spoke of his childhood, unless it was good memories of being with Emmeline and Charles.

"Well, besides the fact that Sébastien was taller than me even though he was younger, and that we both had acne, I'm not sure it's very interesting—" Verlaque stopped speaking and looked down at his cell phone vibrating on the kitchen counter. "It's Bruno," he said.

"You'd better take it," Marine said. "I'll take over the veggies."

Verlaque picked up his phone and took it into the living room, while Marine stirred the leeks, reading the rest of the recipe. She smiled as she imagined her husband as a teenager. She had met his brother, Sébastien, only twice—a week before their wedding, and in Italy on their wedding day. He worked in real estate in Paris, had never married, and Verlaque rarely spoke of him. She turned to get something out of the fridge and saw her husband standing in the doorway, frozen. "What is it?" she asked.

"Père Fernand."

She closed the fridge door and said, "What happened?"

"He's been shot," Verlaque replied, holding on to either side of the door frame.

"Shot?!"

"During vespers this evening. I just had a beer with him last night . . ."

"I vaguely heard the bells at seven o'clock," Marine said, looking out the kitchen window, which had a view of the cathedral's octagonal steeple. "But I didn't hear sirens after. Is he dead?"

"He was rushed to the hospital. When they took him he was barely alive. I'm going to the cathedral. Normally I wouldn't go, as Paulik's there already . . ."

Marine said, "You should go."

Verlaque crossed the kitchen and took Marine in his arms. "Don't wait up for me," he said, but he knew she would.

It was a little after 11:00 when Verlaque returned. He could see a light shining in the living room and he called out, dropping his keys and cell phone on the kitchen counter.

Marine was on the sofa, curled up with a book, covered by a dark red mohair blanket they had bought in Ireland. She quickly set her book down. "How is he?"

"They're operating," Verlaque answered, sitting down and taking off his shoes. "You'll never guess where he was shot from . . ."

"The *logette*?"

"Exactly."

"Why so far away?"

"Why so far away, you ask?" Verlaque said. "So he or she could leave quickly, unseen. It's possible to get from the bottom of Saint Roch's chapel to the front doors through a narrow hallway."

"And not be seen by the congregation," Marine said.

"Because the cathedral is so big, Paulik estimates that by the time one of the younger priests ran down the aisle to the front door, the killer would have been easily out of sight."

"That's so horrible. You must be exhausted. Are you hungry?"

"No, but I'd love a whiskey."

"Sounds good. I'll bring you some almonds and cashews to eat." Marine walked to the kitchen and brought back a tumbler of Lagavulin, placing a bowl of mixed nuts on the side table. She closed her eyes and pictured the square in front of the cathedral and the numerous streets the gunman could have run down. "Rue du Bon Pasteur would be my pick."

"Me, too," Verlaque said, lifting his glass up as a thank-you. "You're most quickly out of sight, and off Bon Pasteur there are three or four subsidiary streets, all of them narrow, quiet, and dark."

Marine asked, "How many people were there? A dozen?"

"Twelve, exactly," Verlaque answered, leaning back and stretching his legs. "Three nuns and four priests, counting Père Fernand. And five obligatory old women. The young priest who was the quickest to run after the assailant was so nervous that he chipped a tooth drinking from an Orangina bottle while we were questioning him."

"How did the gunman get up into the *logette*, anyway? Isn't it closed off?"

Verlaque laughed. "It's blocked off by an old wooden chair sitting at the bottom of the stairs. Remember you saw someone up there during the carol service?"

"Yes, of course I do," Marine said. "I thought it was someone being nosy, or trying to find a better seat." She took a sip of his whiskey and frowned.

"What's wrong?"

"It doesn't taste good tonight," she answered, setting the glass on the coffee table. "Why Père Fernand?"

"We began by asking his colleagues that very question this evening, and will continue tomorrow and all week if we have to."

"And?"

"Tonight, no one had any answers," Verlaque said, finishing his whiskey. "He hadn't argued with anyone, didn't seem to have enemies, was well respected . . ."

"It may be something from his past," Marine

suggested. "Was he ever accused of . . . anything untoward? You hear about priests . . ."

"Not that we know of. That was one of the first things we thought of. But he was an old man, so we'll have to dig around some more."

"To ruin a childhood like that—"

"Marine, don't. It's late."

She went on, "Wouldn't it be wonderful if every couple on earth had one child, and gave them a happy upbringing. Not perfect, because that would be impossible, but happy."

"What would be a happy childhood for you?"

"Much like my own, I suppose."

CHAPTER TWENTY-ONE

Neither Marine nor Antoine slept well that night. They ate breakfast in the kitchen standing up, neither taking pleasure in the good, strong coffee or the buttered toast. Verlaque finished quickly, went into the bathroom to brush his teeth, and came back, kissing Marine. "I'm off," he said. "I'll let you know if I find out anything about Père Fernand."

"Please do," Marine said, loading the plates and cups into the dishwasher. "I'm going to go to the house this morning and check on things. If we're going to have Christmas there, which is right around the corner, I want to make sure the kitchen and larder are well stocked."

"Say hello to the house for me." With that, he was out the door.

Despite herself, France Dubois realized that she was being caught up in what the media referred to as Christmas spirit. She knew, intellectually, that it was all a phony business; a poorly disguised competition among shopkeepers to entice shoppers. The storefronts of Aix were covered in bright green pine branches, with sparkling white lights and touches of artificial snow here and there. The two independent bookshops on the

Cours had each installed gift-wrapping services outside on the sidewalk, and every time France passed there was a queue of buyers chatting happily holding stacks of books. François Mitterrand's *Lettres à Anne* seemed to be a popular choice, and France shrugged at the idea of choosing to read more than a thousand pages of letters that the former president had written to his much younger lover. Letters should be kept private, she believed, especially love letters. Or had the president intended for them to be read one day?

The cafés and bars had turned on their overhead heaters and arranged wool throws on the backs of chairs so that their patrons could still sit on the terrace and have a glass of hot mulled wine while they decided what shop to hit next.

France would be staying here for the holidays. After her parents died she had been invited to an aunt's in Lyon two Christmases in a row, until her aunt's own daughter married a man from Picardy, where the aunt now spent her holidays. For the first few years France had been invited to join them, but she couldn't see the point of traveling to the opposite end of the country for a holiday she no longer enjoyed. Besides, her cousin now had three small children and, as her aunt had reported, a small house.

She walked toward the statue of King René, which stood proudly at the top of the Cours.

She saw Judge Verlaque, his hands in his coat pockets, looking up at the king. "Hello," France said, stopping to stand next to him.

Verlaque turned to look at her. *"Bonjour, Mlle Dubois,"* he said. "Are you out Christmas shopping?"

"No," France answered. In fact, she wasn't doing anything, really. Just walking. Should she make something up? "I heard about the shooting last night. Will Père Fernand be all right?"

"I hope so," Verlaque said. He looked back up at King René. France studied the king, shown here as a young man with long wavy hair and a prominent jawline. "Do you think he liked Christmas?" she asked Verlaque.

"Undoubtedly," Verlaque replied, smiling. "Good King René was one of our most cultured monarchs, and cultured people always go in for Christmas in a big way."

France laughed. "I did a research paper on him when I was young," she said. "I still remember lots of odd facts. For instance, King René hated olive oil so brought his cows with him from the Loire to ensure a supply of milk and butter."

"The Mediterranean diet hadn't got around yet in the 1400s," Verlaque said. "Anything else? I like going home and impressing my wife with facts like these. She has a photographic memory."

"Yes," France said. "René also sponsored Christopher Columbus."

"Really? That's a good one."

"René was fascinated by world maps and globes. Provence didn't have a fleet back then, but they did charter boats between Marseille and Genoa."

"Genoa," Verlaque said. "Hence Christopher Columbus."

"Exactly. In one of Columbus's journals he thanks good King René for his sponsorship."

"No doubt paid for by increased taxes here in Provence."

"No doubt."

"Well," Verlaque said. "I suppose I'd best be getting home, even if I haven't bought any gifts."

"There's always perfume," France suggested.

Verlaque laughed. "I may end up getting that for my father's girlfriend. For my father, I have no idea."

"Brightly colored thin down jackets are the rage in this winter's menswear," France said flatly.

"I know!" Verlaque said, huffing. He hated fads. "What happened to good old wool?" Exactly on cue, two middle-aged men walked by, both with gelled gray hair, both wearing the down jackets, one bright green and the other silver.

"Dare to be different. You could buy your father a traditional wool sweater."

"I think I may," Verlaque said. "From Donegal or Yorkshire, one of those wild places."

"Out on the wily, windy moors," France said in English.

Verlaque did a double take at Mlle Dubois, surprised. Was she referencing that old Kate Bush song? It had always reminded him of a former girlfriend from Edinburgh. He had forgotten all about her.

"Good luck shopping," France said, turning to leave.

"Thanks for the chat," Verlaque said, surprising himself. Mlle Dubois was really quite funny.

France gave him a little wave and crossed the Cours, stepping out of the way of a Diabline, the new electric tiny buses that moved people—mostly seniors—around the downtown area. She smiled as she watched the four occupants, all with shopping baskets balanced on their laps, chat with one another. It made her miss her parents.

Her mind wandered as it usually did when she walked through Aix; she was on autopilot, quickly making her way toward the Place des Cardeurs, passing by the shoppers and cafés and spruced-up boutiques in a whirl of colors and smells that alternated between strong espresso and woodsy perfumes. When she got to the Place d'Albertas she realized that she must have been daydreaming more than she usually did, as she had missed her turn. No problem, she'd walk up the rue Aude for a change. She was about to head up the narrow street when she heard a voice behind her call out, "Mlle Dubois!" She stopped nd saw a middle-aged man wearing a think woolen coat and a wool toque, with a camera hanging from his neck.

"M Abdelhak, good morning," France said, shaking his hand. "Were you taking pictures of the Place d'Albertas before you open up your stall?"

Abdelhak nodded. "This is my favorite spot so far. Such a beautiful building that surrounds this square. But why isn't all of it restored? Only two sides? Such a shame."

"I agree. I'm not sure why they haven't finished. I know it's been a difficult renovation job as the building was very poorly constructed and put up in a hurry in the eighteenth century."

Abdelhak asked, "Why so?"

"The marquis who owned the palace behind us," France said, gesturing to the Hôtel d'Albertas behind them, "wanted something attractive to look at from his windows. He bought the buildings on this street, kicked out the tenants and had the small houses torn down, then commissioned a local architect to build this square with the three-sided building that now surrounds it."

"But he didn't want to spend a lot of money—"

"Exactly, as he didn't care about the people who would live in the new building. It was only for his view."

"That doesn't sound very kind of him. Perhaps the marquis met his end in the revolution."

France smiled. "Worse. Do you want to hear it?"

"Oh, yes," M Abdelhak said.

"One evening, as the marquis was at dinner, he raised a glass of wine to toast his wife on their anniversary, but out of nowhere a young man appeared and brutally stabbed him."

"Whatever for?"

"He was avenging his father," France said. "In those days the nobility had a strong hand in the running of a town, including schools. The young man claimed that the marquis was responsible for the dismissal of his father, who was the much-loved head schoolmaster in a nearby town. The family fell into ruin, and the young man was obliged to learn the butcher's trade instead of carrying on with his studies."

"The marquis died?"

"Yes, as did the young man, who was easily captured."

"Well, it's still beautiful," Abdelhak said, turning to look at the delicate fountain and the small rounded river pebbles that paved the square. "But a sad story for such a beautiful place."

France shrugged. "Some might say the young man did the honorable thing."

Marine walked toward where she had parked her car. As she turned out of the Place de l'Archevêché she considered walking down the narrow medieval streets near the cathedral but realized that was silly—what could she find that the police couldn't? She felt angry as she imagined the assailant walking, not running, away from the church on the streets that she loved and knew by heart. How would he have hidden the gun? A duffle bag, or even a cello case, like something out of a movie? This was *la ville de musique*, after all—in Aix it wasn't unusual to see people carrying musical instruments or hear opera scales being sung from open windows. She felt her muscles tightening as she got close to the cathedral and instead turned to watch the laughing students file into the Sciences Po university building across the street.

She finally relaxed as she drove, avoiding the major roads that led north out of town and instead taking the smaller roads that passed through subdivisions, the roads that her father had taught her to drive on. She traversed the village of Puyricard and was soon in open countryside—most of it vineyards, now barren but still beautiful in their orderly rows—toward their house. She listened to Radio France's classical music station, relieved that it was commercial-free and that there still was such a thing as arts funding.

When a flash of bright yellow—a bicyclist's jersey—went by her on the road she realized just how comfortable she was: She had been driving slower than the cyclist. The cyclist waved as he passed her, rounding a corner just ahead and disappearing. Seeing the corner, she slowed down only to have a large black BMW suddenly behind her flashing its lights. "All right, all right," she said, slowing down and getting as close to the right-hand shoulder as she could so that the car could pass. The BMW zoomed past, and for a second she worried about the cyclist. She, too, now came around the corner and saw the BMW now far ahead of her, amazed that it could have driven that quickly. "The biker!" she said aloud, realizing that the yellow jersey had disappeared. Music played over the radio—a piano piece she loved by Erik Satie—and the melancholic tune felt ominous. She slowed the car to a crawl, scanning both sides of the road. *"Mon Dieu!"* she cried as she saw the cyclist's bent bicycle to the right of her car. She quickly pulled over, stopped, and put on her hazard lights, jumping out of the car. She could hear Satie's piano as she ran to the cyclist, lying in the grass ten feet beyond the bike, his body almost touching the trunk of an ancient vine.

She bent down over him; his eyes were closed and she couldn't see any blood. "Hello?" she asked. From his face he looked to be in his late twenties or early thirties. "Are you all right?"

The young man's eyes opened slowly. "I'm okay, I think," he said.

"Be careful," Marine said. "Do you hurt anywhere?"

He closed his eyes and pursed his lips. He answered, "No, miraculously."

"It may be this tuft of soft grass you landed in."

He lifted his upper body, propped on an elbow. Marine said, "Don't try to stand yet."

He looked at her and smiled. "You're like an apparition," he said. "Saved by Beauty."

Marine blushed despite herself. "Saved by a helmet, is more like it."

He sat up fully and took off his helmet, running his fingers through his hair. "It feels like my head is still attached. Is it?"

Marine laughed at the expression on his tanned, freckled face. "It seems to be. Shall I call an ambulance?"

"No, no. I'm fine, though it's hard to believe," he said. "That was a lucky fall."

"You were hit by that car, weren't you?"

He looked toward the road but didn't answer.

"I can't believe they didn't stop," she said. She read his reaction at once as fear. "What's your name?" she asked, trying to be gentle. She had no idea if he was in shock or would go into shock in the next few minutes. "I'm Marine Bonnet."

"Damien Petit," he answered. He slowly got to his feet, aided by Marine. As she helped him she searched her brain: his name was familiar. But why? Her husband's face came into her head.

She said, "If you don't want an ambulance, then I'm going to take you and your broken bike to a hospital, and then we'll go to a police station to report that BMW."

"No, we mustn't—"

"What were you going to do, walk from here? Can you even walk?"

"Look!" he said, walking in a straight line and forcing a smile.

"Damien Petit," she said. She stared at him, forcing herself to remember. Damien wasn't a common name. Then she had it. "My house isn't far from here. I think you should come back with me, I'll make us some tea, and you'll explain why that driver just tried to kill you."

He laughed again, but it was as forced as his smile.

"You'll have to do better than that," she said. "Your business partner was murdered on Sunday."

Damien's shoulders fell and he sighed heavily, rubbing his eyes.

Marine placed a hand on his shoulder. "Please, come back to the house. You'll be safe. I'll call my husband to come home. . . . You've met him."

"Who are you talking about, Beauty?"

"Antoine Verlaque, the examining magistrate."

"*Merde*. Of all my luck."

"No, your luck was not getting killed five minutes ago," she said.

Marine hung up the phone. "My father is on his way here," she said. "He's a doctor and wants to check on you."

"Your whole family has me covered," Damien said, leaning back in an armchair. "Next, your mother will be coming."

"Oh, you really don't want that, believe me. Here," she said, handing him a small glass. "It's port. My father recommended you drink some."

"Thank you for all of this," Damien said, taking a small sip. "Thank you for the home, and fire in the fireplace, and the drink."

"Are you hungry?"

Damien shook his head. "Is your front door locked?" he asked.

"Yes," Marine said. "You really are frightened, aren't you?"

He closed his eyes. "What crap Cole got us into."

"Wait until my husband gets here to explain your story," Marine said. She wanted to tell him to save his strength, but worried that it sounded overdramatic. Until her father arrived from Aix, she'd have no way of knowing if Damien was really hurt. She looked at the young man, sunk into the chair with a woolen blanket over his bare knees, his bicycle shoes lying at his feet. Could he have been so angry at Cole Hainsby that he poisoned him? But the poisoning, which could have been done by anyone, had nothing in common with a shooting with a precision rifle. And she had just witnessed Damien being run off the road. Or had she? She didn't actually see the car hit him.

"Hello!" Verlaque's voice sounded from the hallway.

"We're in the living room," Marine answered, turning to smile at Damien. She wanted him to feel at ease so that he didn't hold anything back.

Verlaque hung up his coat in the hallway and walked into the warm living room, pressing his hand on Marine's shoulder as he walked by her. He pulled up a footstool and sat beside Damien. "*Bonjour, M Petit,*" he said. "Are you feeling all right? Are you sure you don't need to visit a hospital?"

Damien shook his head. Marine said, "My father is on his way."

"Apparently I should be relieved that her mother isn't coming," Damien said.

Verlaque snorted and laughed. "How about you tell us your story before the good doctor arrives."

Damien sat up straight and sighed. "This may sound childish, but it was all Cole's idea," he began. "I didn't know anything about it. In the beginning, anyway. We desperately need money for our business. I was ready to call it a day; I can easily find work elsewhere. But Cole kept insisting that with a little input of cash we could make the business work again."

"So M Hainsby went to someone for money?" Verlaque asked.

"Yes, and not a bank, as you may have guessed," Damien said. "The banks had already turned us down."

"Did he get the money?"

"Yes, sixty thousand," Damien answered. "That was last Christmas, and we were to start paying it back this Christmas."

"But you haven't—"

"It's impossible," Damien said, rubbing his hands through his hair. "We just didn't make enough."

"Well, technically it's not illegal to lend someone money," Verlaque said. "But it is illegal to try to run someone off the road."

"And you have a witness," Marine said. "Although I didn't get their license plate number. Two men in the front seat."

"So all we have to go on is a black BMW sedan," Damien said.

Verlaque looked surprised. "Do you mean you don't know who Cole approached for money?"

Damien's back went rigid. "Corsicans. Two brothers named Jean-Paul and Michel. I don't know their last name; I figured if I didn't know it I'd be safe, or I could pretend it never happened."

"Would Mme Hainsby know more?" Marine asked.

"I doubt it, but you could try," Damien said.

Verlaque motioned to Marine to move toward

the hallway. "I'll go make tea," Marine said, getting up. She looked at Damien, who was staring into the fire.

"I'll look for something to eat," Verlaque said, getting up and following her. "Do we have any food in the house?"

They walked into the kitchen and closed the door. "How would Hainsby know whom to contact?" Verlaque asked, whispering. "How does a mild-mannered expat go about approaching the underworld for money?"

"Precisely," Marine said. "It's not like they can ask around at church for someone with mafia connections."

They locked eyes and Verlaque put a finger to his lips. "Père Fernand?" Marine hissed.

"Impossible," Verlaque said. "Let's think of another connection."

"An expat friend who's a small business owner," Marine suggested. "Someone who's also gone to the mafia for money."

"Not bad."

Marine started filling the kettle and Verlaque put a hand on her arm. "Gangsta Sorba," he said.

"The school director?"

"Sorba knows Debra Hainsby—"

"I'll say he does," Marine said, putting the kettle on the stove. "Sorba's a good idea."

"I'll ring her after we figure out what to do with our cyclist."

Marine looked at her husband. "We need to be careful with Damien," she said. "He really might be in danger. Cole Hainsby is dead. And Père Fernand?"

"Is out of surgery but still in critical condition," Verlaque said. "I just got the phone call before arriving here."

The doorbell rang and Marine set down her tea towel. "That will be Papa." She passed through the living room, where Damien Petit had drifted off into sleep, his chin resting on his chest. She felt a pang of protection, although he was perhaps only a few years younger than she was. She smiled as she entered the flagstone hallway, realizing that she had also enjoyed Damien's gentle flirting, and being called Beauty.

CHAPTER TWENTY-TWO

Verlaque was grateful that Debra Hainsby had agreed to meet after school, and in downtown Aix. He didn't want to go back to their house, a house that was once home to a complete—happy or unhappy—family. The café he suggested was in the same square as the Palais de Justice, but he was early for their meeting so decided to walk around the block and look in shop windows to clear his head. He passed by a shop selling foie gras, and a sharp memory came to life of Maria, the Verlaque family cook, asking his mother what she wanted to serve that particular Christmas. Mme Verlaque, holding her ever-present menthol cigarette with its ashes about to fall, breezed through their Parisian mansion waving her hand in the air and said, *"Foie gras et vin blanc, comme d'habitude, Maria!"* If Marine did get her way with hosting an elaborate Christmas dinner, which by now he had resigned himself to, they would not have foie gras or white wine, he decided. At least not together.

He walked on, deciding to leave the foie gras for another time, and put his mind back to current-day Aix. This case began with Cole Hainsby, and he realized how little they really knew about the man. It seemed unjust. He was married, with children, had a business, and went to the University of Michigan. Is that all a life adds up to in the end? As he approached the café he felt his mood souring. He walked in and chose a table near the front, where Debra could easily spot him when she arrived.

"Hard day?" the waiter asked as he stood beside Verlaque's small round table, the tray balanced on his hip.

"Not especially," Verlaque answered. "I was just mulling over some thoughts about life and death. What does our short life add up to? And what—"

"Give me your order before I shoot myself."

"An espresso. Please."

The waiter nodded and walked away, glancing over his shoulder and rolling his eyes in Verlaque's direction. Verlaque liked this café but rarely came as it was too close to the Palais de Justice. But no colleagues were here this afternoon. He knew the waiters, but not their names. He was quite sure they knew him, *including* his name. He looked out the window and saw Debra Hainsby parking her car in the square. She got out, locked the door, and strode into the café, her back straight. He had expected her to have the hunched shoulders of the bereaved.

Verlaque shook her hand as she sat down. "Congratulations," he said in English.

Mme Hainsby looked at him, confused.

"On your parking spot."

She smiled. "Once in a while I find a spot on the Place de Verdun." The waiter appeared and Debra ordered an apple juice.

"How are you?" Verlaque asked. "And the children?"

"Fine. My sister and her husband are helping enormously," she replied.

He leaned his forearms on the table. "Did your husband confide in you about his business?"

"Yes and no," she said. "We'd talk about trip ideas, and good restaurants and hotels for clients. But never about the details, like the finances, if that's what you're getting at."

"Yes, that's what I was referring to," Verlaque said. "You told me at your house that M Hainsby was worried."

"Yes."

"But that just before his death he seemed lighter; in better spirits."

She nodded.

"His business partner told me that your husband went to some unsavory characters for a business loan."

Debra laid her head in her hands, shaking her head back and forth. "Stupid, stupid," she muttered. "I was worried that he might have done something like that."

"Do you have any idea whom he may have gone to?"

"He told me a few weeks ago that he had a meeting with Alain . . . M Sorba . . . I think that Cole got it into his head that M Sorba may have connections . . . who would lend him money."

"Do you think that's true?" Verlaque asked. He wondered if it was Debra herself who told her husband of Sorba's friends.

"Probably," she said, sighing. "Alain would hint about the underworld. He idolized the film *The Godfather.* He was constantly quoting from it."

Verlaque said, "That doesn't necessarily mean—"

She waved her hand. "I know. But it was more than that. He'd brag, after a few drinks, about dangerous friends of his, in Marseille. Powerful friends."

"We'll look into this," Verlaque said. "But do you mind my asking why you've turned against M Sorba? And why you held back this information when I visited your house with the commissioner?"

Debra picked up her cell phone. She scrolled through some messages before stopping at one, then showed the screen to Verlaque. Verlaque put on his reading glasses and read aloud, "*C'est fini, chérie. Désolé. Alain.*"

"He ended our affair with a text message," she said, her voice cracking. "That's also why I won't be going back to that school, nor will my children. Cole and I both have very good life insurance plans, so thankfully I won't have to."

"Do you have any idea with whom M Sorba is acquainted? When, as you said, he'd brag about his dangerous friends?" Verlaque asked, already forming an idea in his head of the number-one suspects in Aix and Marseille. He remembered the automobile dealership sticker on Sorba's car, from Marseille, and someone Verlaque knew was linked to the Corsican mafia.

"No," she said. "But I do know that when Alain came into downtown Aix, he always made two stops. He preferred Marseille."

"Where did he go?"

"To a cigar shop on rue Clémenceau," she said as Verlaque tried not to wince. He hated the myth that all mafiosi were cigar aficionados. But he could go and talk to the proprietress, Carole, who was a friend. Debra went on, "And to a men's clothing shop. On the rue Papassaudi. It has an Italian name—"

"I think I know the one," he replied, knowing exactly the shop. "Del Carlo?" The owners were Jean-Paul and Michel Orezza. The names fit with what Damien had told him.

"That's it."

"One last question. How well did Cole know Père Fernand at Saint-Sauveur?"

"Not at all," Debra answered. "He met Père Fernand for the first time on Saturday afternoon when we went to the cathedral for a sort of dress rehearsal."

"And you?"

"The same," she answered, looking genuinely surprised. "Why do you ask?"

"Père Fernand was shot in the cathedral last night."

She put her hands up to her face. "Oh, my God. That's awful. Was he killed?"

"No. He was operated on late last night and is in intensive care."

Debra pushed aside her half-finished juice and sat back, tears forming in her eyes.

Verlaque signaled for the bill and asked, "How did you manage to pay the steep tuition at the Four Seasons?"

She said, "Because I worked there, we got a seventy-five-percent discount."

"And the remaining twenty-five?"

Mme Hainsby blushed and got up to go, collecting her coat and purse. "I think you can work that out on your own."

Verlaque watched her leave the café, a million questions swimming in his head. He got up and walked to the bar and ordered a glass of sherry. Cole Hainsby must have wondered how they were managing to pay even a quarter of the very steep tuition. Did he finally figure it out and threaten Sorba? And did Hainsby confide in Père Fernand? Or did Sorba, who was probably a churchgoer and might have even gone to confession, regretting it immediately after? And what about the Tunisian, who seemed very interested in the chapel of Saint Roch, situated right below the *logette* from where the shots were fired? As he sipped the sherry he stared straight ahead at the glass and brass shelving that held dozens of liquor bottles in need of dusting. He couldn't see any connection between a rug seller from Carthage and an old priest in Aix, and a failing expat businessman.

The waiter stood at the end of the bar and slowly turned the pages of a dog-eared *L'Équipe* while watching Verlaque. Verlaque finished his sherry and put some money on the zinc counter and saluted to the waiter.

"Take it easy," the waiter said. "Have a nice meal tonight, relax, put a log in the fire . . ."

Verlaque smiled as he opened the door. "That's exactly what I intend to do. *Ciao*." He walked out and turned left into the Passage Agard, a shortcut to the Cours Mirabeau that was built by a nineteenth-century lawyer—Maître Agard—who wanted to get from his property in the Quartier Mazarin to the Palais de Justice quicker. One landowner refused to sell, at the end of the passageway closest to the Cours, hence one section of the alley was narrower. Verlaque stopped at the top of the bottleneck to let some people pass through. He thought of the millions of people over the course of almost two hundred years who had also walked through the passageway, stopping at this exact point to wait their turn: lawyers and judges, policemen and thieves, servants and nobility (the nobility albeit rarely, he guessed), students and teachers, mothers and children, tourists, and Paul Cézanne and Émile Zola.

Once out in the wide-open Cours, he looked up at the blue sky and walked south toward the cigar shop on the rue Clémenceau. He quickly walked past the Café Mazarin, not wanting to run into anyone he knew, as it was getting close to 7:00, when the shops closed, and turned right on Clémenceau. Two doors up was Carole's tobacco shop; the smell of it drove him wild. As he opened the front door a small bell sounded, and Carole looked up from where she had been arranging cigars in the glass-fronted humidor. "Well, stranger," she said, grinning. Verlaque's fussiness and Carole's flirting were of equal amusement to them both, as well as to Carole's young trainee, a shy man in his early twenties.

"Hello, dear," Verlaque said, leaning over the counter to give Carole the *bises*. The trainee watched out of the corner of his eye as he pretended to be captivated by dusting the mahogany shelves.

"What can I do for you today?" she asked, still grinning.

Verlaque swallowed. Before he got married, flirting with other women—which was a French pastime—had been easy. Now it only made him nervous. "Two Wide Churchills, please."

She opened the humidor and reached in, pulling out a familiar cigar box. The Romeo y Julieta label was one of his Cuban favorites: a velvet-leotard-wearing Romeo who reaches up to kiss Juliette, who's leaning over her Verona balcony, the image surrounded by a row of gold medals the cigar company had won over the years, beginning in 1885. Carole put the cigars in the palm of her hand and let Verlaque touch them. He did so, smiling. She said, "They're humid, just to your taste. You're my only customer who likes his cigars so humid they've got green mold."

"I can almost smell the dampness coming off of them," he said, putting one up to his nose.

"Is there *anything* else?" she asked. The trainee coughed.

"Some information."

"I should have guessed."

"About a cigar buyer named Alain Sorba," he said.

Carole tilted her head to one side. "Describe him."

"Big Marseillais about my age or a little older," Verlaque said. "Wears cheap—no, expensive but tacky—suits and has a loud laugh. I'd guess buys only Cohibas."

She laughed. "That describes a lot of my clients," she said.

Verlaque smiled, knowing she couldn't explain why without criticizing her own clients: the ones who paid for her one-thousand-square-foot apartment near the Hôtel de Ville. Show-offs who bought the most popular, and most expensive, cigar brands. Verlaque added, "He owns a private bilingual school north of Aix."

"Nope," she said. Her trainee coughed again. "What *is* it, Edouard?"

"I know him," the young man said, shyly approaching the counter. "He was in here the other day, buying a big Cohiba."

Verlaque grinned and winked at Carole. "And how do you know it's him?" Carole asked.

"Because he was talking . . . well, bragging . . . about the school with another man."

"Who was the other man?" Verlaque asked. "Can you describe him?" Was it Damien? Or Cole? Or one of the Orezza brothers, who owned the clothing shop on Papassaudi, which was his next visit?

The trainee answered, "He's easy to describe. He was a priest."

Verlaque turned to Carole and asked, "Do you have today's edition of *La Provence*?"

Carole pointed to the newspaper rack behind Verlaque, beside the front door. He walked over and grabbed the top paper, turning quickly to

260

page 2. He laid the paper out flat on the counter so that it faced Edouard. PRIEST GUNNED DOWN WHILE CELEBRATING VESPERS; IN CRITICAL CONDITION ran the headline. Below was a not-very-flattering photograph of the jolly Père Fernand.

"That's him," Edouard replied.

"Thank you," Verlaque said, paying for his cigars and the newspaper. "For the cigars and the information."

"Come by more often," Carole said, putting his purchases in a small bag. She walked around the counter to give her favorite customer a *bises* good-bye. Edouard went back to dusting, watching them as he slowly spread the dust around with his cloth. Carole opened the door for Verlaque, who walked out into the street and waved.

As he walked up Clémenceau he called Paulik and got a busy signal. He dialed Marine's number and she picked up on one ring. "*Oui?*" she asked.

"How's Damien?"

"My father says he'll be fine," she said. "They both just left. Papa's dropping him off at his apartment."

"Guess what," Verlaque said. "Alain Sorba of the Four Seasons may have helped Cole get that loan, and Sorba was in the cigar shop the other day with Père Fernand."

"Carole's shop?"

Verlaque paused. "Um, yes."

"Is she still crazy about you?"

"Nah," Verlaque replied, trying to sound nonchalant. "I just tried Paulik but his line's busy. Can you find out what the cathedral's head priest and Sorba could possibly have in common?"

"Sounds like fun," she said. "If you take me out for dinner. There's a new restaurant on the rue Lieutaud that's getting good reviews."

"All right. Text me its name and I'll meet you there at eight o'clock." He hung up and turned left onto Papassaudi, quickening his pace, as it was almost 7:00. Del Carlo Men's Clothes was halfway down on the right, and the lights were still on. He walked in, recognizing at once one of the Orezza brothers, Jean-Paul, standing behind the counter talking on the phone. Verlaque looked around; there seemed to be hundreds of thousands of dollars' worth of stock in their shop. He knew they had three other shops in Aix, all with the same amount of merchandise. For years rumors had circulated around the Palais de Justice that the shops were a front for the Corsican mafia, but the slick Orezza brothers had never dirtied their hands to the point of being caught.

"May I help you?" a young man with too much gel in his thick black hair asked. He wore his designer sunglasses propped up on the top of his head, a fashion statement that had always annoyed Verlaque, especially indoors in winter.

"Do you have any Harris Tweed jackets?" Verlaque asked, smiling and faking an English accent.

The salesman snickered, not hiding his contempt for this new customer. "No," he said.

Jean-Paul Orezza barely glanced up from his phone, seeing that Verlaque, while he was wearing Weston brogues and an expensive wool coat, dressed much too conservatively for their crowd.

"Any Burberry?" Verlaque asked, trying on his best idiotic grin. He was enjoying this.

"*Pas du tout*," the young man replied firmly.

Verlaque looked around, waiting to see if the other brother would appear, but then realized he'd be better off heading back to the Palais de Justice, where he could ask Paulik, or another officer, more detailed questions about the Orezzas.

The salesman looked at his watch and walked to the door, opening it. Verlaque smiled and passed through, not bothering to say thank you.

CHAPTER TWENTY-THREE

When Verlaque got to the Palais de Justice, Paulik was at his desk, hunched over, typing on his computer keyboard. "I thought Flamant was looking into all this?" Verlaque asked, pulling up a chair.

"He's on a two-day extra-learning conference," Paulik replied, not looking up.

"What? Can we pull him out?"

"I tried for today but no luck," Paulik answered. "Flamant sent me a text that he'd sneak out early tomorrow. *Q*. Where is the *Q?*"

Verlaque smiled and watched the commissioner one-finger type. "Far left. You didn't take typing, either?"

"It was an option at our high school," Paulik said. "But my parents made me take Spanish instead."

"I had to take Latin. Why are you here so late?"

"Léa has choral practice tonight," he answered. "I'm picking her up at nine."

Verlaque thought of the Pauliks' rustic farmhouse in Puyloubier, about a fifteen-minute drive east of Aix, at the foot of Mont Sainte-Victoire, and the vineyards that surrounded the house, in which he was a silent partner. "What are you looking up?" he asked.

"I thought I'd help out Flamant a bit and get a head start on looking up information about the priest." Paulik stared at the keyboard, with his right index finger hovering over it.

Verlaque ran a hand over his mouth to hide a grin. "Anything?"

"Most of the information is recent, about the cathedral. Touristy stuff." Paulik sat back and sighed. "Flamant will have more luck tomorrow. I got your message about the Orezza brothers and pulled their file." He tossed a worn-out folder toward Verlaque.

Verlaque opened the file and leaned forward, adjusting his reading glasses. He began reading, slowly turning the pages. "Jean-Paul and Michel have never been caught at anything," he said, looking up at Paulik. "As I thought."

"But linked to lots of things," Paulik said. "Read on."

Verlaque turned another page and read. "Well, hello, you." He brought the page up close to his face and examined a mug shot. "Now I really don't like you."

"You know him?" Paulik asked, looking over to get a look at the portrait.

"He's their salesman. He basically just threw me out of Del Carlo."

"What for?"

"For having good taste in clothes." Verlaque read more. "Alexandre Mareschi is the salesman's name. Thirty-four years old, born in Porto-Vecchio. Hello! Three times arrested, twice in Corsica and once in Marseille. First time for theft, age twenty. Second, armed robbery four years later. And in Marseille, pimping. That was three years ago. He just got out."

"Read on," Paulik said.

Verlaque turned a page. "What? There's another Orezza?"

"Gérard. The oldest son. Alexandre Mareschi is a lightweight in comparison."

"Why haven't I heard of him?"

"Because he died ten years ago," Paulik said. "A shoot-out in an underground parking garage in Marseille."

Verlaque looked at the commissioner. "What in the hell does this have to do with a food-loving priest?"

Paulik shrugged. "I can't figure it out. Was Père Fernand responsible somehow? The Orezza brothers finally got their revenge?"

"The shooting certainly had the operatic qualities that the mob loves: during vespers, in a church . . ."

"Père Fernand visited the cigar shop here in Aix with Alain Sorba."

"Carole's place?" Paulik asked dreamily.

Verlaque huffed. Carole was *his* crush. "That's the one. Doesn't that seem weird to you?"

"Yeah, what's he doing with Sorba? It's not like

266

the priest has kids that he sends to the bilingual school." Paulik snapped his fingers. "Some Catholic organization? Some sect. That Opus Dei thing."

Verlaque tilted his head. "I don't know about Opus Dei. I think they're too powerful for our little lot here in Aix." He looked at his watch. "*Merde.* I'm late for dinner. See you tomorrow."

"Right," Paulik said, turning back to the computer. "I'll just do a little more snooping around on the internet."

Verlaque got up and as he left heard Paulik mumbling to himself that he couldn't fine the *E* key. He was still smiling when he walked out the front doors of the Palais de Justice.

"Sorry I'm late," Verlaque said as he sat down across from Marine.

"It's no problem," Marine said. "I ordered a glass of champagne, as you can see."

Verlaque caught the waiter's attention and pointed to Marine's glass and then to himself. He looked around the restaurant. The walls were painted a shade of red that was a little off—was it too bright? Too maraschino cherry? Hanging from the walls were a few not very interesting African masks, a framed photograph of a French village from the turn of the century, and a couple of abstract paintings. "Looks like they're still working out the theme of this place," he said.

"Linen napkins!" Marine said, unfolding hers and putting it on her lap.

He smiled, remembering that it was Marine who had selected the restaurant and made the booking. His mood improved when he looked at the wine list, which had plenty of local beauties—including Hélène Paulik's—and only a few Bordeaux. A waiter in his midthirties with a long, hawkish nose and bright blue eyes recited the chef's daily specials with zeal. They each chose off the daily menu and the waiter left Verlaque to scour the wine list. "This is heaven," Marine said, lifting her glass. "To be in a small charming restaurant, with you, alone."

Verlaque set the wine list aside and let his reading glasses fall to his chest, hanging by their chain. He tapped his champagne glass to hers. "I agree," he said. "I like your first course choice of foie gras with lentils, by the way." He winked. "The queen and her maid. The elegant and the earthy."

Marine laughed. "It's the chef's choice, not mine. He or she invented it this evening. Your warm oysters with fennel and curry are a bit bling, in my opinion. Like they don't know where they belong. In Provence or Brittany or India."

Verlaque couldn't think of a funny reply and was saved by the waiter, who reappeared to take their wine order. "Châteauneuf-du-Pape white," Verlaque said, pointing to the one he wanted. "It's rare to see their whites on a menu."

The waiter straightened his back and smiled. "It's a big favorite of ours. My wife is from Avignon. She's in the kitchen right now."

"She is?" Marine asked. "Is she the chef?"

He bounced back and forth on his heels. "Yes. I'm proud to say we are breaking with tradition. The husband in the front room and wife in the kitchen."

"The menu looks and sounds fantastic. We can't wait to start," Verlaque said.

A new couple entered the restaurant and the waiter excused himself to greet them. "You're getting over your problem with the decoration," Marine said.

"Not quite yet," Verlaque replied, grinning.

"Oh, it's the Italian couple," Marine whispered, leaning over the table toward her husband. "Don't turn around."

"From the sister cities?"

"Yes. But only the wife can see me, and she doesn't seem to recognize me. In fact, why would she? I don't think I bought anything at their stand. It all seemed a bit overpriced."

Just as Verlaque and Marine were finishing their champagne and fighting over the last black olive, their first course arrived. The waiter had brought the white wine, and to their amusement asked which one of them was to taste. "In all the years I've been eating at French restaurants," Verlaque said, "I've seen that question raised only two or three times."

"It's something we're learning now in *hôtelière* school," the waiter, who they now knew must be the owner of the charming restaurant, said. "There are more and more women cooks and sommeliers, even in Europe, although we're way behind North America."

"Have you been long out of school?" Verlaque asked, as the owner looked well into his thirties.

"We went back to school late, both of us," he answered. "Aline was a travel agent, and I worked in a busy Parisian bank. With the disappearance of travel agencies as a trade, and the stress of banking, it was time to change careers." He served them each some wine and then left them to enjoy their first course.

Verlaque lifted a spoon and said, "Travel agent. That explains the weird deco."

Marine murmured in agreement. She looked over her husband's head and said, "The Italians are arguing—"

"That's too bad. Especially when one is out to dinner." He took a bit of the fennel and cream sauce that had obviously been strained through a sieve, and closed his eyes. "Heavenly, and I haven't even tasted the oysters yet."

They ate in silence for a few minutes, savoring, when Marine wiped her mouth with her napkin and said, "Oh, I managed to phone my mother after you called me. She's looking into the relationship between Père Fernand and Alain Sorba."

Verlaque sighed, annoyed. "Why your mother?"

Marine shrugged. "I didn't have time. I'm too busy editing my book. And besides, who but my mother would have reliable access to that kind of information?"

"True." They continued to eat and made plans for their Christmas dinner, to which Marine insisted that Verlaque invite his brother. He in turn argued that Sébastien would never come.

"You'll invite him regardless," she insisted, finishing the last of her foie gras. "*Trop bon*," she said, sitting back.

The restaurant's owner came and whisked away the plates and refilled Marine's wineglass. He was about to do the same for Verlaque when the judge put his hand over the top of the glass. "I'll switch to red now," he said. "Do you have anything open?"

"Well," the owner said, "with the duck you chose, I'd suggest a red from the southwest. I have a Madiran from the Gers that I can open. How's that?"

Verlaque put his hands together in prayer. "Are you sure you don't mind?"

"Not at all," the owner said before leaving their table.

The owner reappeared in minutes with a bottle of Madiran, which he showed to Verlaque before opening. He uncorked it and was smelling the cork when his wife, complete in her chef whites, came out of the kitchen carrying two plates with tea towels. "The plates are hot!" she said as she placed them on the table.

Marine and Verlaque shook her hand and introduced themselves. The chef was also in her midthirties and had a long nose like her husband's, but she had brown eyes. Verlaque and Marine put their noses to their plates and beamed at the chef, all smiles. "Limes?" Verlaque asked. "In my roast duck?"

"I'm crazy about them," the chef answered. "We used to travel to exotic places and now I use limes whenever I can. I put two whole limes in the duck cavity and used lime zest with honey and tarragon in the sauce." She looked at Marine and said, "Your dish is more delicate. The seared pancetta will give a little salt kick and crispiness to the baked cod. I used lemons and capers in your sauce; the limes wouldn't have been a good match for the pancetta and capers."

The chef and her husband left the table. "I love this place," Verlaque said, pulling his chair closer to the table.

Marine laughed. "Too bad the Italians don't," she said. "Now they are silent. She looks really sad."

"Maybe they're breaking up." He picked up his fork and knife and was about to cut into a duck thigh when he heard a familiar woman's voice in the restaurant's small entryway. He set down his cutlery. "Did you happen to mention to your mother where we'd be eating this evening?"

Marine gulped and wiped her mouth with her napkin. "I may have," she said. *It wasn't as if we were having a truly romantic, intimate, evening,* she wanted to add. But she stayed silent, knowing she shouldn't have answered her mother's question about where they were dining if she didn't want this to happen. In fact, there was something Marine wanted to talk to her husband about, but at the last minute she had decided that a restaurant wasn't the right place.

"Hello, you two," Florence Bonnet bellowed as she strode into the dining room.

Verlaque and Marine got up and gave her the *bises*, while the restaurant's owner came and placed a third chair at their table. Florence thanked him and hung her bicycle helmet off the back of the chair while Verlaque smiled at Marine. "Keep eating, keep eating," Florence said.

"Are you hungry, Maman?" Marine asked.

"Oh, gosh, your father and I ate hours ago. I just heated up some soup."

Verlaque looked at Marine with a raised eyebrow and ate in silence, knowing that Florence Bonnet probably opened a tin of soup bought at the supermarket close to their house.

Florence continued, "I'm so excited about this case I just had to ride up here and tell you what I've been finding." Verlaque coughed and held his napkin up to his mouth. She continued, "Besides, you weren't answering your phone, Marine."

"I put it on silent when I walked into the restaurant."

"Well, no matter. Lucky for you I'm in great shape. I made some phone calls and in less than five minutes," she said, snapping her fingers, "I got some great info, very odd."

"Do tell," Verlaque said.

Florence leaned in and looked from her daughter to her son-in-law. "Alain Sorba and Père Fernand certainly know each other," she whispered. "Sorba is on the board of directors of Saint-Sauveur!"

"Wooow!" Verlaque said. Marine kicked him under the table.

"Maman," Marine said calmly. "*Is* that very odd?"

"It certainly adds a whole new chapter to the case, doesn't it?" Florence asked.

"Perhaps Sorba is a practicing Catholic," Verlaque suggested.

"He is, according to my sources, which I'd like to keep anonymous for now—" This time it was Marine who coughed, taking a sip of water to clear her throat. Florence added, "But he's the only nonclergy on the board. My source says that he *forced* his way on."

"But he's on friendly terms with Père Fernand?" asked Marine.

"They had a falling-out recently," Florence said. "Just before the carol service. But no one knows what about."

Marine looked at Verlaque and raised an eyebrow. She thought her mother might be onto something.

"Thank you, Mme Bonnet," Verlaque said flatly. "I'll go and talk to Sorba again."

Marine shot Verlaque a glance; she knew he was being sarcastic and wouldn't speak to Sorba.

Florence smiled and reached behind her, grabbing her helmet. "Glad to help." She stood up and said, "Don't get up. Carry on with your dinner."

"Please thank Papa again for helping out with the cyclist," Marine said.

"Yes," Verlaque quickly added. "We'll have to come here again sometime, the four of us!" He immediately regretted it.

But Florence leaned in once again and said, "*Tsss*. Can you imagine all the food I can buy at the supermarket for the price of one of these meals?"

Verlaque was about to reply when Marine beat him to it. "Yes, we can imagine," she said, cutting into her fish and taking a mouthful, smiling at her husband.

CHAPTER TWENTY-FOUR

The next morning Verlaque left for work later than he usually did, stopping on the landing to kiss Marine, who was standing in the doorway of their apartment. "What are you doing today?" he asked.

"Oh, editing and some Christmas shopping, perhaps," she replied. "And I'm having lunch with Sylvie."

"Let me know if you have any gift ideas for my father or Rebecca."

"Will do," she said, waving to her husband. She listened to Verlaque skip down the stairs as she closed the door, then walked to the living room windows, where she could see the narrow rue Adanson down below. In about two minutes she saw the top of her husband's head, and his shoulders covered in a navy wool coat. He walked down the street toward the Palais de Justice.

She cleared the breakfast dishes. She'd arranged to meet her best friend, Sylvie, for a coffee and then visit some of the shops, looking for Christmas presents. She hadn't seen Sylvie— who taught photography at the Beaux Arts—in ages, as she knew that Sylvie would be busy with end-of-term grading and meetings. Sometimes the friends saw each other every day, and sometimes only twice a month, but it never worried Marine. They always picked up where they had left off, sometimes laughing so hard that if they were out in public they got stares, or, more often than not, Aixois smiled back, sharing in their happiness.

Grabbing her purse and keys, Marine left the apartment and walked the same way that Verlaque had, toward downtown.

Verlaque sat at his desk, sipping an espresso from his favorite demitasse and reading over, a second time, Mme Girard's resignation letter, which she had left on his desk late Friday night. It didn't surprise him that his secretary—always so elegant and of an indeterminate age—was leaving the Palais de Justice. He'd plan a going-away party for her, although he couldn't imagine Mme Girard tipsily swaying back and forth with a glass of inexpensive champagne in her hand, tears in her eyes, telling her colleagues how much she'd loved working with them and that they *just had to* stay in touch. Perhaps a lunch, just the two of them, would be better? Or a dinner, with M Girard and Marine, at last night's restaurant? He was mulling these ideas over, playing with the letter, when Paulik walked through the open doorway, knocking on the door frame as he did.

"Is everything okay?" Paulik asked, sitting down across from the judge, who had a faraway look in his eyes and was twirling a piece of paper around on his desk.

Verlaque pointed in the direction of the outer-office area, where Mme Girard worked from a spotless desk. "She just resigned," he whispered.

Paulik got up and closed the door, then sat back down. "*Merde*," he said.

"Well, it's not that bad," Verlaque said. "And it's hardly surprising. She's been here forever."

"Exactly," Paulik said. "You'll have no say in who HR sends up here to replace her."

Verlaque stared at Paulik. "*Merde*. I hadn't thought of that. I'm now realizing how much good work she did for me . . ." He let his voice trail off, feeling guilty that he had rarely thanked Mme Girard for her efficiency and, at times, the discreet background checks or delicate phone calls he had asked her to handle. How could she be replaced?

"I'm just here for a short visit. I have a meeting in ten minutes, but I wanted you to know that last night I got hold of that guy from Lyon who wasn't happy with Hainsby and Petit's bike tour."

Verlaque said, "I can't remember his name. Did he tell you anything interesting?"

"Cédric Farou," Paulik replied. "And, yes, he did. He complained about the usual tour hiccups—some of the days starting too late because of bicycle problems, not liking the lunches or dinners, that kind of thing. He was a real whiner, actually. But his biggest beef was with Cole Hainsby."

"What about?"

"Reckless driving."

"Did he file a complaint?"

"No, he just didn't sign up for any more tours." Paulik looked at his watch and got up. "I'll be through in an hour or so," he said. "Then I'll check whether Flamant is back."

"Are you free for lunch?" Verlaque said. He'd suddenly had the idea to go back to last night's restaurant. Perhaps they had a decent lunch menu?

"Sure. See you in a bit." Paulik opened the door and asked, "Did you find any interesting connections between Sorba and Père Fernand?"

An image quickly came into Verlaque's head in Kodachrome color: a small, neat Art Deco–era white stone building with a neon sign swinging back and forth in the wind that read DR. FLORENCE BONNET, PRIVATE INVESTIGATOR. "No," he answered. "Nothing interesting."

Verlaque sat at his desk for another minute, but when more details of the detective agency began to appear in his head, including Mme Bonnet's bicycle propped up against one of the walls of her stately office, all shiny mahogany and glittering glass, he got up and put on his coat and scarf. He had no idea where he was going, but it was better than waiting for information to come to him.

The minute he was outside, the cold, crisp air and wind heightened his senses. He stood on the steps and looked at the Place de Verdun with its agreeable, old-fashioned café; the clothing store that hadn't changed its look since the 1950s that sold sensible sleepwear and lingerie for grandmothers; and, on the corner, the Hermès shop that had replaced one of the city's independent bookstores (there were still three or four in Aix, he consoled himself). From here he could also see the top of the Protestant church's steeple. He walked down the steps, now sure that he had to go back and start at the beginning: the APCA. Cole Hainsby and Père Fernand had both been present the day of the Anglo church's carol sing service. He traversed the square and began trudging up the rue Emeric David, his upper body bent into the oncoming wind. He shoved his hands into his pockets and flinched as he felt the soft wooly head of the elf, having forgotten that he had bought it. In less than three minutes he was ringing the doorbell of the APCA offices.

"Good morning, Judge," Dave Flanagan said as he shook Verlaque's hand, which was red and cold from the walk.

"Good morning, Reverend," Verlaque said. "I just have a few more questions, if you don't mind."

"Of course," Dave said, motioning toward his office.

"I'd like to speak to Mlle Dubois as well."

Dave shrugged. "She isn't in this morning."

"Still off sick?"

"*Non*," Dave said. "I mean, she did come in, but then left."

Verlaque looked surprised. "Is that normal?"

"Oh, yeah. But since she's such a good worker I leave her to it."

Verlaque sat down opposite Dave. He began, "I understand that on the evening before the carol sing the Hainsbys argued here, during a potluck dinner."

"That's right."

"Can you remember what about?"

Dave rubbed his chin. "I'm afraid not. It happened often, you see." He looked through a small window in his office door and said, "My wife, Jennifer, just walked in. Perhaps she'll remember." He got up and opened the door, calling to his wife.

"*Bonjour, Judge*," Jennifer said. She continued in French, "I've been delivering cakes to Fanny's."

"Lucky Fanny, and lucky Aix," Verlaque said, smiling. He motioned for Mme Flanagan to sit down beside him.

Dave said, "Honey, Judge Verlaque wants to know if you remember what the Hainsbys were fighting about last Saturday night."

"Here, at our dinner?" she asked. She crossed

her arms and looked at the floor for a second or two. "Cole broke a wineglass," she said, looking up.

"Oh, yes!" Dave said.

Verlaque asked, "Is that the only reason Mme Hainsby was cross with her husband?"

"No, there was something else," Jennifer continued. "I remember now. Cole ate off someone else's plate. That was it. He picked up the plate of someone else and started eating."

Verlaque looked at Mme Flanagan, stunned. "Thank you so much," he said, getting up.

"Oh, my!" Jennifer said. "Do you think?"

"I'm a bit slow," Dave said, puzzled, looking from his wife to the judge for an answer. "Oh!" he said after a few seconds. "Do you think it's possible?"

"It's entirely possible," Verlaque said from the door. "Thank you both. I'll see myself out."

Five minutes later Verlaque was back in his office, thankful that downtown Aix was so small. He hung up his coat and sat down, dialing Paulik's number and getting his voice mail. He called Flamant's number with the same result. He signed off on Mme Girard's retirement letter, then began pacing around his office, wondering why, despite everything pointing at the Orezza brothers, he found France Dubois's behavior so strange.

Paulik arrived and watched Verlaque from the

open doorway. "You're going to wear out the carpet."

"Let's go," Verlaque said, getting his coat. "We can have lunch at my apartment, if you don't mind leftovers."

"Your leftovers are going to be just as good as any restaurant lunch."

"I may have a few surprises down in the cellar, too."

"Let's not waste any time, then," Paulik said, turning to go. As much as he loved his wife's wines, he loved when his boss used the words *surprise* and *cellar* in the same sentence.

As they walked, Verlaque filled Paulik in on his visit to the APCA. Paulik called Flamant's phone and left a message to call him as soon as he got back to his desk. It seemed that Père Fernand might have been the intended victim all along. A car pulled up behind them as they strolled up the rue Gaston de Saporta. "Okay, okay," Verlaque said, standing aside so the car could pass on what was normally a pedestrian street, save for merchants or residents who had passes. The car was a black BMW, and he caught a glimpse of the driver as it passed. It was the salesman from Del Carlo, gesturing to a group of tourists in front of him to get out of the way. "Look!" Verlaque said to Paulik. "The Orezzas' thug."

Paulik grabbed Verlaque's right arm. "The right-hand side of the car is smashed up."

They walked behind the car, which was still driving slowly, creeping up the road because of the heavy pedestrian traffic. "Look at the bumper sticker," Verlaque said. "It's the same auto dealer that Sorba bought his giant four-by-four from."

"He's getting through," Paulik said as the road cleared and the BMW picked up speed. He got out his phone and typed in the BMW's license plate number.

"Let's follow him." Verlaque had started jogging. "My car is parked up the road, in the square," he said, thankful that he had been too tired to park his car in the garage. When had he used it last? He couldn't remember; he just remembered parking it, turning off the engine, and putting his magistrate's permit on the dashboard so the traffic police would see it. Everyone knew his car anyway, but you never know.

They turned into the square and Verlaque was relieved to see his beautiful green car still there. He fumbled for his key and found it, opening the doors. They jumped in. Verlaque put the key into the ignition and turned. The Porsche made a sad, whining sound, then stopped making the noise altogether. He looked at Paulik, who said nothing but couldn't help grimacing. Verlaque tried again, and not a sound came out.

"No worries," Paulik said. He took his phone out of his pocket and called the police station, giving them the license plate number. He ordered someone to follow the car and stop it for a routine check. "Hopefully they'll be able to match the scratches on the car's right-hand side with the paint of Damien Petit's bike," he said, glancing over at Verlaque, who had let his hands drop from the steering wheel and was staring straight ahead.

"I think I'll upgrade our lunch wine to a Grand Cru," Verlaque said, opening his car door.

Paulik shrugged and got out of the car. He wasn't about to argue.

CHAPTER TWENTY-FIVE

Marine and Sylvie, on the other hand, did eat lunch at the restaurant she and Verlaque had so enjoyed the previous evening. Marine sipped sparkling water, feeling tired. Although she loved Sylvie dearly, shopping with her was an Olympic sport. Every time Marine had picked out an object, Sylvie came up with two or three reasons why it would be an inappropriate gift. Sylvie's choices, on the other hand, Marine found too expensive, too luxurious. Her parents didn't care about luxuries, nor did Antoine's father, who had lived surrounded by luxury, and now, in his old age, appreciated simpler things. And what to buy Rebecca, the elder Verlaque's American girlfriend, thirty years his junior and who looked like Naomi Campbell? In the end Marine chose for Rebecca a showy coffee table book about Venetian palaces—"With recipes!" the sticker on the book boasted. She was sure Rebecca would never use the recipes, but she could imagine the supermodel lookalike curled up by the fire in winter, enjoying the dreamlike images of the palaces. After two hours of shopping, that had been Marine's only purchase.

Marine ordered the winter *soupe au pistou*, and Sylvie, a *pot-au-feu*. "You can have a glass of wine if you want," Marine heard Sylvie saying. "Just because I'm not having one doesn't mean you can't."

Marine said, "No, but thanks. I don't feel like wine."

Sylvie rubbed her temples and moaned. "Who would have thought that the older I get, the more fun end-of-semester parties are? Never mix gin and vodka cocktails." She looked at her friend and expected a laugh, but instead Marine was staring off into space.

Their meal arrived, and Sylvie took a piece of bread and dipped it into her broth. "This *pot-au-feu* will cure my hangover," she said. "Nothing like beef broth and veggies on a cold day." She looked at Marine, who was slowly twirling around her bean and vegetable soup with a large spoon. Marine sighed. Sylvie ate her bread, delicious now that it had soaked up the salty broth. She swallowed and said, "What's going on with you?"

Marine took in a big breath and blew it out. She told Sylvie of her recent fatigue, the unusual impulse to stay clear of coffee and alcohol, the nonconversation that she had had with her husband about children, and her current self-diagnosis. And for the rest of the lunch they talked of nothing else.

Less than hour later they said good-bye at the restaurant's front door. Marine found herself walking toward the Place des Cardeurs, hoping some of the stands would still be open. She might find something interesting from Italy or Tunisia for her parents. She smiled, thinking that she could surprise Antoine with a Tunisian carpet, since he was hinting so badly about wanting one the other night. She walked with a purpose now, feeling better about so many things.

She was glad to have had such a good talk with Sylvie; in contrast with Sylvie's gift-buying opinions, her advice was constructive and thoughtful. "I have only your best interests in mind, Marine," Sylvie had said. "But you need to tell Antoine as soon as possible. Once you do, you'll feel relieved, and you can discuss the options and make a decision that's right for *both* of you."

Marine got to the Cardeurs and stopped to tighten her scarf as the wind ripped through the big open square. She saw the man from Philadelphia holding on to a section of his tent's canvas while a woman quickly retied it to a pole. Marine looked across to get her bearings; she couldn't quite remember where the Tunisian's stall was, and then she saw France Dubois standing in the wind alone, staring at the Americans. Marine waved and yelled France's name. France saw Marine and turned her back, running behind another stall. "France, wait!" Marine hollered. Marine began to run and noticed the German woman watching the whole thing. Anna Rösch saw Marine and quickly looked down, pretending to furiously scrub down her counter.

"*Bonjour*," Marine said as she approached the Tübingen stand. "What's going on? I saw you watching Mlle Dubois."

"Perhaps," Anna said quietly.

"Why is she behaving like that? In this cold wind?"

Anna shrugged.

"Listen," Marine said. "Mlle Dubois may be in trouble . . ."

Anna looked up, surprised. Marine continued her bluff. "Mlle Dubois is a prime suspect in Cole Hainsby's murder. I need to know why she keeps watching the stand from Philadelphia. It may help her case." Marine leaned in and explained that Hainsby had been responsible for the death of France's parents.

"Well, I don't know very much," Anna whispered. She looked over at her husband, who was chatting with a customer. "Come, follow me," she said as she led Marine to a spot out of the wind in the back of their tent. "Mlle Dubois is watching monsieur. The man."

"The American?" Marine asked. "Why?"

"Last year he was here, and he accosted Mlle Dubois."

"You mean he harassed her?"

289

"Yes, in a . . ." She paused, putting a finger in the air. "An inappropriate way," she said, having found the correct word in French. She took hold of Marine's arm. "I told mademoiselle to report it, but she's afraid to. So she comes and watches him."

"Did you witness it?" Marine asked. "Last year?"

"No, this is our first visit to Aix," Anna said. "But I saw him grab France this year, trying to talk to her, and it was clear to me she wanted nothing to do with him. When he was gone I took her a cup of warm tea with some schnapps and she broke down, crying, and told me everything."

"He sees her watching him, obviously," Marine said.

Anna nodded. "I think that she is trying to wear him down, make him feel guilty. That, or she's trying to decide what to do. Waiting."

"Thank you," Marine said. "It makes sense now, her strange behavior."

"She's a sweet girl," Anna added.

"Yes," Marine said. "I'll let you get back to your work."

They parted and Marine walked slowly up the path, keeping an eye out for France Dubois. She saw the stand from Carthage and went up to it, smiling at the owner, who was folding a large piece of bright yellow fabric. She touched it and said, "It's beautifully soft."

"And perfect for a bed in the summer, when

it's hot but you still need a coverlet," Mehdi Abdelhak answered. He looked at Marine and asked, "Don't I recognize you from that evening at the cathedral?"

"You have a good memory," Marine said. "I did help myself to some of your food more than once."

Abdelhak smiled and introduced himself. "I never forget a client, especially one who loves Tunisian food." But the truth was, she was so beautiful he could hardly take his eyes off her. Like his wife, whom he dearly missed. He wished they could have afforded to buy a plane ticket for her to accompany him to Aix.

Marine asked to look at some of the carpets, and Abdelhak was only too glad, as he had sold only three so far. "And the priest?" he asked as he held up one of his favorites. "Is it true he was shot?"

"Yes, he wasn't killed," Marine said. "But he may not live."

Mehdi dropped his head and clasped his hands.

"I'll take this one," Marine said. "It will be lovely in our kitchen."

He brought his head back up and looked at her, relieved and happy. This sale would help pay for part of his flight. It was then that Marine noticed a thin gold chain around his neck, with a small crucifix hanging from it. "You're a Christian?" she asked.

Mehdi nodded. "Here, I can wear this chain,

but not back home. It would cause too many . . . misunderstandings. My wife is Muslim."

"She knows about your faith, I take it."

"Oh, yes, I told her when we met. She didn't mind then, and doesn't now."

"That's the loveliest thing I've heard all week," Marine said, getting her wallet out of her purse. She paid, and then helped him to roll up the rug and tie it with a piece of rope at either end.

"Will you manage?" he asked. "I can bring it to your apartment after I close the stand, perhaps? If it's downtown . . ."

"Thank you, but I'll be fine," Marine answered. "We live near the cathedral, and it's a small rug."

"I will go to the church this evening," he said. "And light a candle for the priest."

Marine nodded and thanked him. She took the carpet and hoisted it up on her right shoulder, holding on to its bottom end with both her hands. "Good-bye, and happy holidays if I don't see you again!" she said.

Halfway home she began wishing that she had taken up M Abdelhak's offer of bringing the carpet to her apartment. But it was a surprise for Antoine, and it wasn't that heavy. She just hadn't counted on the wind. Every so often she looked at a shop or a landmark and told herself, *Not far now. You just passed the Museum of Old Aix . . . now the shop that sells expensive scented candles from Paris . . .*

Once inside their building she set the carpet down and rested, sitting on the cane chair that had always stood in the corner, waiting for someone to use it. She had never sat in it before. She felt like an old woman. After a few minutes she picked the carpet back up—it really wasn't that heavy—and ascended the four flights to their apartment. She put her key in the lock and opened the door with her hip but stopped when she heard voices. "*Merde,*" she mumbled as she made straight for the back of the apartment and their bedroom.

"Marine!" Verlaque yelled. "We're in the dining room!"

"I'll be right there!" she answered, walking into their walk-in closet and shoving the carpet behind a row of her colorful summer dresses. She closed the closet door and walked down the long hallway, past the kitchen, to the dining room, where Antoine and Bruno Paulik were sitting.

Paulik jumped up and gave Marine the *bises*.

"Marine, you have to try this wine," Verlaque said, grabbing the bottle. "Oh, sorry, there isn't any left." Paulik smiled sheepishly.

"That's all right," Marine said, sitting down. "I have some information for you." She told them about France Dubois and Jason Miller, and about Mehdi Abdelhak's Catholicism. "Now we know why Abdelhak was taking pictures of Saint Roch's chapel," she said as she finished.

"Yes," Verlaque agreed. "But France Dubois . . ."

"Oh, she's harmless, Antoine," Marine said. She looked over to Paulik for support but he was now standing in the doorway, listening to a message on his cell phone.

"The BMW was pulled over," Paulik said as he hung up. "Alexandre Mareschi's license is no good, too many traffic violations, so they've been able to impound the car and are checking it with Damien Petit's bike."

Verlaque clapped. "Perfect."

Marine yawned. "You can fill me in later about this BMW," she said. "I'm off to bed."

Verlaque gave her a sideways look; Marine never napped, unless on summer holidays after a sea swim. He was about to ask her about it when Paulik said, "Flamant is back and already has some info for us." Verlaque leaned back in his chair so he could watch Marine walk down the hallway, and he noticed she hadn't even bothered to take off her winter coat.

CHAPTER TWENTY-SIX

When she heard the front door close, Marine hopped out of bed and phoned Margaux, who was waiting at a nearby café for the go-ahead. Margaux arrived in ten minutes and soon Marine found herself sitting in front of the bathroom mirror wearing a dressing gown, her hair tightly gathered into a bun and secured with netting. She grimaced without her thick auburn-colored hair framing her face. It made her features come into sharper view.

Margaux begged Marine to sit still as she applied foundation, eye shadow, and mascara, none of which Marine normally wore. "Stop flinching," Margaux said as she rubbed—violently, in Marine's opinion—the foundation onto her cheekbones. "You're lucky that this isn't taking hours, as it can sometimes take in my business."

"*Mon dieu*," Marine said.

"It's a long process, but it can be fun, too," Margaux continued, "because with makeup and a wig you're completely transformed. You're suddenly a different person. You can pretend to be anybody; change your accent, country, or even era."

Marine muttered something in agreement,

seeing the appeal of it for some people, but not for her. She looked at herself, her dozens of freckles now hidden by the sand-colored foundation.

"Time for the wig," Margaux said. "Wait until you see this." She put her hands into the wig and placed it firmly on Marine's head, tucking in any loose hairs.

Marine turned her head from side to side, grinning. It looked rather good. The wig was made from jet-black hair cut with blunt bangs, or, as Margaux had described, "Uma Thurman in *Pulp Fiction*." Marine thought that it would have been impossible to get all of her thick wavy hair tucked up into the wig, but Margaux obviously knew what she was doing.

"Now for the clothes," Marine said, sounding a little more excited than she meant to.

"The outfit is hanging for you in the bedroom," Margaux said. "Luckily we're the same size."

Marine got up, tightening her bathrobe, and entered her bedroom while Margaux packed away her makeup and went to the kitchen to get a glass of water. Five minutes later Marine walked into the kitchen and Margaux flinched, spilling some water onto the floor.

"No longer Uma Thurman," Marine said, turning around. "Even better."

"True," Margaux replied. "More like Julia Roberts in *Pretty Woman*."

"The skirt's a little short, isn't it?"

"You're taller than me, that's why."

"I do like the blouse," Marine said, walking around the kitchen and wondering what Antoine would think if he were to walk in.

"Leopard prints are classic," Margaux said. "And that blouse is good and tight on you. But I just have to fix something." Margaux walked over and undid one of the buttons on the blouse, revealing more of Marine's chest. "Leave it like this for him."

"All right," Marine said.

"Can you walk in heels that high?"

"I'll manage."

Margaux looked at her watch. "It's time to go," she said. "I'll drive you and wait down the road in the car. Are you sure you're up for this?"

Marine said, "It was my idea. He knows you, and even if he does remember me from the carol sing, we've never met and I'm very nicely disguised." Marine walked around the apartment a bit more, getting used to her new height, hair color, and clothes. Margaux watched, smiling, as she saw her new friend embracing the role, as she herself had done dozens of times. She knew as she had applied the makeup that Marine was going to try to resist—as many nonactors did—the idea that they could so easily be physically changed, and that they might enjoy the transformation, even revel in it.

"Take me to the car," Marine said in a strange

voice, grabbing a coat and purse, also specially chosen by Margaux for the occasion. "I don't want to be late."

"I like the Sophia Loren accent," Margaux said, trying not to laugh.

Marine was thrilled that Margaux recognized it. She lowered her voice and said, "I was born in Aix but raised near Naples in my mother's family villa." She closed her front door, locked it, and shook her head so that her new black hair swished back and forth as she slowly descended the stairs, holding tightly to the handrail. She turned around and continued her story, adding huskiness to her newly acquired voice. "I've just had a terrible divorce and have come back to Aix to raise my children. No more money to repair the villa. I'm feeling so sad, so sad."

"Perfect," Margaux said, privately thinking the repetition of "so sad" was overacting a bit. "We'll rehearse more in the car. What's your name?"

"Valentina," Marine answered slowly.

"All right, Valentina, just try not to break your neck in those heels."

Thirty minutes later Margaux dropped Marine off at the Four Seasons bilingual school, parking the car down the road under a leafy plane tree. She brought a film script about the painter Cézanne to read, sent by her agent. She would be auditioning for the part of his ill-treated wife,

Hortense. Margaux felt that she was too pretty to play frumpy Hortense, but with makeup these days . . . She frowned, doubting it would be an interesting role, but at least much of the story took place in Aix, so she wouldn't have to leave her family during filming. And costume dramas were popular, so perhaps the film would be profitable. She tried to concentrate on the script and not worry about Marine.

Marine managed to walk into the school, introduce herself to the ambivalent secretary, and make it up the narrow stairs to Alain Sorba's office without falling. While she waited for her appointment she squirmed, feeling the microphone that Margaux had wired her up with, the cord running through the inside of her blouse and a tiny battery pack hidden, she hoped, by her velour blazer. She yawned, wishing she had a taste for coffee these days.

"*Bonjour, madame,*" Sorba said, opening the door to his office and gesturing for her to enter.

Marine jumped up, her short skirt lifting up even higher than it already was. Sorba's eyes were fixed on her elegant long legs. "*Bonjour,*" Marine said, shaking his hand. "Thank you for seeing me at such short notice. My life is . . . crazy . . . these days."

"Come in," he said. "Please take a seat and tell me about your situation."

Marine sat down, leaning forward slightly so

that her blouse revealed a view of her chest. "I'm here because I have two children," she began. "They are both in middle school, both boys. Very smart boys, you will see. They speak Italian and French and I want them to learn English."

"You've come to the right place, Madame . . ." Sorba cast a glance at a piece of paper on his desk. "Madame Abbona."

Marine smiled, hopping that Sorba didn't pick up on the fact that Abbona was a northern name. She got it from the label of a wine bottle, one of Antoine's favorite Barolos.

"Do you offer scholarships?" She leaned forward a little more.

"Rarely, I'm afraid. Except in exceptional circumstances."

"Those are my circumstance," Marine replied. "Exceptional ones."

"Tell me about them," Sorba said, making a not very good attempt to not stare at her cleavage.

"Long story, as they say." Marine let out a small laugh. "I was born in Aix, but we moved to my mother's family villa near Naples when I was very small. Beautiful villa. Frescoes on the ceilings and walls, so many rooms, and views of the sea. But it takes so much money to keep up. The staff is so expensive these days . . ." She tried her hardest to look sad. "So I marry a wealthy man . . ."

"M Abbona?"

"*Si*. Only he's not as wealthy as he pretends. He has some shady businesses, with a friend of his who's a crooked accountant. And then they get caught, and both get thrown in jail."

"Oh, I'm so sorry," Sorba said, leaning forward.

"No, not sorry!" Marine replied, trying her best to play an angry Neapolitan woman. "I ask for a divorce, but I find out from our family lawyer that in this crooked business everything has been tied to me, without my knowing it. Those papers they made me sign, they told me they were investments. His businesses have so many debts, and I will lose everything, even the family villa . . ."

"Oh, no!"

"*Si!*"

"If your sons have very good grades," Sorba said, "we may be able to help them out a bit."

Marine looked at him, dabbing the corners of her eyes with a tissue. "*Grazie*. But it's not enough . . ."

"The villa."

"My lawyer tells me that if I can pay off one of the debts very quickly, I may be able to save the villa, at least. How do I help my poor unmarried sisters? Eva, Clara, Rosa . . ."

Sorba's eyes enlarged and he got up and walked around his desk. Marine got a lump in her throat, realizing she had gone a bit far with the sisters, but it just slipped out. It was as if she had *become* Valentina, and she really did have three unmarried sisters. Marine could even see them in her head.

Sorba sat on the edge of his desk, beside Marine. She shifted a bit, revealing more leg. "Do you think you can help us?" she asked, almost whispering. "You would be our guest at the villa anytime. Clara is a dancer in a nightclub . . ."

"I do have friends here who may offer you a loan," Sorba said, smiling. "To get you out of your troubles. I'll talk to them this afternoon. Tell me more about your villa, and your poor sisters . . ."

Marine smiled and the stories flowed out of her. The villa and its glazed tile floors, the fountain outside with an eighteenth-century sculpture of Leda and the swan, the palm trees framing the views of the sea. The ancient roses in the garden, and the hunchbacked gardener named Giuseppe. Equally enjoyable for her were the stories she made up about her sisters: Rosa wanted to be a nun but was kicked out of the convent for being "too wild"; Eva had been a model but now just wanted to perfect her ravioli recipe . . .

Just before leaving Marine gently stroked Alain Sorba's cheek, thanking him. By the time she got back to Margaux's car she was wild with excitement.

"Whoa, slow down," Margaux said, looking at Marine, who was flushed and gesticulating with her hands much more than she normally did. "Let's get that microphone off of you." She helped Marine pull the wires out of her blouse and took the tape recorder. She turned it on and replayed a few seconds; the sound was perfect. "Well done, Valentina!"

CHAPTER TWENTY-SEVEN

Flamant was standing at the printer when they walked into his office, a large open space shared with dozens of other officers. He waved a paper in the air, and gestured to a desk to his right. Paulik and Verlaque found two spare chairs and brought them to the desk, by which time Flamant was back.

"Once I started searching on the computer," Flamant began, flipping through his printouts, "it was easy. Père Fernand Janin has had a busy career."

"Did you find any connections with the sister cities?" Paulik asked. "They were the ones who cooked and served the food on Sunday evening, and we're quite sure now that Père Fernand was the intended victim."

Flamant looked confused and Verlaque told him about the Hainsbys' fight over Cole helping himself to someone else's food. Flamant pulled out the paper he was looking for and said, "Yes, there are a few connections. Fernand Janin worked in Tunisia for a while."

Verlaque and Paulik exchanged looks. "He loves Tunisian food," Verlaque said. "He kept talking about it on Sunday. I don't suppose he was in Carthage?"

"No, Tunis," Flamant said.

Paulik pulled out his notebook and read through the names he had written down. "Does the name Mehdi Abdelhak come up anywhere?"

"That name doesn't ring a bell," Flamant answered. "But you'll want to look over these more closely. I only skimmed the Tunisia stuff, as what comes next is fascinating. I would have called you sooner, but I was engrossed. Janin's Tunisia stay was uneventful. Unlike his stay in Africa, which is why I called you—"

"Where in Africa?" Paulik asked.

"Ethiopia. Which was once a colony of—"

"Italy," Verlaque cut in. "What happened there?" He tried to picture the faces of the Italians from Perugia: He was a big guy, bald, and his partner was a small, thin woman with reddish hair. Sort of like Bruno and Hélène Paulik, he mused.

Flamant read from one of the pieces of paper and showed it to Verlaque and Paulik. "Janin was there ten years ago," he said. "In a village north of Addis Ababa. He was mobilizing the villagers to protest against multinational groups selling used clothing in Ethiopia. It's a huge business in Africa; I had no idea."

"Isn't that a good thing?" Paulik asked. "Don't they need used clothes in Africa?"

"Not when there's local clothing manufacturing, as there was in the village where Janin was a priest."

"Used clothes from the West would put them out of business," Paulik said.

"Exactly." Flamant went on, "The used-clothing industry is worth more than three hundred million dollars in sales yearly. The clothes come from the West and are sorted and resold in East Africa. They create jobs for the guys selling clothes in markets but devastate local clothing companies. Janin was working with two small clothing factories, leading protests against one of the local used-clothing importers, called Elite. He was trying to ban all imported used clothes in Africa by 2019."

"Will it happen, the ban?" Verlaque asked.

"Unlikely. There's too much resistance, especially from the USA, which unloads large quantities of secondhand clothes all over the world."

"And you feel so good, donating your used clothes to those charities," Paulik said.

"Yeah," Flamant agreed. "My girlfriend just cleared our closet last week, and she went out of her way to go to a Catholic charity to drop off our old clothes. We were patting ourselves on the back."

"And this Elite company?" Verlaque asked. "What happened?"

"The workers of the two small factories went on marches, led by Père Janin," Flamant said. "But one of Père Janin's followers was a real militant, a bit of a nutter. One night he set fire to the Elite warehouse, and all those cheap T-shirts and old jeans went up in flames." He passed a photocopy of a newspaper article to them. "The problem was, Elite's owner, Vito Giraldi, was inside the warehouse that night. His family said he was paranoid—with good reason, it seems—and the smoke and flames were so strong he couldn't get out. Giraldi died in there."

"What kind of fallout was there?" Paulik asked.

"Fernand Janin came back to France a few months later," Flamant said. "He was in a church in Paris, then got transferred down here. And Elite, without its founder, folded."

"Plus it lost all of its inventory that night, one would assume," Verlaque suggested. "Elite was an Italian company, I take it, given the founder's name."

"But they weren't from Perugia," Flamant said. He picked up one of the pieces of paper and read from it. "Bari, down in Puglia."

Paulik checked his notebook. "Matteo Ricci is the name of the guy running the Perugia stand."

"And his partner?" Verlaque asked.

Paulik read aloud, "Vittoria Romano."

"No direct connection, it seems," Flamant said. "But I thought it was interesting."

"It certainly gives someone a motive to try to kill Père Fernand," Paulik said. "Although it was hardly his fault that some loony set fire to the warehouse."

"We just have to find out *whose* motive it was," Verlaque said. "Good work, Flamant." He looked at the floor for a few seconds and then asked, "Is it possible that Matteo Ricci is using a fake name?"

"I thought of that, too," Flamant said. "So I called the city worker in charge of booking the Christmas stands. She told me that the stand renters have to provide their passports and fill out a whole bunch of paperwork and permits. She checks their references, too. They are especially careful because of the threat of terrorist attacks. When I suggested someone could slip through the cracks using an alias, I thought she was going to bite my head off."

"That doesn't sound like a city worker," Verlaque said, laughing.

Verlaque sat at his desk, writing down a list of possible restaurants he could take Mme Girard to for her good-bye lunch. Much to his relief, and as expected, she rejected the suggestion of an office party and accepted his offer to lunch. The problem was, none of the restaurants in Aix seemed fitting for such a grand lady. Aix's only Michelin-starred restaurant had just closed, the chef having retired. Avignon and Les Baux-de-Provence were too far away—what would they talk about for more than an hour in the car? That left Marseille—and its famed three-star restaurant on the sea. He looked in his wallet and couldn't find their business card so he looked them up on the computer. He found the website quickly, with its sparkling photographs of the white mansion surrounded by emerald-green water, and the young chef with shoulder-length hair who recently took over the reins from his father. The restaurant had been a family affair for almost a century, the old man's grandmother having been a Marseillaise cabaret singer at the turn of the twentieth century. Verlaque looked at the current chef, who was handsome enough to be an actor, and mused at how much things had changed in the restaurant business. Good looks were so important now. He shook his head back and forth when he noticed the chef's tattoos running up and down his forearms. It seemed that even handsome young men now had body art. He picked up the phone and dialed the number listed on the website. While he was on hold he stared at the photograph on the screen, trying to make out why the chef had thought it so important that he had to drill with permanent ink an image of it on his arms. Verlaque had recently wondered the same thing here in Aix, fascinated—or repulsed—by someone's tattoos, but he couldn't remember where. In a café? The restaurant employee came back online and he was able to reserve for the following Friday. He hung up and remembered who and where it was—the Italian woman at the Sister City stand. He remembered her name, too: Vittoria Romano. Beautiful name.

He looked at the clock; it was almost time to leave, and now he couldn't get the image of the tattooed Vittoria Romano out of his head. The only link she had with Père Fernand was the fact that she was Italian, as was the warehouse owner in Ethiopia. His phone rang and he picked it up. "*Oui, Verlaque ici.*"

"Judge Verlaque," said a high-pitched male voice on the other end. "It's Collot at the lab. We've tested the paint scratches on the BMW with the bicycle involved in the hit-and-run north of Aix."

"And?"

"Perfect match, sir."

"Excellent," Verlaque said. "The BMW driver, where is he now?"

"Alexandre Mareschi is in interview room two, sir."

"Thank you, Officer." Verlaque hung up and walked out of his office, appreciating the formality used by Officer Collot, whom he had never met. Mme Girard was gone for the day, her desk cleared, as usual, of all paper and debris. He looked down at the framed photograph of her three smiling children and thought of Marine's comment the other evening about perfect childhoods. In his opinion, the chances of a perfect childhood greatly diminished with the arrival of each new child in the family. Having three was a risky business. His parents had even messed up two. How was that possible? He thought of himself and Séb as children. They hadn't been demanding; all they wanted was love and affection and a certain number of stories at night. And good food, on his part. Séb didn't care one way or the other. Why had that been so difficult for his wealthy, well-educated parents? He continued through the empty office and suddenly felt his forehead begin to sweat. He sat down in an empty chair, holding his head in his hands with his elbows on his knees. He took a few deep breaths, trying to wipe certain images out of his head. Instead, he thought of Marine, her grin, her freckles, her long narrow fingers, one of them that wore his grandmother's Cartier engagement ring. He got up and patted his forehead with a tissue that he took from a box on Mme Girard's desk, and then looked at his watch. It was almost 6:00; the Christmas stands would be closing soon, and he was still consumed by thoughts of Vittoria Romano's tattoos. He called Marine as he walked down the stairs and asked if she wouldn't mind going to the Italians to buy some cheese, and if, by chance, she got a look at the woman's forearm tattoos, that would be great. "I'll explain later," he said. "It's just a hunch." She agreed but she sounded flustered and slightly annoyed at his request. He hung up just as he got to interview room two.

"*Bonsoir*," he said as he opened the door, more to the waiting police officer than to Mareschi, who sat back in a chair with his arms folded. The police officer nodded and Verlaque sat down across from his favorite clothing salesman.

"I'll get right to the point," Verlaque began, "as it's almost dinnertime. The red paint on your black BMW matches the red paint of an expensive road bike that was hit north of Puyricard." He saw Mareschi's shoulders fall and his face crumple. Up until now Mareschi had thought he was here because of a traffic violation. "Why would you hit a cyclist? Why Damien Petit, a young man whom you've probably never met?"

"I have never met him."

"So why run him off the road?"

"He owes me money."

Verlaque asked, "How does he owe you money if you've never met him?"

"His partner owes me money."

"You should speak of Cole Hainsby in the past tense; he's dead." Verlaque thought he could see fear in the young man's dark eyes.

"I didn't kill him."

"Really? It's a very good motive. How much money did they borrow from you?"

"Sixty thousand euros."

Verlaque whistled and sat back. "That's a lot of cash for a store clerk to have."

Mareschi stared at the table and said nothing.

Verlaque tried again. "Who was lending the money, exactly?" The young man stayed silent. "Do you want to add murder to your rap? It's already impressive—"

"We didn't murder Hainsby!"

"We?"

"We heard that the American keeled over at the church after being poisoned. We didn't do it! He owed us money!"

"So you tried to kill his partner, too?" Verlaque asked. "To give others a warning? Or just to make amends."

"No! We just wanted our sixty thousand back. How would we get it back if they were dead?"

"How does a nice guy like Cole Hainsby find out about guys like you?" Mareschi didn't answer, but Verlaque figured it was through Alain Sorba. He pictured Cole Hainsby going to Sorba for advice. "Where were you last Sunday afternoon?" he asked.

"Nowhere near the cathedral," Mareschi answered. "And I can prove it. The three of us, me, Jean-Paul, and Michel, went for lunch in Marseille—the Miramar, you can check, we left around four o'clock—then we drove back up here to the casino. We played cards there until late at night."

Verlaque nodded; he'd have someone call Aix's gambling joint and check.

"And I wasn't trying to kill Petit the other day,"

Mareschi offered. "I was just reminding him . . ."

"Reminding him not to get involved with guys like you?"

"Hey! Jean-Paul is always saying that it's guys like us who help others out. That's why they come to us, whining about needing money."

"Jean-Paul? Michel? Who *is* us, exactly?"

Mareschi sat back and pursed his lips together.

On his way back home Verlaque called Marine but got her voice mail. He walked up Gaston Saporta and was about to turn left to go home when he saw, just past the cathedral, one of the Orezza brothers standing in the door of Père Fernand's favorite bar. Orezza was speaking to someone inside the doorway, and gesturing as if angry. He then swung around and walked away, up the street toward the ring road. Verlaque quickened his pace when he saw that it had been Pierrette who was taking the brunt of Orezza's anger. By the time he got to the bar she was behind the counter, busying herself with loading the small glassware dishwasher. He walked up to the bar and sat down on an available stool, next to an old man with a yellowed mustache who was drinking a pastis and reading *La Provence*.

"I'll have what he's having," Verlaque said, gesturing to the pastis.

The old man overheard and held up his glass, smiling. "To pastis in winter," he said.

"It was almost warm out today," Verlaque said, smiling.

"Positively," Pierrette said, placing a glass of the alcohol, a bowl of ice cubes, and a small pitcher of water before him.

"No wind, that's why," the old man added, and then turned back to the newspaper.

"Peanuts?" she asked.

"Sure, thanks," Verlaque said. As he watched Pierrette he thought of Florence Bonnet again, and her news that Sorba and Père Fernand had had a falling out. And why did Sorba so badly want to be on the cathedral's board of directors? It's not as if that would help him get more students into his school, as the parents were mostly expats. Pierrette slid a small bowl of peanuts to Verlaque and he took a handful, half surprised that they were fresh.

He poured water into his pastis and added two ice cubes, wondering if she remembered him from the other evening. She looked at him, hesitated a little, then came over and put her hands on the linoleum counter. "I heard Père Fernand might make it," she said.

So she does remember me, Verlaque thought. "Yes," he answered. "I'm not religious but I did consider lighting a few candles in the church for him."

"I thought of doing that, too," she said. "And although I'm against what the Catholic church preaches for so many reasons, they do good work, too."

Verlaque looked at her Castro T-shirt and the rainbow across it and nodded.

She went on, "Especially priests like Père Fernand."

Verlaque looked toward the old man, but he was gone. Verlaque then spotted him at the back of the bar, watching two other old-timers play chess. He took the opportunity to be direct with Pierrette. "I just saw one of the Orezza brothers here," he said. "It looked like he was threatening you. Or he was angry—"

Pierrette looked toward the old men and then turned her gaze to Verlaque. "I can handle him."

"I'm afraid you might not be able to, Pierrette." She turned slightly and he went on, afraid that he would lose the opportunity to speak frankly with her. "There's some ugly business going on in Aix. One person has died in the cathedral, and another has been shot, and the cathedral is your neighbor. This bar is almost built up against it."

"I've always loved the irony in that," she replied. "As did my grandfather, who was a Communist and an atheist."

He went on. "The Orezza brothers are connected to one of the men who came to harm in that church, an American businessman. But what do the Orezza brothers have to do with our friend the jolly priest?"

"Père Fernand was helping me," she said quietly and quickly. She rubbed her eyes and muttered, "I'm so tired of all of this." She poured some pastis into a glass and added half the water Verlaque had put in his own.

Verlaque asked, "What do they want? How was Père Fernand helping?"

"They want this bar, of course."

Verlaque breathed out. "Of course. It's so well located."

"Across from Science Po, where rich bourgeois kids learn politics," she said. "And it's on the way down into town, with hundreds of well-heeled tourists walking by daily."

"And you won't sell?"

"Not on your life," she said. She looked around and whispered, "Where would these old guys go?"

At that moment he wanted to jump up and embrace her. Instead, he raised his glass to hers and they toasted. He asked, "And Père Fernand stood up to them?"

She blinked twice and nodded.

"Would you testify against them?" he asked. "We can protect you, and the bar."

She nodded again, this time smiling.

The old man came back to the bar and said, "That chess game is going to go on all night. You'd better fix me another pastis while I wait to play the winner."

"Coming right up, Yannick." Pierrette said.

Verlaque finished his drink and put a couple of coins down on the bar. "I'll see you around," he said.

Pierrette nodded and busied herself with Yannick's drink and he left, anxious to see Marine.

Verlaque got home to find Marine upstairs, in a loft that she used as an office, surrounded by books that she had pulled off the shelves. He sat down in an armchair and watched her as she scanned the shelves, sometimes pulling books out or making an opening in the middle of a row with her hands to see what was behind. "I knew one day I'd regret doubling up all these paperbacks," she said without turning around.

"You mean there are two rows on those shelves?" Verlaque asked. "One in front and one behind?"

"Yep. At least they're sort of in order, theme-wise. I thought when I quit the university and emptied out my campus office I'd have lots of time to sort out my books."

"I take it that you're looking for something for a text you're writing," Verlaque said, getting up and stretching. "I'm going to have a glass of white wine. And you?"

"Nothing, thanks."

Verlaque looked at Marine with raised eyebrows. "What? No wine?"

"And I'm not looking for this book for me," Marine said, changing the subject. "It's for you. For the case."

Verlaque sat down again. "You sound like your mother."

Marine laughed and then snapped her fingers. "Bingo!" She reached behind a row of books and picked one out, holding it up and waving it in the air. It was a thin paperback with a yellowed cover. She walked over and kissed Verlaque, then sat down behind her desk, opening the book and hurriedly flipping to the contents pages.

"What's the book?" Verlaque said, intrigued.

"Italian short stories from the nineteenth and early twentieth centuries."

"I married you partly for your reading choices."

"Here it is," she mumbled, ignoring his joke. "Page 145. 'The Reverend Walnut' by Luigi Capuana. Sicilian, born in Catania in 1839."

"Is it in Italian or translated into French?"

"French," she said, turning the pages. "My Italian wasn't good enough then. I bought it in junior high."

Verlaque grinned, amazed that he had married someone who bought books like this one when she was not yet sixteen. "Hold on, I will get that glass of wine. Nothing for you? Are you sure?"

"I'm fine, thanks," Marine said. "Hurry up, though."

"All right, all right," Verlaque called from the

stairs. A few minutes later he came back up to the loft, carrying a large glass of wine the color of straw. He sat back down, took a sip, and said, "Ready."

Marine said, " 'Walnut' is a nickname for the young man in this story, Lucio, born prematurely. The midwife holds him up and says, 'He's as small as a walnut,' and the nickname sticks."

"Even when he becomes a priest?"

"Yes," Marine answered.

"So are we talking here about Père Fernand? Listen I have some news about him—"

"No. We're talking about Lucio Somebody-or-other, the name tattooed on Vittoria Romano's lower arm. There's a small walnut tattooed there, too."

"I saw that walnut too. It looked so odd. . . . Listen, Marine," he said, holding his hand up. "I was wrong about the importance of the tattoo. The Orezza brothers and Alain Sorba are behind all of this." He went on to tell her of Pierrette's story.

Marine sat back in the chair and sighed. "The tattoo is a better angle."

Verlaque snorted. "The Reverend Walnut?" He took a big gulp of wine.

"Do you really think that small-time thugs like the Orezza brothers would shoot someone? In a church? Just because they want to buy a bar?"

"It's more plausible to me than the walnut short story. The bar owner just confirmed . . ."

"The Italians are somehow connected to this," Marine said as she rubbed her eyes.

Verlaque knew he had spoken unkindly. It had been his idea to send Marine on that wild-goose chase, and she had done it, even though she had sounded so tired on the phone. "How did you manage to see the tattoo? Was it difficult?"

"Yes." She didn't tell him that when he called her she had been struggling to remove all of the war paint Margaux had applied to her face, and despite the fact that she had secretly loved dressing up and acting in front of Sorba, it had exhausted her. It was a little like teaching, she reflected, with all those young eyes on you. She continued, "It's cold out, so she had a long-sleeved sweater on. I bought my cheese, then asked for a glass of water, which she kindly gave me. I then purposely spilled some water on her arm. What do you do when your arm gets wet but you're wearing long sleeves?"

Verlaque set his glass down and looked at his right arm. He shook it and immediately pulled up his jacket sleeve. "You're smart," he said, laughing.

"I grabbed some paper towels that had been lying on the counter and tried to help her dry her arm," Marine said. "It was then that I could see the walnut, with its distinctive little ridges, and the name. It triggered memories of this short story, as his name is the same in the story—Lucio."

"You remembered all of this because of the name Lucio?" Verlaque asked, doubting the importance of this bizarre short story but not wanting to offend Marine.

"Yes, because Lucio became one of my favorites."

"Favorites?"

"Favorite names. You know, when teenage girls pick out their future baby names."

"I wouldn't know about that." He took a sip of wine and looked at Marine over the top of his glass. She had closed the book and was holding it in her hands, smelling its pages with her eyes closed. "Did you have any other favorites?" he asked quietly.

"Rosa," Marine answered.

CHAPTER TWENTY-EIGHT

Verlaque met Paulik on the steps of the Palais de Justice. He shook Paulik's hand and said, "We seem to arrive at the same time most mornings."

"Mental telepathy," Paulik said, smiling.

"No, it means I'm slower than you are, as my apartment is a three-minute walk away and your house is a fifteen-minute drive."

"To be honest, having a kid helps," Paulik said. "Léa starts school now at eight o'clock."

"Right, I forgot," Verlaque replied.

"Flamant sent me a message," Paulik said. "He got here early and found out more information on that Italian family."

"Forget about that," Verlaque said, opening a door for the commissioner. "Père Fernand was helping the owner of the little bar next to Saint-Sauveur fight off the Orezza brothers, who were trying to threaten her into selling."

"So Père Fernand was at it again, helping the little guy."

"Yeah, in this case *girl,* a woman named Pierrette Lapierre."

Paulik said, "What? She has Pierre twice in her name, poor thing."

"I know, Bruno," Verlaque said, smiling in spite of himself.

"Is she willing to testify?"

"Yes." He thought of Vittoria Romano's tattoo, the name Lucio, and the walnut, and didn't bother telling Paulik. It was too inconsequential next to Pierrette and the threats of the Orezza brothers that he had seen with his own eyes last night.

"Does Mlle Lapierre know for a fact that one of the Orezza brothers shot Père Fernand?" Paulik asked.

"No."

"How did they poison Cole Hainsby?" Paulik asked as they walked up a flight of stairs.

Verlaque stopped and looked at the commissioner. Before he could say "I don't know" they ran into a magistrate from Marseille, shook hands, and exchanged pleasantries. The magistrate, a thin, gaunt man with white hair and a hawkish nose, was also a lover of old cars. He asked Verlaque about his Porsche.

"It's in the shop," Verlaque replied. "I think I may have to make that decision one always faces with old cars. Do I sink a lot of money into it, or sell it and buy a newer model? I stayed up late last night smoking a cigar and making one of those pros-and-cons lists."

The magistrate wished Verlaque good luck and excused himself; he had to get back to Marseille.

Paulik chuckled as he and Verlaque walked on. "Hélène and I do those lists, too. The last one was a long time ago, though; maybe twelve years or so."

"That's a long time," Verlaque said. "You obviously make decisions more easily than I do."

"We were trying to decide whether to have children or not. We talked about it for five years after we got married. It wasn't an easy decision; or, I should say, it was one we didn't take lightly."

Verlaque nodded and mumbled, "*Merci.*" It was a little too much information; a Parisian would never have been that forthcoming. He didn't need to ask Bruno Paulik if the decision had been a good one. The Pauliks openly adored their daughter, as did he.

"I'll meet up with you in a few minutes," Verlaque said suddenly.

"All right," Paulik said, hoping he hadn't gotten too personal. "I'll be with Flamant if you need me."

Verlaque turned around and headed toward his office. Once inside, he closed the door and picked up his telephone.

"*Oui, cheri?*" Marine answered on the first ring. Verlaque couldn't see his wife, but she was standing in the kitchen, smiling.

"We've already checked, and the man who died in the warehouse fire in Ethiopia, Vito Giraldi, isn't related to either of the Italians running the Perugia stand."

"Vittoria Romano's never been married?"

"No."

Marine paused. Verlaque could hear her

breathing. "My mother's maiden name was Ardevol . . ." she said.

"Yes . . ."

"And when I was little she'd sometimes joke that Bonnet and Ardevol were such dull names compared to her maternal grandfather's name."

"Which was?"

"Voltaire."

Verlaque burst out laughing. "No relation to the philosopher I take it?"

He could hear the smile in Marine's voice as she replied, "None whatsoever. But you see what I'm getting at . . . names can go back several generations."

"It's worth a try. Thank you." He hung up and walked quickly out of his office, heading down the corridors and flights of stairs that took him to the office where Flamant was hunched over his computer.

Flamant saw Verlaque and jumped up, waving him over.

"Any news?" Verlaque asked as he sat down.

"I just found a connection between Elite Clothing and those people from Perugia," Flamant said. "We were waiting for you to arrive, sir, before I explained."

"Is the connection through Vittoria Romano?" Verlaque asked, almost missing a breath.

"Yes," Flamant replied. "Her maternal grandfather was Vito Giraldi."

"The man who died in the fire," Paulik said.

"Exactly," Flamant said. "I didn't make the connection right away because their last names are different. The business closed, as you know, and her father went into a depression and committed suicide."

"Ah," Verlaque mumbled.

"And *his* son, Lucio Romano, also went into a downward spiral and has been in and out of jail, down in Bari."

"Lucio?" Verlaque asked, thinking of the tattoo. Apologies to Marine were in order. No, champagne. Except she seemed to be off wine at the moment.

"Yes," Flamant answered.

"How did you manage to dig all this up so fast?" Paulik asked.

"This Google Translate thing is amazing," Flamant said, trying and failing to suppress a yawn. "It was easy enough at first when I was just looking for names. But when the names started appearing in small Italian newspapers, I had entire articles translated. That got me onto the Romano family, and then I was able to double-check everything with Interpol and the carabinieri down in Bari."

Verlaque thought of the city employee who hadn't liked Flamant's questions about the stall renters. "Is it possible that Matteo Ricci is really Lucio Romano?" he asked, again thinking of Vittoria Romano's tattoo.

Flamant shook his head. "I thought of that, too, as I can't see Vittoria shooting a priest, especially from far away. But, no, Matteo Ricci is a real person and seems to be her boyfriend." He held up a finger. "But," he went on, "I dug some more and found out that Matteo and Lucio are best friends. One of the officers down in Bari told me; everyone knows them."

"There's Matteo Ricci's motive," Paulik said.

"Call *her* in first, before him," Verlaque said, looking at Paulik. "What do you think?"

"Excellent," Paulik replied, picking up his cell phone. He spoke to another officer and gave him instructions to pick up Vittoria Romano as soon as she appeared at her stand and to accompany her to the Palais de Justice. He hung up and said, "Flamant, go home and get some sleep, or take a nap downstairs in the quiet room."

"Yes, sir," Flamant said, yawning again.

"This new information doesn't make things easier, does it?" Verlaque asked Paulik once Flamant was gone. "On the way here I was convinced that the Orezza brothers were responsible for Père Fernand's attempted murder, and the accidental murder of Cole Hainsby."

"Will the bar owner testify against them?" Paulik asked.

"Yes, she agreed last night."

"We can't accuse them of murder just because they threatened her."

"We can at least link them to trying to run a cyclist off the road."

"Only one of them, unfortunately," Paulik pointed out. "And it isn't either Orezza brother."

Marine made herself tea and was carrying it upstairs to the loft when the downstairs buzzer sounded. She looked at her watch, perplexed and annoyed that someone might be out selling useless products, or insurance, or a new cell phone subscription, before ten in the morning. "*Oui?*" she said into the intercom, trying to sound harsh.

"Mme Bonnet?" a woman's voice sounded. "I'm so sorry to bother you. May I come up and talk with you? Oh, sorry, it's France. France Dubois."

"France, come right up. Fourth and last floor." She quickly filled the kettle with water and put it back on the stove, lighting the gas burner. She was still mildly annoyed; she had a chapter to edit in her book, and then had a doctor's appointment right after lunch. But still, she liked France and was curious as to why she was visiting.

France arrived at the door and the two women shyly gave each other the *bises*. "Please call me Marine," Marine said, stepping aside to let France into the apartment. "Mme Bonnet is my mother."

France giggled. "Your mother is Professor,

or Dr., Bonnet to me," she said. "But okay. It was your mother who gave me your apartment address. I hope you don't mind."

"No, of course not," Marine replied, half lying. The location of their apartment, on a small dead-end street, wasn't known to many people except close friends and family. "Come into the kitchen while I make some tea." France followed Marine and looked around, wide-eyed, at the marble counters and expensive German appliances that she had only ever seen in magazines. "I have some LU cookies somewhere," Marine said, opening a cupboard. "If my husband didn't sneak them all."

France politely laughed, easily imagining Antoine Verlaque sneaking cookies. She felt that she knew him better now, after their talk by the King René statue. He wasn't as intimidating as people in Aix said he was.

Marine made more tea and carried it into the living room while France carried a mug for herself and the cookies that Marine had found and put on a plate. "Please excuse the lingering cigar smell, France," Marine said. "I think my husband was up late last night, smoking."

"Oh, I quite like the smell, I always have," France replied, smiling. "My mother's father smoked Cuban cigars." France looked around the living and dining rooms. After all, Marine had probably done the same the first time she came to Antoine's apartment. "Is that a real one?" France asked, pointing to an oil painting of Venice that hung near the dining room table.

"No," Marine said, smiling and pouring France some tea. "I mean yes, it's a real eighteenth-century painting, but by the *school* of Caneletto, not by *him*." Marine looked at the small oil, knowing very well that although this painting was beautiful, the large black abstract in their bedroom, by Pierre Soulages circa 1983, was worth a lot more money than the view of Guidecca done by an apprentice.

"Wow," France said. "Well, I suppose you're wondering why I'm here."

"It had crossed my mind. Did you want to talk about someone at the Sister City fair?"

"More than one person," France said. "I'm not sure where to begin."

"Why don't you begin with the more difficult story?"

France blew on her tea. Tea made by someone else was so much better than at home, she mused. "All right. I'll tell you about Jason Miller. Anna told me you were asking about him. About what happened."

Marine nodded. "Yes, you've been watching him."

"I only wanted to make him think about what he'd done; make him feel remorse."

"What did he do, France?" Marine asked, leaning forward.

She sighed. "Last Christmas he'd follow me around the Place des Cardeurs. Once he grabbed me behind one of the tents. And another time I could swear that he followed me home."

"Why didn't you report it?"

"Because he really didn't do much."

Marine nodded again. "And you confided in Anna?"

"Yes," France replied. "She saw what was going on and asked me about it. She's very kind."

"And Cole Hainsby," Marine said. "Did he bother you in that same way?"

"M Hainsby? Why, no. I had never met him until just before the carol sing."

Marine breathed out a sigh of relief.

France went on, "Your husband thought I might have wanted to kill him, because of my parents. But that wouldn't have changed anything, would it?"

"No."

"Jason Miller's sister said they won't be coming back next year, so that's that."

"Really? Why not? Although I'm not sad about it."

"The rent for the stand was too high, she said, and they're too busy at home."

"So, what's the other story you have?" Marine asked, taking a cookie but not really wanting it.

"It's the Italians," France said. "From Perugia. I wanted M Verlaque to know."

"Go on."

"They're not from Perugia, for one." France sat forward, pleased with her information. "I used to go to Perugia, with my parents. I speak a bit of Italian—"

Marine smiled; a kindred spirit.

France said, "I asked them a few questions about the city, at first in innocence, excited to speak to Perugians. But it was obvious to me they didn't know much about it. So then I asked them a few specific questions, trying to trap them, which I did. They answered incorrectly every time."

Marine got nervous. "Did they catch on?"

"Oh, no, I was discreet. It's easy, as most people don't notice me."

Marine was about to argue and France waved her hand. "I thought you should tell your husband about the Italians, since he's investigating the murders. I'm not saying they are guilty, but they're lying about something. Plus, this may be unimportant, but on the first day I went to say hello and ask about the carol sing dinner, they had lots of photographs up in their stand. You know, like all the stands do. A few of the pictures were of him, the man, hunting. He was holding a very big gun, with a dead boar at his feet. There were some prize ribbons hanging from the photographs."

"That's not unusual, France," Marine said. "Hunting is popular in Italy, like here."

"Oh, I know. But the next time I went, after Père Fernand was shot, the photographs had been taken down."

"Now, that's interesting." Marine handed France the plate of cookies. "Eat some LUs before my husband eats all of them."

Paulik turned on the recording machine. Verlaque sat to his left and a uniformed officer stood behind them, his back to the wall, watching. Vittoria Romano played with a package of cigarettes. Verlaque remembered Marine's reportage of the Italian couple in the restaurant, and of their arguing, and he was glad that Romano was here on her own. He also knew he owed Marine an apology for last night; he had brushed off her hypothesis about the Italians and the walnut tattoo.

"Why don't you start at the beginning," Paulik said. "Whose idea was it to put crushed-up acetaminophen in Père Fernand's dinner?"

She stayed quiet. Verlaque could see that she was actually biting her tongue.

"It had to be done quickly," Paulik went on. "As there was a lot of commotion at the buffet table. But you couldn't know that Père Fernand would be in line next to someone notorious for his absentmindedness and lack of attention. Cole Hainsby somehow managed to take Père Fernand's plate. Then Hainsby fell ill and died that evening. So you needed a plan B, and quickly. Matteo Ricci is a hunter; there's good hunting in Provence, especially at this time of year. He had his gun with him."

"Ricci has won hunting tournaments," Verlaque added. "We spoke with hunting colleagues of his who have confirmed to us what a good long-distance shot he is." Verlaque was bluffing here, having just received France Dubois's information via text message from Marine a minute before walking into the interview room.

Vittoria Romano held her head in her hands.

Paulik pressed on, "Your grandfather, then your father, and now your brother. All victims, in your opinion, of Père Fernand's meddling."

She still wouldn't look at them. Verlaque had stayed up late reading Luigi Capuana's short story while he finished his cigar. Little did he know how useful that short story would be. Marine's intuition and exceptional memory were once again spot-on. He now tried a different tactic. "The walnut," he said. "Your brother, Lucio. Born prematurely, no? He was named after the character in the Capuana short story, wasn't he? And you protected him, like Sister Celeste in the story. But unlike the story, your Lucio doesn't turn to the priesthood, desperate to give his life a purpose, but to petty crime. And like Capuana's Lucio, he's always being taken advantage of; he's too meek, and kind. Easy for bigger crooks to frame him. So he's taking the rap, in and out of jail—"

She kept her head down, staring at the top of the table that separated them. "Go to hell with your walnut story," she whispered in Italian.

"If Vittoria Romano won't speak," Verlaque said as he and Paulik walked together fifteen minutes later, "then we'll go have a chat with Matteo Ricci. He must be beside himself, wondering why we are still keeping her."

"The longer we keep her," Paulik said, "the more nervous Ricci will be."

Verlaque said, "Call a team to search his stand as well. If he's a prize hunter, then he might not be able to tear himself away from his prize rifle."

"Although it would be a million times easier to dump it in the sea," Paulik said. "But I agree."

When they got to the fair, Ricci was putting fresh pasta into a plastic container for two elegantly dressed elderly Aixois. Verlaque watched Ricci, who, despite his smiles, didn't look like the other Sister City hosts. His heart wasn't in it. Would he have been able to see that before? Verlaque wondered. Before he knew the background story of the clothing warehouse in Ethiopia?

The couple left, and Ricci saw Verlaque and Paulik. "Where is Vittoria?" he asked in rough French.

"We are keeping her in custody a bit longer,"

Paulik answered. "In the meantime, we'd like to ask you a few questions."

"I'm working."

Verlaque turned around; there was no one else there. "You don't have any customers at the moment," he said. "We won't take long."

Paulik began, "You've taken down the hunting photographs and your medals."

Ricci shrugged. "So many people are against the hunt these days. I thought it best."

"May we see them?"

"I threw them out."

"Threw out medals, and photos of you winning shooting prizes?" Verlaque asked. "That's odd."

"Maybe to you."

"Your hotel room and truck are being searched," Verlaque said.

"Without a warrant?" Ricci asked, his eyes direct.

"I don't need one," Verlaque replied. "As a magistrate."

Ricci shrugged. "Good for you," he replied. "You won't find anything."

"I'd suggest that you pack in here for the day, as a team is on their way to search this stand," Verlaque said.

"Here they are now," Paulik said, turning around to see the two police vehicles that had just parked at the top of the square. "We'll keep Mlle Romano with us a bit longer, until we hear from the officers searching your possessions."

Verlaque and Paulik swung around and walked away before Ricci could reply. They heard him cuss and set down his knife with a thud. He lit himself a cigarette and walked out of the tent, leaning against a pole as he watched six officers walk into his tent and begin working. Verlaque and Paulik watched from the opposite side of the tent as the white-gloved officers carefully picked up objects—blocks of cheese, cartons of plastic dishes and utensils—looked at them, turning each object over in their gloved hands, and setting them back down. Verlaque's eyes scanned the stand's interior, searching for a long, thin object that could conceal a gun. He rocked back and forth on his heels to stay warm, wishing they could be drinking one of the Italian's Illy espressos. The officers continued searching, and after fifteen minutes one of them gave Paulik a worried *I give up* look. "*Merde*," Paulik whispered. Verlaque looked over at Ricci, smoking his third or fourth cigarette, playing some video game on his phone.

Verlaque's eyes took in the scene, beginning at the top of the stand, its sides, then its interior, from the back wall to the front counter. His eyes then moved outside the stand, to the makeshift bar area that most of the sister cities had set up—except those from Bath and Carthage— where customers could eat or at least set down their drinks. He then said, "Bruno, do you see something different about the columns today?"

Paulik was startled at the judge's use of his first name. "Yes," he said. "One of them doesn't have a tabletop on it anymore."

"That's what I thought," Verlaque replied.

Paulik walked up to the stand and spoke to one of the officers inside. The officer turned to a colleague, said something, and they came out of the tent, one of them leaving to walk up to their vehicle. In a minute she was back with a pickax. Matteo Ricci looked up from his game and his face went pale. The officers laid the column gently on its side and the female officer began to tap at its top. Verlaque walked over to watch and Paulik whispered, "The top looks like it's been recently plastered."

Verlaque whispered back, "He would have broken the tabletop—either on purpose or accidentally—to get at the inside."

Paulik nodded and they watched as she continued gently picking away while her colleague took pieces of broken plaster with a gloved hand and set them aside. With a final tap she broke a large piece from the top third of the column and Paulik said, "Okay, that's enough." They set the column back upright and Paulik leaned over and reached in, pulling out a rifle. Ricci turned to flee, but it was no use. There were four officers standing beside him, one with handcuffs ready.

CHAPTER TWENTY-NINE

The first thing Verlaque did when they got back to the Palais de Justice was telephone Debra Hainsby. Much to his relief she answered on the second ring and he told her about the Italians, and that Cole had not been the intended victim. He could hear her breathing heavily, a gasp, and then he heard nothing.

"Are you still there, madame?" he asked.

"Yes," she said, almost in a whisper.

"So your husband did nothing wrong."

"Except be his usual absentminded self," Debra said. "Eating off the wrong plate."

"I'm sorry."

She sniffed and said, "Thank you for calling."

"How are you? The children?"

"Mary won't get her head out of her books, and Sean won't leave his room," Debra said. "But they're starting a new school next week so I think that will help. And I have good news . . ."

"Really?"

"I start a new job in two weeks," she said, "at HeliIndustries."

"That's fantastic!"

"Yes, I'm quite thrilled. They advertised a position on the internet, I applied for it, and at the interview they said they had been impressed with me when I visited their offices earlier this year with . . . Alain Sorba."

Verlaque smiled, happy for her, knowing that she wasn't bragging, but just needing to share this good news with someone. Verlaque said, "They're a great company. Again, congratulations." Before saying good-bye they joked about running into each other at the café across from the Palais de Justice. He did not tell her of Alain Sorba's involvement with the Orezza brothers, or their threats on both Damien and Pierrette. Debra Hainsby had enough to deal with, and for some reason he couldn't explain, despite the fact that he had never met them, his heart ached for Mary and Sean. He hung up, and much to his relief Paulik came into his office.

"Espresso?" Verlaque asked.

Marine walked out the front door of her doctor's office on the rue Espariat and stared, her eyes trying to adjust to the late-afternoon sunlight, at the Place d'Albertas across the narrow pedestrianized road. It was a three-sided square with a not very interesting fountain in the center, but it was paved with river stones that veered off in every direction, forming wonderfully organic patterns that made it charming. Two sides of the eighteenth-century three-story buildings had been renovated and painted a bright, deep yellow; the third façade, in the back, was waiting its turn, and not very elegantly: Its dull dark brown paint chipped and flaked off the walls, and the whole building looked like it was leaning inward, about to topple over into the fountain.

She stepped into the street and began to walk toward the Palais de Justice. She felt at once queasy, elated, and in shock. She had felt this way two other times in her thirty-seven years—when she knew that she would marry Antoine (although on their wedding day, in their beloved seaside Italian village that she and Antoine nicknamed Paradiso, she had felt extremely calm) and on the day she passed the bar.

When she got to the front doors and the small glassed-fronted office of the security guards, she showed her ID and asked them to tell her husband that she would like to see him. The officer smiled, recognizing Marine, gave an obligatory glance at her identification, then put it in a tray with the cards of other visitors. He picked up the phone and spoke to Verlaque, but Marine couldn't hear their conversation through the glass. She rocked back and forth on her tiptoes, impatient. The guard slid open a small glass window and said, "You can go on up, madame. He's expecting you in his office. Do you know where it is?"

"Yes, thank you," Marine said as she turned around and crossed the vast interior courtyard to a gray set of double doors. Up three floors, she thought she remembered, then left and down a hallway, until she reached Mme Girard's office, which was connected to a small waiting room. She walked through, said hello to Mme Girard, and then saw her husband standing in the doorway of his office.

"What a nice surprise," he said. "Come on in. Bruno is here, too."

"Oh," Marine said, trying to hide her disappointment. She walked into Verlaque's office and gave Paulik the *bises*. She said, "I was in the neighborhood . . . at my doctor's office on the rue Espariat, and thought I'd swing by."

"Huh?" Verlaque asked.

"I'll go," Paulik quickly said.

"No, you just got here," Verlaque said, pulling out a chair from against the wall for Marine. "Marine will want to hear all this; *chérie*, we found the gun at the Perugia stand."

"Excellent! Did the Italians confess?" she asked.

"Not yet, but Vittoria Romano is still downstairs and will confess soon. We're waiting to hear if the gun's been fired recently and if it matches the gun and bullets used on Père Fernand." She knew that now was not the time to confess that she had dressed up in disguise and recorded Alain Sorba. She had the tape safe and sound in her loft office and could show it to Antoine later.

"Père Fernand is out of danger," Marine said. "My mother called me this morning, after my strange visit with France Dubois."

"Mlle Dubois did well to notice those hunting photographs," Paulik said.

"She's very smart," Marine said. "She speaks English and a bit of Italian and who knows what other languages, and she's so discreet."

"Reverend Dave said she basically runs the APCA," Verlaque said.

Marine titled her head. Verlaque looked at his wife and said, "You have an idea, don't you?"

"Could you hire her here?" she asked. "To replace Mme Girard?"

Verlaque smiled. "That's not a bad idea."

Paulik laughed. "No chance."

"Why not?" Marine said.

"Mme Girard started eons ago," Paulik said. "Anyone you interview for the job will now have to come from our own HR."

"I'll slip her CV on the top of the pile," Verlaque said, smiling.

Paulik guffawed. "Good luck! It's not as easy as that. And you'd have to get Mlle Dubois's application approved by that battle-ax who's in charge of HR."

Verlaque swung his head around to look at Paulik, his smile gone. "Not her. On the first floor at the end of the hall?"

"Oh, yes."

"She terrified me when I got the job here," Verlaque said. "My hand shook when I was filling out the paperwork."

Marine and Paulik laughed. Marine said, "Antoine, have Mme Girard print out the hiring instructions and bring them here."

Verlaque picked up the phone and did as he was told, and two minutes later Mme Girard appeared at the door wearing, Marine would have to tell Sylvie, a red knit Sonia Rykiel dress. "Here you go," Mme Girard said, handing the papers to Verlaque. "And I'm sorry about all this."

"No, no, no," Verlaque, Marine, and Bruno Paulik all protested at once.

Verlaque said, "Mme Girard, you will be difficult to replace, but you deserve your retirement."

"Thank you," Mme Girard answered. She turned to Marine and said, "Mme Bonnet, you look ravishing today."

Marine put her hands up to her neck. "Thank you."

"She does, doesn't she?" Verlaque agreed. Something was bothering him, though. He remembered: Why was she at the doctor's?

Mme Girard left and Marine sat down with the paperwork and began reading while Verlaque and Paulik spoke of the Italians and now the complications involved with having foreigners, albeit EU member citizens, involved in a court case in France.

"What are you doing, Marine?" Verlaque asked after a moment.

"Looking for loopholes," she replied.

"I can do that—"

"No need. Found it," she said.

"Really?"

"Section 3.6, 'On hiring someone with external qualifications not found in the roster of available municipal employees,'" she read, bringing the sheet of paper up close to her face to read the fine print. "This is really interesting. The next point, section 3.7: 'Language skills are one example of a quality an external candidate may be interviewed and hired for.'"

"English!" Verlaque said.

"Yes!" Paulik said in English, laughing and giving the air a fist pump. He continued, but in French, "We need someone who can speak English. When we deal with Interpol in Brussels, that's often the common language everyone speaks even if there are four official ones."

Marine went on, "Listen to this. The interview may be held in the language the candidate is being hired for."

"I can interview Mlle Dubois in English!" Verlaque said.

"Battle-ax wouldn't understand a word," Paulik said. "You could talk about what you had for breakfast."

"Well, I could be jumping ahead of myself. Mlle Dubois may be perfectly happy where she is now," Verlaque said.

"No," Marine said. "She told me she was looking for a change, a new job. She talked about fixing up her apartment, things like that. Would you like me to phone her?"

"Would you? Right now?"

Marine smiled, knowing that once her husband had a thought, he couldn't let it go. "Sure," she said, stepping out of the office. She saw that Mme Girard was away from her desk so she quickly dialed France's number. In less than two minutes she was back in Verlaque's office.

"Well?" he asked.

"I gave her your email address and she's sending her CV."

"Perfect," he said. "Thank you so much."

"I should go," Paulik said.

"No, I'll go," Marine said, looking at her watch. "Antoine, dinner at seven sharp tonight. Sound good?"

"Perfect," he said, getting up to kiss her good-bye. "You know what? Let's invite France Dubois to our place for Christmas."

Marine stopped at the door and turned around, smiling. She looked at Bruno Paulik, who stood with his hands on his hips and a quizzical look on his face.

Marine said, "With our two families? Your uptight father and my bossy mother?"

"She's all alone."

"I'll call her when I get home," Marine said,

giving her husband a kiss. "It's a wonderful idea, Antoine."

"The spirit of Christmas!" Paulik said with forced glee.

"Don't you start," Verlaque said, pointing his fountain pen at Paulik.

His telephone rang and he quickly said to Marine, "See you later!" and answered the phone, gesturing for Paulik to sit down. Marine waved good-bye, frustrated that she'd have to wait a few hours more, but it was better that way, she realized. She'd buy flowers and champagne on the way home. She walked out, closing the office door behind her.

"It's Bari," Verlaque whispered with his hand over the receiver. Verlaque continued to speak into the phone using a mixture of English and Italian, and then hung up. "I had a hard time explaining in my pidgin Italian how we found the rifle. I had to make up the Italian words for *tabletop* and *column* by using the French word and adding an *o* and the end." He glanced at Paulik, who in turn was looking out the window and smiling and then let out a little laugh. Verlaque asked, "What's so funny?"

"Those columns! Here I am, someone trained to watch people, look for clues, be diligent; like today, remembering that there should be four tabletops on those columns. We both saw it right away, didn't we? But with my own family I can completely miss the signs."

"What are you going on about?"

"I was so blind, for example, when Hélène was pregnant," Paulik said, turning to look at his colleague. He gave Verlaque a raised eyebrow.

"What kind of signs?" Verlaque asked. At least it was a story about Hélène, someone he knew well, and not one of Paulik's numerous cousins from the Luberon.

"Hélène was so tired all of a sudden. And she's always been the first out of bed in the morning."

Verlaque rolled his fountain pen around on the desk. "What else?" he asked, his throat suddenly dry.

"The most obvious one was the wine. She'd stopped drinking it. I'd offer her a glass and she'd put her hand over the glass and refuse. Hélène's a winemaker, and I still didn't put two and two together!" He almost added *What an idiot I was!* but he didn't want to overdo it.

Verlaque felt his forehead and upper lip begin to perspire. "Why didn't she tell you? Didn't you want kids?"

"Oh, yeah, we both did. After we did that pros-and-cons list that I told you about, the pros column won out by a mile. But Hélène wasn't sure yet at first. She wanted to be sure, you know, before she told me. A few days later she got the yes from her doctor . . . whose clinic is on the rue Espariat . . ." he said, adding a cough for extra effect, "and boy did we celebrate—"

"Rue Espariat?" Verlaque got up, almost knocking his chair over. Paulik leaned back and watched Verlaque grab his coat and then do up the buttons, missing at least three of them. Paulik tried not to grin. "Where are you going?" Paulik asked. "Don't you want to wait for the ballistics report? They'll be calling any minute."

"You can take the call, Bruno," Verlaque said, quickly tying his scarf around his neck. "I have to go. . . . Besides, we both know what the results are going to be."

"Yes, that's true," Paulik said, getting up. He walked across the room and shook Verlaque's hand, something they always did when a case was closed. "And it's going to be good news, Antoine."

M. L. LONGWORTH has lived in Aix-en-Provence since 1997. She has written about the region for *The Washington Post*, *The Times* (London), *The Independent* (London), and *Bon Appétit*. She is the author of a bilingual collection of essays, *Une Américaine en Provence*. She is married and has a daughter.

Books are produced in the United States using U.S.-based materials

Books are printed using a revolutionary new process called THINKtech™ that lowers energy usage by 70% and increases overall quality

Books are durable and flexible because of Smyth-sewing

Paper is sourced using environmentally responsible foresting methods and the paper is acid-free

Center Point Large Print
600 Brooks Road / PO Box 1
Thorndike, ME 04986-0001 USA

(207) 568-3717

US & Canada:
1 800 929-9108
www.centerpointlargeprint.com